For Grace Fredericks, with love and gratitude

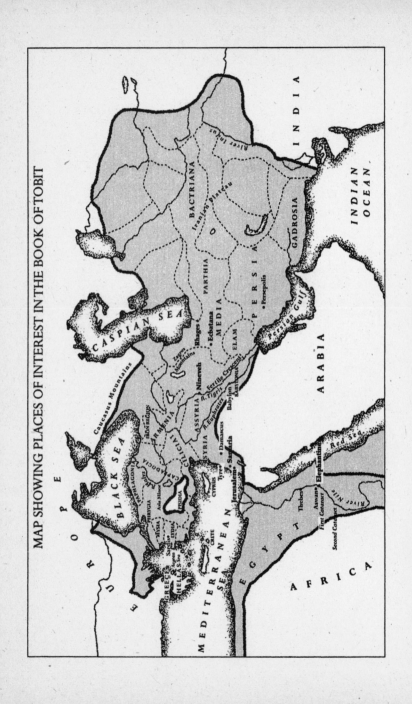

MAP SHOWING PLACES OF INTEREST IN THE BOOK OF TOBIT

Miss Garnet's Angel

SALLEY VICKERS

A PLUME BOOK

PLUME
Published by the Penguin Group
Penguin Putnam Inc., 375 Hudson Street, New York, New York 10014, U.S.A.
Penguin Books Ltd, 80 Strand, London WC2R 0RL, England
Penguin Books Australia Ltd, Ringwood, Victoria, Australia
Penguin Books Canada Ltd, 10 Alcorn Avenue, Toronto, Ontario, Canada M4V 3B2
Penguin Books (N.Z.) Ltd, 182-190 Wairau Road, Auckland 10, New Zealand

Penguin Books Ltd, Registered Offices: Harmondsworth, Middlesex, England

Published by Plume, a member of Penguin Putnam Inc. This is an authorized reprint of a
hardcover edition published by Carroll & Graf Publishers, a Division of Avalon Publishing
Group Incorporated. For information address Carroll & Graf Publishers, a Division of Avalon
Publishing Group Incorporated, 161 William Street, 16th Floor, New York, New York 10038.

First Plume Printing, March 2002
1 3 5 7 9 10 8 6 4 2

℗ REGISTERED TRADEMARK—MARCA REGISTRADA

Library of Congress Cataloging-in-Publication Data is available.
ISBN (hc.): 0-7867-0823-9
ISBN (pbk.): 0-452-28297-7

Printed in the United States of America

Acclaim for *Miss Garnet's Angel*

"*Miss Garnet's Angel* is a most impressive debut, and one eagerly
looks forward to Vickers' next book."
—*San Francisco Chronicle*

"Charming . . . subtle and discerning . . . This beguiling
redemptive novel has a touch of the miraculous."
—*The Orlando Sentinel*

"Reveals itself as a surprising exploration of the mysteries of
imagination and faith."
—Joanna Trollope, author of *Marrying the Mistress*

"A lovely book, an affecting story of loss, personal exploration,
and redemption."
—*The Denver Post*

"Vickers has taken myth, religion, and secular humanism and
turned them into substantial life-affirming fiction."
—*The Philadelphia Inquirer*

"The novel alights in the heart softly, with rustling wings, and a
reader cannot help but be enchanted by Miss Garnet's
beautifully decaying Venice."
—*The Baltimore Sun*

SALLEY VICKERS has worked as a university professor of English and
as a Jungian psychologist. She lives in London and Somerset. *Miss
Garnet's Angel* is her first novel.

Visit the author's website at www.salleyvickers.com
or e-mail the author at reception@salleyvickers.com

'If some people really see angels, where others see empty space, let them paint the angels . . .'

JOHN RUSKIN

ACKNOWLEDGEMENT

The peculiar charm and poetry of The Book of Tobit has endeared it to artists through the ages; many people will have seen paintings of the boy carrying a fish, accompanied by a dog and an angel, without recognising the source of these images.

In my retelling of the tale I have retained certain anachronistic features of the original, but the variations — imaginative reconstructions of the story's sources — are my own, and for those I must take responsibility. To the anonymous author, or authors, however, I most gratefully acknowledge my debt.

I
EPIPHANY

1

Death is outside life but it alters it. It leaves a hole in the fabric of things which those who are left behind try to repair. Perhaps it is because of this we are minded to feast at funerals and it is said that certain children are conceived on the eve of a departure, lest the separation of the partners be permanent. When in ancient stories heroes die, the first thing their comrades do, having made due observances to the gods, is sit and eat. Then they travel on, challenging, with their frail vitality, the large enigma of non-being.

When Miss Garnet's friend Harriet died, Miss Garnet decided to spend six months abroad. For Miss Garnet, who was certainly past child-bearing years and had lost the only person she ever ate with, the decision to travel was a bold one. Her expeditions abroad had been few and for the most part tinged with apprehension. As a young woman straight from college she had volunteered, while teaching the Hundred Years' War, to take a school party to Crécy. On that occasion she had become flustered when, behind her back but audibly, the boys had mocked her accent and had intimated (none too subtly) that she had brought them to France in order to forge a liaison with the large, sweating, white-faced coach driver.

'*Mademoiselle from Armentières*,' they had sung hilariously in the back of the coach. '*Mademoiselle from Armentières. Hasn't had sex for forty years!*' And as she had attempted to convey to the coach driver the time she considered it prudent to start back for Calais, wildly and suggestively they had chorused, '*Inky pinky parley vous!*'

The experience had left its mark on Miss Garnet's teaching as well as on her memory. Essentially a shy person, her impulses towards cordiality with her pupils, never strong in the first place, were dealt a blow. She withdrew, acquired a reputation for strictness, even severity, and in time became the kind of teacher who, if not loved, was at least respected. Even latterly, when in terms of pupils' taunts *Mademoiselle From Armentières* would be considered very small beer, no member of Miss Garnet's classes ever thought publicly to express a view about her intimate life.

Julia Garnet and Harriet Josephs had lived together for more than thirty years. Harriet had answered Julia's advertisement in the National Union of Teachers' monthly journal.

'Quiet, professional female sought to share small West London flat. No smokers. No pets.'

Harriet had been, in fact, the only person to respond to the advertisement, which had not prevented Julia from giving her what her friend later described as 'a toughish interview'. 'Honestly,' Harriet had used to say, on the few occasions when together they had entertained friends, 'it was worse than the time I tried to get into the Civil Service!'

Generally Harriet had laughed loudly at this point in a way her flat-mate had found irritating. Now Miss Garnet found she missed the laugh just as she missed Stella, Harriet's cat. The prohibition against pets had been relaxed seven years earlier when late one night after choir-practice Harriet had been followed from the station by Stella. Stella, then an anonymous black kitten with a white-starred throat, had waited all night on the stairs outside the front door of their fourth-floor flat, whereupon, on finding her, the soft-hearted Harriet had fed the kitten milk. After that, as Julia had observed, there was 'no getting rid of the animal'.

Alongside the two school teachers Stella had grown into an elderly and affectionate creature but it was Harriet to whom the cat had remained attached. Two days after they had both retired (they had arranged the events to coincide in order, Harriet had suggested, that the New Year could see them setting off on 'new feet') Julia returned from the shops to find her companion, apparently asleep, stretched out upon the sofa, her romantic novel face down on the carpet. Later, after the doctor and then the undertaker had been, Stella disappeared. Julia had placed milk outside first the flat door and then, worry making her brave the neighbours' ridicule, downstairs by the main entrance to the block. The milk she left outside was certainly drunk but after a few days she was forced to accept that it was not Stella drinking the milk but, more likely, the urban fox who had been seen rootling in the communal dustbins.

Perhaps it was not just the loss of Stella, but also her incompetence in the face of it – so soon after losing Harriet – which finally determined Miss Garnet's abrupt decision. She and Harriet had made plans – or rather Harriet had – for it must be said that, of the two, she was the more given to planning. ('Flighty' was sometimes her companion's name for Harriet's tendency to cut out advertisements from the *Observer* for trips to faraway and exotic places.) Harriet's (now permanent) flight had rendered the plans pointless; a kind of numbness had dulled Miss Garnet's usual caution and she found herself, before she was quite aware what was happening, calling in on one of the numerous local estate agents which had sprung up in her locality.

'No worries, Mrs Garnet, we'll be able to rent this, easy,' the young man with the too-short haircut and the fluorescent mobile phone had said.

'*Miss* Garnet, it's Miss,' she had explained, anxious not to accept a title to which she felt she had never managed to rise. (There had never been any question of Miss Garnet being a Ms: her great-aunt had had some association with Christabel Pankhurst and the connection, however loose, with the famous suffragette had strengthened Miss Garnet's views on the misplaced priorities of modern feminism.)

'*Miss*, I'm sorry,' the young man had said, trying not to laugh at the poor old bird. He'd heard from Mrs Barry, the caretaker, that there had been another old girl living with her who had just died. Probably lezzies, he thought.

Miss Garnet was not a lesbian, any more than Harriet Josephs had been, although both women had grown aware that that is what people sometimes assumed of them.

'It is very vexing,' Harriet had said once, when a widowed friend had opined that Jane Austen might have been gay, 'to be considered homosexual just because one hasn't been lucky enough to marry.'

'Or foolish enough,' Julia had added. But privately she believed Harriet was right. It would have been a piece of luck to have been loved by a man enough to have been his wife. She had been asked once for a kiss, at the end-of-term party at the school where she had taught History for thirty-five years. The request had come from a man who, late in life, had felt it was his vocation to teach and had come, for his probationary year, to St Barnabas and St James, where Miss Garnet had risen to the position of Head of the History Department. But he had been asked to leave after he had been observed hanging around the fifth-form girls' lockers after Games. Julia, who had regretted not obliging with the kiss, wept secretly into her handkerchief on hearing of Mr Kenton's departure. Later she plucked up courage to write to him, with news about the radical modern play he had been directing. Mr Maguire, Head of English, had had to take over – and in Miss Garnet's view the play had suffered as a consequence. Timidly, she had communicated this thought to the departed Mr Kenton but the letter had been returned with 'NOT KNOWN AT THIS ADDRESS' printed on the outside. Miss Garnet had found herself rather relieved and had silently shredded her single attempt at seduction into the rubbish bin.

'Where you off to then?' the young estate agent had asked, after they had agreed the terms on which the flat was to be let (no smoking, and no pets – out of respect to Stella).

Perhaps it was the young man's obvious indifference which acted as a catalyst to the surprising form she found her answer taking – for she had not, in fact, yet formulated in her mind where she might go, should the flat prove acceptable for letting to Messrs Brown & Noble.

Across Miss Garnet's memory paraded the several coloured advertisements for far-flung places which, along with some magazine cuttings concerning unsuitable hair dye, she had cleared from Harriet's oak bureau and which (steeling herself a little) she had recently placed in the dustbin. One advertisement had been for a cruise around the Adriatic Sea, visiting cities of historical interest. The most famous of these now flashed savingly into her mind.

'Venice,' she announced firmly. 'I shall be taking six months in Venice.' And then, because it is rarely possible, at a stroke, to throw off the habits of a lifetime, 'I believe it is cheaper at this time of year.'

*

It was cold when Miss Garnet landed at Marco Polo airport. Uncertain of all that she was likely to encounter on her exotic adventure she had at least had the foresight to equip herself with good boots. The well-soled boots provided a small counter to her sense of being somewhat insubstantial when, having collected her single suitcase with the stout leather strap which had been her mother's, she followed the other arrivals outside to where a man with a clipboard shouted and gestured.

Before her spread a pearl-grey, shimmering, quite alien waste of water.

'Zattere,' Miss Garnet enunciated. She had, through an agency found in the *Guardian*'s Holiday Section, taken an *appartamento* in one of the cheaper areas of Venice. And then, more distinctly, because the man with the clipboard appeared to pay no attention, 'Zattere!'

'*Si, si, Signora, momento, momento.*' He gestured at a water-taxi and then at a well-dressed couple who had pushed ahead of Miss Garnet in the shambling queue. '*Prego?*'

'Hotel Gritti Palace?' The man, a tall American with a spade-cut beard, spoke with the authority of money. Even Miss Garnet knew that the Gritti was one of the more exclusive of Venice's many expensive hotels. She had been disappointed to learn that a Socialist playwright, one whom she admired, was in the habit of taking rooms there each spring. Years ago, as a student teacher, Miss Garnet had, rather diffidently, joined the Labour Party. Over the years she had found the policies of succeeding leaders inadequately representative of her idea of socialism. Readings of first Marx and then Lenin had led her, less diffidently, to leave the Labour Party to join the Communists instead. Despite all that had happened in Europe over the years she saw no reason now to alter her allegiance to the ideology which had sustained her for so long. Indeed, it was partly Venice's reputation for left-wing activity which had underpinned her novel notion to reside there for six months. Now the long plane flight, the extreme cold rising off the grey-green lagoon waters and the extremer fear, rising from what seemed more and more like her own foolhardiness, joined force with political prejudice.

'Excuse me,' Miss Garnet raised her voice towards the polished couple, 'but I was first.' As she spoke she lost her footing, grazing her leg against a bollard.

The woman of the couple turned to examine the person from whom these commanding words had issued. She saw a thin woman of medium height wearing a long tweed coat and a hat with a veil caught back against the crown. The hat had belonged to Harriet and although Miss Garnet, when she had seen it on Harriet, had considered it overdramatic, she had found herself reluctant to relegate it to the Oxfam box. The hat represented, she recognised, a side to Harriet which she had disregarded when her friend was alive. As a kind of impulsive late gesture to her friend's sense of the theatrical, she had placed the hat onto her head in the last minutes before leaving for the airport.

Perhaps it was the hat or perhaps it was the tone of voice but the couple responded as if Miss Garnet was a 'somebody'. Maybe, they thought, she is one of the English aristocracy who consider it bad form to dress showily. Certainly the little woman with the delicately angular features spoke with the diction of a duchess.

'Excuse us,' the man spoke in a deep New England accent, 'we would be honoured if you would share our taxi.'

Miss Garnet paused. She was unaccustomed to accepting favours, especially from tall, urbane-mannered men. But she was tired and, she had to own, rather scared. Her knee hurt where she had stupidly bashed it. And there remained the fact that they had, after all, pushed in front of her.

'Thank you,' she spoke more loudly than usual so as to distract attention from the blood she feared was now seeping observably through her thick stocking, 'I should be glad to share with you.'

The American couple, concerned to undo any unintentional impoliteness, insisted the water-taxi take Miss Garnet to the Campo Angelo Raffaele, where the apartment she had rented was located. Miss Garnet had chosen the address, out of many similar possibilities, on account of the name. Devout Communist as she was, there was something reassuring about the Angel Raphael. She found the numerous other saintly figures, whose names attach to Venice's streets and monuments, unfamiliar and off-putting. The Angel Raphael she knew about. Of the Archangels of her Baptist childhood, Gabriel, Michael, Raphael, the latter had the most appeal.

The water-taxi drew up at shallow broad stone steps,

covered in a dangerous-looking green slime. Miss Garnet, holding back the long skirts of her coat, carefully stepped out of the boat.

'Oh, but you have hurt yourself!' cried the American woman, whose name, Miss Garnet had learned, was Cynthia.

But Miss Garnet, who was looking up, had caught the benevolent gaze of an angel. He was standing with a protective arm around what appeared to be a small boy carrying a large fish. On the other side of the angel was a hound.

'Thank you,' she said, slightly dazed, 'I shall be fine.' Then, 'Oh, but I must pay you,' she shouted as the boat moved off down the *rio*. But the Americans only waved smiling and shouted back that it could wait and she could pay what she owed when they all met again. 'Look after that leg, now,' urged the woman, and, 'Come to our hotel,' boomed the man, so loudly that three small boys on the other side of the canal called out and waved too at the departing boat.

Miss Garnet found that the departure of the newly met Americans left her feeling forlorn. Impatient with what seemed a silly show of sentimentality in herself, she caught up her suitcase and her hand luggage and looked about to get her bearings. Above her the angel winked down again and she now took in that this was the frontage of the Chiesa dell'Angelo Raffaele itself, which lent its name not only to the *campo* but also, most graciously, to the waterfront before it.

'*Scusi*,' said Miss Garnet to the boys who had crossed the brick bridge to inspect the new visitor, 'Campo Angelo

Raffaele?' She was rather proud and at the same time shy of the '*Scusi*'.

'*Si, si,*' cried the boys grabbing at her luggage. Just in time Miss Garnet managed to discern that their intentions were not sinister but they wished merely to earn a few lire by carrying her bags to her destination. She produced the paper on which she had written the address and proffered it to the tallest and most intelligent-looking boy.

'*Si, si!*' he exclaimed pointing across the square and a smaller boy, who had commandeered the suitcase, almost ran with it towards a flaking rose-red house with green shutters and washing hanging from a balcony.

The journey was no more than thirty metres and Miss Garnet, concerned not to seem stingy, became confused as to what she should tip the boys for their 'help'. She hardly needed help: the suitcase was packed with a deliberate economy and the years of independence had made her physically strong. Nevertheless it seemed churlish not to reward such a welcome from these attractive boys. Despite her thirty-five years of school teaching Miss Garnet was unused to receiving attentions from youth.

'Thank you,' she said as they clustered around the front door but before she had settled the problem of how to register her thanks properly the door opened and a middle-aged, dark-haired woman was there greeting her and apparently sending the boys packing.

'They were kind.' Miss Garnet spoke regretfully watching them running and caterwauling across the *campo*.

'*Si, si, Signora*, they are the boys of my cousin. They must help you, of course. Come in, please, I wait here for you to show you the apartment.'

Signora Mignelli had acquired her English from her years of letting to visitors. Her command of Miss Garnet's mother tongue made Miss Garnet rather ashamed of her own inadequacies in Signora Mignelli's. The Signora showed Miss Garnet to a small apartment with a bedroom, a kitchen-living room, a bathroom and a green wrought-iron balcony. '*No sole*,' Signora Mignelli waved at the white sky, 'but when there is . . . ah!' she unfolded her hands to indicate the blessings of warmth awaiting her tenant.

The balcony overlooked the *chiesa* but to the back of the building where the angel with the boy and the dog were not visible. Still, there was something lovely in the tawny brick and the general air of plant-encroaching dilapidation. Miss Garnet wanted to ask if the church was ever open – it had a kind of air as if it had been shut up for good – but she did not known how to broach such a topic as 'church' with Signora Mignelli.

Instead, her landlady told her where to shop, where she might do her laundry, how to travel about Venice by the *vaporetti*, the water buses which make their ways through the watery thoroughfares. The apartment's fridge already contained milk and butter. Also, half a bottle of *syrop*, coloured an alarming orange, presumably left by a former occupant. In the bread bin the Signora pointed out a long end of a crusty loaf and in a bowl a pyramid of green-leafed clementines. A blue glass vase on a sideboard held a clutch of dark pink anemones.

'Oh, how pretty,' said Miss Garnet, thinking how like some painting it all looked, and blushed.

'It is good, no?' said the Signora, pleased at the effect of her apartment. And then commandingly, 'You have a hurt? Let me see!'

Miss Garnet, her knee washed and dressed by a remonstrating Signora Mignelli, spent the afternoon unpacking and rearranging the few movable pieces in the rooms. In the sitting room she removed some of the numerous lace mats, stacked together the scattered nest of small tables and relocated the antiquated telephone – for, surely, she would hardly be needing it – to an out-of-the-way marble-topped sideboard.

The bedroom was narrow, so narrow that the bed with its carved wooden headboard and pearl-white crocheted coverlet almost filled it. On the wall over the bed hung a picture of the Virgin and Christ Child.

'Can't be doing with that,' said Miss Garnet to herself, and unhooking the picture from the wall she looked about for a place to store it. There were other pictures of religious subjects and, after consideration, the top of the ornately fronted wardrobe in the hallway seemed a safe spot to deposit all the holy pictures.

Going to wash her hands (in spite of the high cleanliness of the rooms the pictures were dusty) she found no soap and made that a reason for her first shopping expedition.

And really it was quite easy, she thought to herself, coming out of the *farmacia* with strawberry-scented soap, because Italian sounds made sense: *farmacia,* when you heard it, sounded like pharmacy, after all.

After three days Miss Garnet had become surprisingly (for she was unused to forming new habits) familiar with the neighbourhood. She shopped at one of the local greengrocers who spoke English, where the stacked piles of bright fruits and vegetables appeared, to an imagination nourished among the shops of Ealing, minor miracles of texture and colour. At the husband and wife grocers, the parmigiano cheese and the wafer-sliced prosciutto made her stomach rumble in anticipation of lunch and at the bakers she dithered almost frivolously over whether to buy one of the long crusty loaves which must be consumed within a day's span or the olive-bread, doughy and moist, which lasted if wrapped tight in a polythene bag.

Miss Garnet had not, so far, done more than wander around the neighbourhood and sleep. Before her departure she had gone to Stanfords of Covent Garden where she had purchased a learned-looking book, *Venice for Historians* by the Reverend Martin Crystal, MA (Oxon.). A brief survey suggested the content was sensibly historical and in view of the MA (Oxon.) she was prepared to overlook the title of 'Reverend'. But when with a sense of sober preparation she opened the Reverend Crystal, on more than one occasion she found herself falling asleep. She was rather ashamed of this new tendency for sleeping: nine or ten hours a night and, in addition, often a doze in the early afternoon, but nothing worked to abate it. In an effort to rise at eight, she set her alarm and woke at ten to find, defiant in half-sleep, she had depressed the switch to turn the ringer off. After that she succumbed to the narcolepsy and allowed it to overtake her.

It was after one such heavy afternoon doze that Miss Garnet woke to voices in the *campo* outside. Pulling on a cardigan she went to the window. A procession. Children running, singing, blowing speakers like rude tongues and toy trumpets; mothers with babies in their arms and older children in pushchairs. Amid them, magnificent in scarlet, blue and gold, walked three crowned kings.

One of the kings turned back towards her window and she recognised him. It was the tallest of the three boys who had helped her on her first day. She had half looked for the boys since. Seeing one of them now gave her her first sense of belonging. The boy-king smiled and waved up at her and she tried to open the window to the balcony. But, oh how maddening, it was stuck. She wrestled with the catch, pulled and wrenched, swore quite violently and had torn her thumbnail before she heaved her way outside and onto the balcony.

But the procession had left the *campo* and the last edges of it were already trailing over the brick bridge which crossed the Rio dell'Angelo Raffaele.

'Damn, damn, damn.' Miss Garnet was almost in tears at the disappointment of having missed the spectacle. She wondered if she ran downstairs at once and across the square after them all whether she could perhaps catch up with the colourful parade. But she felt fearful of making a fool of herself.

The loss of the procession produced a sudden drop in Miss Garnet's mood. She had been proud of her acquisition of local information which had produced a competence she had not foreseen. The regular, easy trips to the shops had begun already to create for her a stability, a base which had taken thirty-five years to build in Ealing. But now, the image of the smiling scarlet-robed boy, who had conducted her so courteously to Signora Mignelli's, threatened that security. Miss Garnet was not given to fancifulness but she felt almost as if the boy had picked up a stone from the dusty floor of the *campo* and hurled it deliberately at her. The laughing and chattering of the locals had about it the sharp ring of exclusion. It was not, she was sure, that they intended to exclude her — the few days Miss Garnet had already spent were sufficient to establish that these were not excluding people — but that she was entirely ignorant of what was of real importance to them. The event that had passed so vividly over the bridge had some meaning, to be sure, but what that meaning was remained a blank to her.

There was no refuge in a return to the soft, sagging bed from which she had recently awakened. She had slept too much already and the heavy-limbed lethargy, which had become familiar and acceptable, was replaced by a different quality of heaviness. Unpractised at introspection Miss Garnet nevertheless began to suspect she might be missing Harriet. The faint insight stirred a desire for physical activity.

Miss Garnet, who had been enjoying what Harriet would have called 'pottering about', had so far not ventured beyond the area around the Campo Angelo Raffaele. But now she felt it was time to assert her position as visitor. It was naive to pretend, as she had been doing, that in so short a space of time she had somehow 'fitted in'. She was a foreigner, after all, and here principally to see and learn about the historic sights of Venice.

The light afternoon was filled with mist, and Miss Garnet hesitated a moment before taking down Harriet's hat. 'A third of body heat is lost through the head,' her father, a fund of proverbial wisdoms, had used to say. It was cold and Harriet's hat, with its veil, might, after all, prove serviceable. Glancing at the looking-glass in the tall yellow wardrobe she gained a fleet impression of someone unknown: the black-spotted veil falling from the sleek crown acted as a kind of tonic to her herringbone tweed. The once unfashionably long coat, bridging the gap between one well-booted and one veiled extremity, had somehow acquired a sense of the stylish rather than the haphazard.

Miss Garnet was the reverse of vain but the sight of herself framed in the speckled looking-glass boosted her spirits. She felt more fortified against the sudden sweeping sense of strangeness which had assailed her. Taking from the bureau drawer the map of Venice she had purchased along with the Reverend Crystal, she unfolded it to plot a route.

But where to start? The glint of introspection which had just been ignited began to illuminate an insecurity: her parochial tendencies had been born of timidity, rather than a natural aptitude with the new locality. For all its apparent clarity she found the map bewildering. One location alone had any resonance for her: the Piazza San Marco, Venice's focal point. At least she knew about that from her teaching of history. She would go to the Piazza, from where the doges had once set out to wed the seas with rings.

Miss Garnet had chosen one of the further reaches of the almost-island-which-is-Venice to stay in and from this remoter quarter the walk to the Piazza San Marco takes time. Despite Signora Mignelli's instructions Miss Garnet did not yet feel equal to experimenting with the *vaporetti* and besides, exercise, she felt, was what was called for. She walked purposefully along the narrow *calle* which led down to the Accademia (where, the Reverend Crystal promised, a wealth of artistic treasure awaited her). At the wooden Accademia bridge she halted. Ahead of her, like a vast soap bubble formed out of the circling, dove-coloured mists, stood Santa Maria della Salute, the church which breasts the entrance to Venice's Grand Canal.

'Oh!' cried Miss Garnet. She caught at her throat and then at Harriet's veil, scrabbling it back from her eyes to see more clearly. And oh, the light! 'Lord, Lord,' sighed Julia Garnet.

She did not know why she had used those words as she moved off, frightened to stay longer lest the unfamiliar beauty so captivate her that she turn to stone, as she later amusingly phrased it to herself. But it was true it was a kind of fear she felt, almost as if she was fleeing some harrowing spectre who stalked her progress. Across another *campo*, then over bridges, along further alleys, past astonishing pastries piled high in gleaming windows, past shops filled with bottled liquor, alarming knives, swathes of patterned paper. Once she passed an artists' suppliers where, in spite of the spectre, she stopped to admire the window packed with square dishes heaped with brilliant coloured powders: *oro, oro pallido, argento, lacca rossa* – gold, silver, red, the colours of alchemy, thought Miss Garnet, hurrying on, for she had read about alchemy when she was teaching the Renaissance to the fifth form.

At the edge of the Piazza she halted. Let the spectre do its worst, for here was the culmination of her quest. Before her stood the campanile, the tall bell-tower, and behind it, in glimmering heaps and folds, in gilded wings and waved encrustations, emerged the outline of St Mark's. People might speak of St Mark's as a kind of dream but Miss Garnet had never known such dreams. Once, as a child, she dreamed she had become a mermaid; that was the closest she had ever come to this.

Measuring each step she walked across the Piazza. Although still afternoon the sky was beginning to darken and already a pearl fingernail clipping of moon was appearing, like an inspired throwaway gesture designed to point up the whole effect of the basilica's sheen. Reaching the arched portals Miss

Garnet stopped, wondering if it was all right to go on. But it must be, look there were other tourists – how silly she was, of course one didn't have to be a Christian to enter and inspect a renowned example of Byzantine architecture.

Inside the great cathedral before her a line of people shuffled forward. Above her, and on all sides, light played and danced from a million tiny surfaces of refracted gold. A dull smell of onions disconcertingly filled her nostrils. What was it? Years of sweat, perhaps, perfusing the much-visited old air.

There appeared to be a restriction on where one might walk, for barriers and ropes were prohibiting entrances here, blocking ingress there. 'But why are *those* people allowed?' queried Miss Garnet. For there were men and women but mostly, it must be said, the latter, moving into the great interior space from which the swaying line of visitors was debarred. She stopped before an official in navy uniform. '*Vespero?*' he enquired and '*Si, si,*' she found herself replying for whatever it was she was not going to be shut out a second time that day.

The official detached the wine-coloured rope from its catch and ushered the Signora in the black veil through. 'Look, it's our little duchess,' Cynthia Cutforth exclaimed to her husband. 'She's joining the service, she must be a Roman Catholic. See how cute she looks in her veil.'

But Miss Garnet was oblivious to all but the extraordinary surroundings in which she now found herself. Silver lamps burned dimly in the recesses. Above her and on all sides loomed strange glittering mosaic figures, in a background of unremitting gold. A succession of images – lions, lambs, flowers, thorns, eagles, serpents, dragons, doves – wove before her startled eyes a shimmering vision, awful and benign. Like blood forcing a route through long-constricted arteries a kind of wild rejoicing began to cascade through her. Stumbling slightly she made her way to a seat on the main aisle.

There was a thin stapled book of paper on the seat and picking it up she saw 'Vespero Epifania'. Of course! Epiphany. How stupid she had been. January the sixth was the English Twelfth Night when the Lord of Misrule was traditionally abroad and one took down one's Christmas decorations to avert ill luck. But here, in a Catholic country, the journey of the Magi, who followed the star with their gifts for the baby who was born in the manger, was still celebrated. That was the meaning of the three kings who had graced the Campo Angelo Raffaele that afternoon.

Later, as Miss Garnet emerged from the service the crescent moon had vanished from the sky and instead a lighted tree was shining at the far end of the Piazza. Along the colonnades, which framed the square, hung lavish swags of evergreen, threaded and bound with gold and scarlet ribbon. They do not bother to avert ill luck here, thought Miss Garnet as she retraced her way home. There was a peace in her heart which she did not quite understand. But, as she paced unafraid towards the Campo Angelo Raffaele she understood enough not to ask the meaning of it.

*

When she had returned to Signora Mignelli's apartment, Miss Garnet, who had never in her life gone to bed without first hanging up her clothes, had simply stepped out of them, shoes, coat, hat, blouse, skirt, petticoat, underwear, all, and left them, an untidy pool, in the middle of the marble floor. They were the first thing she found the following morning. Reaching up to the top of the wardrobe to put away Harriet's hat, her hand knocked against something and the picture of the Virgin and Child crashed to the ground.

The picture itself seemed unharmed but the glass was broken. Dismayed, Miss Garnet examined it. The Virgin's calm visage stared out through shards of glass. I will have to find a glass-cutter, determined Miss Garnet.

Outside some boys were kicking a football and among them she recognised the tallest Magi. 'Scusi,' called Miss Garnet from the balcony and the boy ran across and stood politely below. She held up the fractured glass. 'Scusi. Broken.'

Surprisingly, the boy appeared to comprehend. He beckoned vigorously, indicating that she should join him. Miss Garnet bundled herself back into her coat and hat. Shoving the Virgin and Child into a polythene bag she hurried down the stairs. Some letters on the mat caught her attention; two had British stamps and she pushed them into her pocket, adjusting Harriet's veil with her other hand.

Outside, in the cold sunlight, the boy was waiting.

'You want glass?' he asked.

Miss Garnet was astonished. 'You speak English!' she cried

and then, thinking this sounded too like an accusation, 'you speak very well.'

'Thank you.' The boy lowered his eyelashes in appreciation. 'My father say if I speak English good he send me to *Londra*.'

'Oh, then perhaps you would like to speak it with me?'

She spoke slowly but the boy did not immediately understand. Then he favoured her with a perfect smile. '*Si, Signora*, I speak with you. My name is Nicco.'

Miss Garnet, unused to such physical charm, blushed. 'Hello, Nicco, my name is . . .' but how was the child going to manage 'Miss Garnet'? So, 'Julia,' she concluded and blushed again.

Nicco smiled showing stunning teeth. 'You want glass, Giulia?'

With a child's acceptance he did not ask her how the accident had occurred but simply led her over bridges and along a *calle* until they reached a shop on the *fondamenta* where a man with a workman's rubber apron and a red woollen hat sat over a wide sheet of brilliant blue glass. Nicco turned to his companion. 'Here,' he said, proudly, 'glass.'

Miss Garnet offered the broken Virgin awkwardly to the man in the hat to whom Nicco was speaking rapidly. 'Please,' she said, 'can you mend?'

Seeing the picture the man smiled broadly. Miss Garnet was relieved to notice that his teeth, unlike Nicco's, were in a state of bad repair. 'Bellini!' he exclaimed, '*Bellissimo* Bellini,' and he kissed his fingers in a way that Miss Garnet had seen only in films or on TV.

'He likes very much,' Nicco gravely explained.

'But he can do it, he will mend the glass?'

In reply the man with the woolly hat held up a thick forefinger. '*Si, Signora,* in wan ower, OK?' He spoke with exaggerated enunciation, displaying his tarry teeth.

What a relief, Miss Garnet said to herself and then, because she was jubilant that she had negotiated her first Venetian disaster, 'Nicco, may I buy you lunch?'

Nicco, who did not at first understand her suggestion, became enthusiastic when the penny dropped. He led her to a Trattoria-Bar where he ordered a toasted cheese and ham sandwich and a Coke. Miss Garnet, daringly, chose gnocchi. The gnocchi came in a pale green sauce and was the most delicious thing she thought she had ever tasted. '*Carciofi,*' Nicco said, when asked for the name of the green ingredient and cupped his hands in an effort to mimic an artichoke. She did not understand and then became distracted by the sudden appearance of a large glass of what appeared to be brandy.

'For you,' Nicco said proudly. 'Is my cousin.' He pointed at the young man who had produced the drink. 'He say "Hi!".'

'*Freddo!*' Nicco's cousin clapped his arms around himself to indicate cold.

Miss Garnet was not a teetotaller but she rarely drank. A lifetime of abstemiousness had bred in her a poor head for alcohol. Nevertheless it seemed impolite to decline the courtesy. And really the brandy was most acceptable, she thought, as she sipped the contents of the big-bellied glass.

'My cousin say, you like another?'

'No, please, it was delicious. Please thank him, Nicco, just the bill.'

Miss Garnet felt unusually jolly as she and Nicco walked single file along the side of the green canal back to the glass-cutter. The light, refracting off the water on to the shabby brick frontages of the houses, bathed her eyes. The brandy had warmed her and a sense of wellbeing suffused her body.

Re-entering the glass-cutter's Miss Garnet nearly knocked into a man on his way out and almost dropped the purse she had ready, so eager was she to complete the transaction which would restore Signora Mignelli's picture. The glass-cutter had the repaired Virgin out on his bench but when Miss Garnet began to count the notes from her purse Nicco, who had been exchanging some banter with the departing customer, stopped her.

'Is free,' he explained.

Miss Garnet did not comprehend. 'Three what, Nicco? Thousand, million?' She prided herself on her mental arithmetic but the huge denominations of Italian currency still tripped her up.

'No, no, is free.'

'Oh, but I can't . . .'

The glass-cutter was holding up the picture, excitedly stabbing at the Virgin's face. '*Bellissimo*,' he insisted, '*per niente* – is now charge. I give yow.'

*

Following Nicco back along the *fondamenta* Miss Garnet felt both subdued and elated. The refusal of the glass-cutter to accept a fee troubled her; and yet his powerful assertion of his own autonomy was also exhilarating. Karl Marx, she couldn't help thinking, would have approved even if he would have deplored the glass-cutter's motive. A love of the Virgin Mary would have struck Marx as a sign of subjection and yet one could not, really one could not, Miss Garnet mused, trying to keep up with Nicco's pace, describe the man she had met as subject to anyone.

'He like this artist,' Nicco had explained. But Miss Garnet, in whom insight, like an incipient forest fire, was beginning to catch and creep, sensed suddenly there was more to it than that. The glass-cutter, she guessed, also liked the subject of Bellini's painting and his love of Mary, and the *bambino* in her arms, was stronger than his love of money. How would Marx or even Lenin have explained that, she wondered as they arrived on the *fondamenta* alongside the Chiesa dell'Angelo Raffaele.

The Archangel smiled down at her and she remembered she had questions about the boy with the fish and the hound.

'Nicco, who is the boy up there with the dog?' She pointed to the stone effigies which were lodged two-thirds up the church's façade.

But Nicco had other appointments. His pride in his new role as translator and guide was now giving way to peer anxiety. There was a football fixture he could not afford to miss. He shrugged.

'Tobiolo?' he said, uncertainly. 'I see you again. *Ciao*, Giulia!'

And, *'Ciao!'* Julia Garnet called after him watching his young shoulders as he ran across the bridge and disappeared behind the church.

The sun was a pale gold disc in the sky. Some words filtered into memory.

*When the Sun rises, do you not see a round disk of fire, somewhat like a Guinea? O no, no, I see an Innumerable company of the Heavenly host crying, 'Holy, Holy, Holy!'
. . . I question not my Corporeal Eye any more than I would Question a Window . . . I look thro' it and not with it.*

William Blake. Years ago she had been invited to contribute a chapter on Blake for a book on Radical Thinkers but somehow the project had never got off the ground. William Blake had been a revolutionary but had he not also been whipped by his father for seeing angels in the trees? *Oro pallido*, she thought to herself, crossing, in the lowering light, the bridge where Nicco had sped before her. This was not a morning sun on fire, like Blake's, but pale wintery gold — *oro pallido*.

The letters which had been delivered from England were from Brown & Noble, the estate agents who had let the flat and her friend, Vera Kessel. Vera, a fellow member of the Communist Party, had been at Cambridge with Julia Garnet.

They had not been close as students but a few years later had recognised each other at a Party meeting and, thereafter, had occasionally gone on holidays to Dubrovnik or to the Black Sea together. The holidays had been bleak affairs, nothing like the trips Harriet had planned for their retirement.

The letters had been, in fact, forgotten until looking for her left glove she found them stuffed into the pocket of her coat. She opened them while the kettle boiled for tea.

Dear Miss Garnet,

This letter confirms a tenancy of six months to Mr. A. D. Akbar at a rental of £1,200 p.c.m. We remind you of our terms of 12% to include insurance and collection fees. £1,006.00 (plus one month's deposit) has been transferred to your account today and thereafter £1,006.00 until 3 June. Trusting in your continued satisfaction.

Yours etc.

'To the eye of a miser a Guinea is more beautiful than the Sun,' murmured Miss Garnet, recalling some more of the words of the visionary poet which had come to her by the canal, and she opened the other envelope.

Dear Julia,

Just a brief card to wish you well in benighted Italy! How are you getting along with the RC God squad? Pretty oppressive I should imagine but I hope the history makes up for it.

We had a disappointing meeting about the unions last week.

*Ted spoke well as usual but much of the life has gone out of
the comrades. All send greetings and solidarity.*

Best, Vera.

For a moment Julia Garnet remembered the impoverished
little ceremony with which she had bidden Harriet a final
farewell, and the utilitarian stone with the severely practical
information carved upon its stony face, with which she had
chosen to mark the passing of her closest friend's life. She
wished now she had paid the funeral more attention. Harriet's
large, mild face hovered before her – somehow she could
not quite get used to the idea that Harriet was no more.

She turned down the flame beneath the saucepan of water
and added two tea bags. The kitchen was equipped with
neither kettle nor teapot. At first she had minded, her cup
of tea being a regular point in her routine, but now she
enjoyed the slightly Bohemian feel to her saucepan tea-making.
No 'love' in Vera's letter. After nearly forty-five years'
acquaintance 'Best' was all Vera could manage.

The following morning Julia Garnet, this time with the Rev.
Crystal in the pocket of her tweed coat ('For really I must,'
she insisted to herself, 'find out about this city'), returned to
the basilica of St Mark. She entered not by the main door
but by a less frequented doorway on the north side. It did
not deter her that this side-slip into the cathedral was marked
'Per Pregare' – 'For Prayer'.

Inside, by long, hanging red and silver lamps, a door was

open onto a side chapel. With no special thought in her mind she entered.

About a dozen people sat, in the vaulted, ancient-looking surroundings, listening to a priest reading from a leather book. Julia Garnet looked around. At one end of the chapel a blue mosaic of a huge Madonna gazed down; at the other, a tomb on which rested an inclined marmoreal figure observed by an angel. Twelve candles burned on the table before the tomb.

The priest came to the end of his reading and sat down. There was a pause during which Julia Garnet waited for something to happen. After a while it became apparent that nothing was going to happen, except the silence.

Her first response was annoyance. The Vespers in St Mark's had been dramatic: the flute voices of the clerics, the melodic bells, the incense, the enthralling rhythmic passing and return of the litany-chant thrown between priest and congregation – compared with the threnodic splendour of all that, this abrupt nothingness felt like a cheat. But after a while she began to enjoy the silence. She looked round at the mosaics which seemed to depict some awful martyrdom – certainly there was a body and a tomb and, yes, surely that was the same body being removed from the tomb, and here how eagerly it was being hauled away. There was a kind of ebullience in the narrative which she made out on the chapel walls as if the dead man had, if not enjoyed, at least participated energetically in his own persecution.

She twisted her neck to look back at the blue Madonna and found a man in a serge suit staring beadily at her, as if his was the task of checking her credentials to be present at the ceremony and was hopeful of finding them wanting. Abashed, she turned from the Madonna to examine the other attenders.

All were women and one, two, three, four, five, six – no seven of them in furs. Now there was a thing! Feeling in the pocket of her own tweed she remembered Vera's letter and almost she started to laugh. What would Vera make of her sitting here in church among seven furs? And which would Vera abhor most? The chapel or the wealth? All the furs were elderly save one: a woman with a long daffodil pony-tail and high gold heels. 'Tarty,' Harriet would have called her. (Vera very likely would not have known how to use the word.) But Mary Magdalene had been a tart, hadn't she? It was surprising how much you remembered of your school scriptures, thought Julia Garnet.

There was a disturbance now at the door and three nuns dressed in white robes entered. They looked like an African order with their smooth brown skins – but so young! The nuns, and really they were no more than children, heavily crossing themselves knelt, so that Julia Garnet could see their thick-soled boots. Now one of them was elaborately prostrating herself and kissing the ground while the grave fur-clad ladies sat decorously in impeccable silence. How irritating the young nuns were, and how out of place the kissing and the boots amid the unspeaking elegance. She was relieved to see them depart, noisily snatching at the water in a carved high stoup by the door. Around the bowl more angels.

One of the silent furred ones was wearing a wide-brimmed emerald hat. The woman was no younger than herself and. Julia Garnet found she wanted just such a hat too. But surely this was not what the silence was for? Designing a wardrobe! Gently, like dripping honey, the quiet filled her pores, comforting as the dreamless sleeps she had fallen prey to. The angel over the inclining man gestured at the heavens; beneath. him, another angel on the tomb looked with all-seeing, sightless eyes towards the angels on the holy-water stoup . . . *I see an Innumerable company of the Heavenly host crying, 'Holy, Holy, Holy!* . . .' The silence was holy. What did 'holy' mean? Did it mean the chance to be whole again? But when had one ever been whole? Silently, silently the priest sat and in the nameless peace Julia Garnet sat too, thinking no thoughts.

A slight stir on her right and someone had entered and was wanting to take the place beside her. A man crossing himself, but discreetly, thank God. Removing the Rev. Crystal from the seat she smelled tobacco and instantly her father was there, not in the days when he would remind her that cleanliness was next to godliness but in those last days when he was losing his mind and could smoke only under supervision. She had had to apologise to the nurses. 'I am so sorry, he doesn't know what he is saying,' she had said, hearing with shame her self-righteous father's demonic curses. And they would smile and tell her not to worry, it was all in a day's work. But he did know what he was saying, Julia Garnet thought. And the nurses knew he knew.

And now the priest had risen to his feet and they were all on their feet a little after him and a man with a bell had arrived and incense. Fervently, praise was given to 'Signore', (how nice that God should be a humble mister!) and there was singing and the amen. And then the furs were chatting to each other while she stood and drank in the blue Madonna and her stiff, truthful baby.

'You like our treasures?'

It was the man who had sat beside her.

'How did you know I was English?'

As if it were a reply the man said, 'I have friends in England.' Then, nodding at the mosaics, 'Do you know the story?' and enlivened for her the story of the removal of the saint's remains. 'We Venetians always take what we want,' he laughed, and his eyes crinkled; a tall man, with white hair and a moustache.

Coming down the steps beside her into the darkening Piazzetta he said, 'Look, another example of our looting,' pointing to the two high columns. 'St Theodore with his crocodile was once our patron saint. But in fact this is not St Theodore at all — it is a Hellenistic statue which we have taken for our own. And opposite, you see, the lion of St Mark is not a lion at all — a chimera from the Levant we stuck wings on. All stolen! The columns too. Would you honour me by taking a glass of prosecco, perhaps?' and he smiled, so that she omitted to say she had suddenly remembered she had left the Rev. Crystal behind on the chapel floor.

Instead, why not? she decided, for no one waited for her

return but aloud she said merely, 'Thank you very much. That would be delightful.' and felt proud of herself that she had added no objection.

'Good. I take you to Florian's.'

'But is this not very expensive?' she could not prevent herself saying ten minutes later, as they sat, all gilt fruit and mirrored warmth, under the wreathed colonnades surrounding the Piazza.

'But of course!' The man who had introduced himself as Carlo crinkled his eyes again. 'Next time I shall take you to the bar where the gondoliers meet. But for a first meeting it must be Florian's.'

Julia Garnet felt something she had felt previously only under pressure or fear. It was as if the bubbles in the pale gold glass had passed through her stomach up into her heart. '*Oro pallido*,' she said speaking the words aloud.

Her companion frowned. 'Excuse me?'

'Oh, I'm so sorry. I was trying to say the words for pale gold – the drink. It is delicious.'

'Ah! *Oro pallido*, I did not understand. Prosecco is our Italian secret. I think it is nicer than champagne but my French friends will kill me if they hear this!'

'Your English is very good.'

He was, he explained, an art historian, who had worked at the Courtauld Institute in London for several years. Now he was a private art dealer, buying and selling mainly in Rome, a little in London, sometimes Amsterdam. But Venice was his home. His mother was dead but he had kept on her old *appartamento* – he returned when he could – he had cousins, an aunt.

'And you?' he asked. 'You have a husband, children?' and she was grateful for she felt sure he could see that she did not. 'But what a shame!' He spoke lightly. 'You are such a pretty woman,' and she hardly blushed at all but said, 'Thank you very much,' gravely, as if he had opened a door for her, or gathered up a dropped parcel. And she did not ask if he were married.

Carlo asked where she was staying and she explained about Signora Mignelli and the Campo Angelo Raffaele. Perhaps it was his enquiry about the husband and children she did not have which found her telling him also about Nicco. 'I seem to have acquired a young pupil here,' unaware of the covert pride in her voice. And when he nodded and smiled encouragingly, 'I am teaching him English,' she explained, conscious of some exaggeration in this claim, for Nicco so far showed little enthusiasm for learning her language.

Carlo, however, listened with polite attention. He gave her his card, and insisted on escorting her home by the *vaporetto* which dropped them at S. Basilio, the stop nearest to her new home.

'I won't ask you in.' Julia Garnet spoke carefully. The combination of the water-journey and the prosecco had gone to her head (that was twice in two days she had been tipsy). 'I have nothing to offer you but tea and I am sure you have a supper to go to.'

'Another day I should be charmed. You stay in one of the most beautiful *campi* in Venezia!'

Easy, murmured Julia Garnet inwardly, and she thanked her handsome host and hurried across the bridge past Veronese's church where they were too poor to have a sacristan. 'Easy, girl,' she said aloud later, taking off her stockings. It was a manner of address the rag-and-bone man, who had driven about Ealing when she was still a young teacher, had used to his horse. A white horse, called Lily, she seemed to think, as she stood, barefoot on the cold floor, running a bath.

The following morning, passing the side-door of the *chiesa*, she saw a man with an oversized key unlocking the church.

In reply to her finger pointing questioningly at the interior, he indicated that she should enter. *'Prego!'* He shuffled ahead of her, attending to duties in the dimness of the interior.

One by one small pools of illumination flicked on and Julia Garnet stood amid the gathered half-light. She turned around. It was the first time she had been in a proper church (you couldn't really count St Mark's) since she didn't know when. The funeral of a colleague at school in an ugly C. of E. church in Acton; that must have been the last time. And how cold it had been then, and how she had resented the Actonish odour of bourgeois sanctity. But why was this different? For a second her mind flickered guiltily to the Reverend Crystal. He, to be sure, would have had safe and solid information to convey on such points.

She sniffed the hazy air. The odour here was dry and musty

too but there was a fragrance about it. How sensible to scent your place of worship. The incense, of course, it was the incense, like the frankincense brought by one of the kings. Gold, frankincense and myrrh. Were there reasons for the gifts? She couldn't remember.

The sacristan came forward now, pointing to an organ above the door which opened on to the water-front and then at an assortment of leaflets on a small table. To please him she picked one up from the pile marked 'English'. 'Tobiolo and the Angel Raffael.' Looking up, painted on the organ loft, she saw an angel with azure wings.

Despite his wings the angel seemed to be marching forward, grasping the hand of a young man who, in turn, was looking back, his hand stretched beseechingly after an old man who stood staring after the departing pair. Beside him, her head averted, a woman – perhaps his wife? And look! Before them all a small black and white spotted dog. She followed the story round.

Now the boy Tobiolo appeared to have caught a giant fish in his handkerchief while the dog looks on admiringly. And the angel, this time wearing a handsome and surely anachronistic blue waistcoat, stands rather like a proud parent at speech day in the background.

Here was another scene: the young man kneeling with a young woman now, she dressed in gauzy clothes. And now the young pair are kneeling before the angel by a bed, a mysterious fire burning in a pan while the dog huddles as if scared in a far corner.

In the next scene the young man is back with the older man, who lies back as if in astonishment, and now the young woman is there too. Over them the angel broods with azure wings.

In the final scene the angel seems to be taking his leave: unfurled and aloft, a cloud of pink and blue; his lovely limbs and sturdy feet are displayed in glory, as the young and the old man marvel and the dog looks longingly after him.

Something rusty and hard shifted deep inside Julia Garnet as she stood absorbing the vivid, dewy painting, the joyfulness of the conception and the unmistakable compassion in the angel's bright glance. Her eyes filled. The door of the church opened and light streamed into the interior, bringing with it a tall figure. To her horror she saw that it was the man she had met the previous day at St Mark's and hastily she pushed away tears.

'My friend!' He was smiling again and for a second she was irked: it wasn't, well, *manly* to smile quite so often. Then, ashamed of her xenophobic instincts, she tried to smile back herself.

'I was looking at these.' Such feeble language to describe the treasures she had stumbled on.

'Ah! The Guardis!'

'You know them?' But why should she be surprised? He was an art historian and probably everyone in Venice knew of the paintings. Julia Garnet was annoyed to find herself possessive of her new discovery.

'Oh, indeed. They are famous. There exists a famous

quarrel, also, about their authorship. There are two Guardis, you see, an elder by many years, Giannantonio, and a younger, Francesco, who never did any known painting of a religious nature. Some authorities, because of the superb style, ascribe it to the younger, better-known brother. But others, of whom I am one, are passionate for the elder. It is a great dispute!'

'And the story?' She did not so much care who painted the angel – it was the fact that he had been painted that was so miraculous.

'It is from the Jewish Scriptures – you call it, I think, Tobias and the Angel?'

He took the crook of her arm and they walked about the tall, theatrical, shabby church while he recounted the story of the young Tobias who travels, unaware he is accompanied by the Archangel Raphael, seeking a cure for his father's blindness.

'The cure is found in a great fish but before this Tobiolo has married and saved a young woman, cursed by a demon. The demon rests inside her, killing, on their wedding night, the young men who try her virginity. Seven men have died before Tobiolo arrives but, of course, he has the Angel Raphael to help him.'

'And does he help?'

'Certainly. He instructs Tobiolo how he must burn the heart and the liver of the fish and so' – like a conjuror, Carlo waved a hand – 'the demon is driven out, *cursing*.' He grimaced, imitating the departing spirit.

'And this is in the Old Testament?' Surely this was some

racy Catholic version of the Bible. His sudden impersonation of the demon slightly disconcerted her.

'Oh, indeed, I assure you. It is a tale of wonder, is it not?'

'More like magic, I should think. Why does the angel help?'

But Carlo gave a little shrug as if he had become bored with the topic. He had called, he explained, to find out how she was and to invite her, if it would amuse her, to a concert that evening. Julia Garnet could think of no reason why she should not accept the invitation. The Reverend Crystal could never have instructed her so entertainingly – nor, perhaps, with such authority. Later, as she stood before the sparse collection which made up her wardrobe, exercised by what to wear for the evening's entertainment, she allowed herself to wonder what so personable a man wanted with so dowdy a companion as herself?

 I am an old man near the end of my life – although my son lies and protests this is not so. (He is a good son, in spite of the lies.) You may ask what an old man of one hundred and eighty-five years can have to say to interest you? The secret of my longevity, perhaps? Well, it may be that our years are not reckoned as you reckon yours. But even allowing for differences I would say we live close to the cycle of the sun and moon, we rise and go to bed with

the birds, labour hard, eat frugally and these things conspire towards longevity; but I will hazard there is another thing more important than these: it may be we may live long because there is something we value above human life – I shall not give it a name!

Among our people the old are respected for their wisdom – I hope it may be the same with yours. However it is with you, if you are young now you might hold it in your mind that one day you too will be old and may find yourself glad then to be heard; if you are already old, perhaps like me you already have a story to tell (for all lives, I think, have some sort of a story in them)? Yet I do not tell my own because I wish it, or because I wish to instruct you in how to live, though I'll admit that might once have been my purpose. No, I tell you this because I was told to tell it – by what you might call 'a higher authority' – and truth is, the thought of how to tell it has taxed me for many years.

I promised so long ago to set all this down but you know how it is when you make a promise? There is that small serpent voice inside which says, 'No need to bother about it now,' or 'Later will do better,' or (most true in my case) 'Give me time to understand.' Thinking leads to a kind of weighing of words which holds back action. But now I feel the shadow of the Angel of Death upon me and I do not think I have much more time.

At first it was not only that I did not understand but that I did not even know *how* to begin to understand. What happened to me and my family was so remarkable that I believed I should bungle the telling of it. But I was only a third through my life when these events took place. Nowadays I have come to see that bungling is what all of us do; perhaps bungling is what we are here for?

I would like to begin at the beginning if I only knew when the 'beginning' starts. Some might say it was when we were first fashioned out of the mud of the great River Tigris, before our wives were pulled out of our ribs to create a source of perpetual reproof to us! (That is my little joke: I call my wife, Anna, 'Rib'; I have an idea this oft-repeated joke of mine annoys her but she is a generous woman and mostly puts up with her husband's trying ways.)

Or maybe the 'beginning' was later, when our first parents lost their paradise (which some say was here between the two rivers, which the traders still call 'garden' on account of its great fertileness) and had to make their way in the world? From the time of our first parents our people were wanderers – until the patriarch Abram came from Ur into the land which was then called Canaan. Later our people found their way into Egypt – and out again, through the vision of Moses, who we call 'Liberator', by a path through the Sea-of-Reeds. In time we returned to the land which was promised us, provided we did not 'play the harlot' with other gods.

In those days the twelve tribes inhabited two kingdoms and there was bad feeling between the northern country and the south. Perhaps northerners will always be slow to toe the line where the south is concerned? Among the northern tribes there were many who did play the harlot. In my own young days already my own tribe of Naphtali had begun to sacrifice in secret to the old gods (more persuadable than our own with gifts of oil or barley) and I alone travelled to the kingdom in the south, to Jerusalem, the holy city, to the temple with the brazen pillars, the ornaments of gold and ivory and lapis lazuli, and the walls lined in cedar-wood from Lebanon by Solomon, son of David, who ruled over both our kingdoms. I alone kept faith and went with my first fruits and firstlings and the first shearings of sheep and one tithe of all my corn and wine and oil and pomegranates; but my kin openly gave their tithes to the heifer Baal, and in the end my own tribe was led captive, to Nineveh, in the land of Assyria, and the other tribes were scattered among the far cities of Media, a proverb of reproach to all the nations among whom we are dispersed. But you see, from the first it was our way to be sojourners and strangers!

2

When Julia Garnet looked back on this period of her life she remembered it as a time in which she discovered excitement. The concert to which Carlo took her, that first evening, was in an old *scuola*, with dark, painted ceilings, coffered, gilded and carved. She sat listening to Vivaldi, Albinoni, Corelli – triumphant musical spirits of Venice – played by a quintet of pretty girls in long frocks and wild-haired young men.

The musicians looked too young to understand the gaiety of the music they played. Yet when they attacked their fiddles, their violas and their cellos they communicated an energetic vibrancy which sent the blood around the body leaving one, Julia Garnet reflected, positively tingling. Thinking of the dismally picked out hymns of her childhood piano lessons she became humble. 'I could never have played like that!' She stood, slightly chilly, in the marble hall during the interval. Beside them, around white Venetian necks, luxuriated copious fur tippets and wraps.

'This I do not believe.' Carlo took off his jacket and whisked it, with the adroitness of a matador, around her shoulders and when she tried to demur: 'No, no,' smiling as ever, 'this is our Venetian way. The woman is for cherishing!'

This was the first of many outings – more than she could ever have believed anyone would want to take with her, let alone this tall, cultivated man who – though nearing seventy, he assured her – was, in the old-fashioned style, undeniably handsome. Sometimes they would go to a concert and afterwards they would dine at one of many out-of-the-way restaurants where he was greeted like a long-lost son; or he would suggest a visit to a church where in rich glooms he pointed out altarpieces with obscure stories from the Catholic scriptures, unknown to Protestant histories; or he steered her, always charmingly holding the crook of her arm, through rooms of the Accademia, where she learned to look at painters whose names were formerly not even names to her, Bassano, Longhi, Vivarini. Their reds and golds and blues, in tones she had been used to deriding as 'showy' (for the paintings of Lowry had formerly been her highest notion of art), somewhat dazed her eyes. In one room she stopped, overcome by the eight great canvases which lined the four walls. 'Carpaccio,' he said, amused at her evident delight. 'Carpaccio, I always say, is the prosecco among painters — he is another of our Venetian secrets!'

One of the canvases in particular held her attention: a high, square room infiltrated with a quiet dawn light; on one side of the painting a simple bed, with a woman tranquilly asleep — opposite, at the threshold of a lighted door, an angel in blue with dusky wings, just standing. Looking at the angel waiting with such stillness, Julia Garnet felt something like a small shudder pass through her.

On another occasion, at the Peggy Guggenheim museum, he had made her blush horribly by pointing out the tumescent angel who exposes his proud member in all its glory to the passing watercraft. ('Oh, I assure you, it unscrews when visitors from the church come!') Afterwards he had bought her marigolds from a narrow shop crammed with flowers, and she knew it was by way of apology for having embarrassed her. That night she lay awake, hating herself for her damnable strait-laced upbringing, so that by morning she had schooled herself not to expect him (for how could so urbane a man put up with such unsophistication in a grown woman?). But he had appeared, as usual, across the *campo*, smiling as if nothing had happened, and her heart had turned over and over in joy as she stood waving from the balcony.

Once she had succumbed to a fit of sneezing and he had pressed his handkerchief upon her, warm from his trouser pocket. She had tried not to use it, trusting to his impeccable manners not to ask for its return, aware already that later she would put it away unwashed in her drawer beside the book which pressed one of the embarrassing marigolds.

Although she kept his card in her handbag, she held back, unwilling to put his desire to see her to the test, from ever initiating their meetings. And yet he gave ample proofs of seeking out the friendship.

Usually it was the afternoons when Carlo would come by looking for her. Signora Mignelli, made familiar by the leveller of sex, got to teasing her about her 'friend'.

In Carlo's company Julia Garnet felt herself become more feminine: she bought a black skirt and a daringly wide-lapelled cream silk blouse – to wear at the concerts. She even patrolled the back streets, half-looking for an emerald hat such as she had seen on the woman in the little chapel in St Mark's, but found nothing she liked well enough to fuel the courage necessary for the purchase.

One day, returning home after such a search (she had hovered over a red hat but prudence finally had overruled her) Julia Garnet paused outside a shop which sold linen and embroidered tablecloths. The tablecloths reminded her of her mother, whose only acts of rebellion against her husband had been expressed in an obsessive purchase of linen. Julia Garnet had stood, rather yearningly, gazing at the flowers picked out in coloured silks, until the proprietor, sensing a sale, had come out and pestered her and she had hurried on down a small alley which ran beside the shop.

It was many years since Julia Garnet had risked taking a short cut (short cuts she associated with laziness) and she felt a slight agitation at having left her familiar route. And yet there was that sense of exploration too, which had been developing since her arrival in Venice.

The first month had almost passed, accelerated by the novelty of her new companion. And he had aided that adventurousness which the loss of Hariet had first sparked. Almost, Julia Garnet thought as she hurried down the dark alley (as if the tablecloths had taken off and were in ghostly pursuit), almost it was as if Harriet's soul had poured down Harriet's own meagre stock of boldness upon her, a last gift to the friend she was leaving for ever.

Goodness, how fanciful she was getting! And yet the idea of possessing a soul no longer seemed quaint. And, to be sure, if one had a soul how much nicer to let it wander here in Venice. As she ruminated upon the desirability of a good environment for one's afterlife, the alley turned into a narrow *campo*, one which she had never penetrated before.

One of the old stone-carved wellheads with which Venice is endowed was situated slightly off the centre of the area, and to its left stood a small, rounded Romanesque building, with what seemed to be a statue of an angel on the roof, half-covered in scaffolding.

Miss Garnet, moved by her new spirit of adventure, walked slowly round seeking some clue to the building's function. It was unclear whether it was a church, although the general shape of the architecture indicated that it was built for some devotional purpose.

Moving closer to determine the purpose of the building better, Julia Garnet was startled by a shout.

'Hey, watch it! Mind Out!'

The voice came from above her head, and for a second it flashed across her startled mind that the angel himself had addressed her, before a blue-clad pair of legs brought a distinctly human shape into sight.

'Didn't you see the notice?'

'Notice?' Julia Garnet's first reaction was one of annoyance. For the second time she had been 'found out' as English: the stranger who had descended in so surprising a way from the scaffold above had instinctively addressed her in her own tongue — but with none of the courtly civility of Carlo. Who was this person in the dirty overalls? It was not even possible to discern their sex, for whoever it was wore goggles and the wooly hat beloved of Venetian workmen.

'Look! See!' The blue-clad person pointed at a yellow sign indicating falling stones hanging on the scaffolding which Julia Garnet had failed to take in. 'If you get hurt there's hell to pay. We're working here.' The person pulled down the goggles to reveal indignant pale blue eyes.

'I'm sorry.' Though in truth she wasn't. 'I didn't see the notice.'

'What's the trouble?' A second voice, lighter than the first. A figure also wearing goggles swung down. Pulling off an almost identical hat and pushing down the goggles it revealed itself as a fair-haired young woman. 'What's up, Tobes?'

'I fear I am trespassing.' Julia spoke coldly.

'Don't worry,' the girl spoke soothingly. 'He was just worried we might drop something on your head. We were breaking for lunch anyway. I'm Sarah, by the way. This is Toby.' She gestured at the other figure and then as Julia Garnet made no remark, 'We work together.'

The tone was propitiating and Julia unbent. 'It was silly of me. I didn't think.' Really she wanted to scuttle away from the aggressive young man but the girl seemed pleasant enough. She struggled to find an answering politeness. 'What is your work?' She found, as she asked the question, she indeed wished to know.

'We're restorers. This is one of the English restorations.'

'And do you work always together?' How exhilarating it might be to work high up. One could look out over the city, like a bird – or an angel.

'We're twins,' said the girl as if in explanation and indeed her eyes were the self-same pale blue as her brother's.

Julia Garnet had taught twins and the experience had not been comfortable. For the whole of one fraught year the Stevens twins had reduced a class to chaos by answering in unison when either was asked a question or (worse) singing in a peculiar toneless syncopation when neither was. There was a brazenness and self-sufficiency about twins which challenged her composure. Instinctively, she made as if to depart.

'Would you like to see round?' Again it was the girl who spoke while her brother only watched silently. His lashes, Miss Garnet noticed, were long and fair.

'How kind of you but I must –'

'If you want, you can come up on the platform and see Himself.' It was the young man speaking and he had also pulled off his woolly hat to reveal long blond locks and an earring.

'Himself?' Julia Garnet found her face was reddening. How provoking that she should blush so easily before these young people.

But the young man, who appeared to have forgotten his former discontent, was not looking at her face but was extending a gloved hand. 'Here, it's quite safe.' And to her own surprise Julia Garnet found herself being gripped by the elbow and swung up and onto a wooden-planked platform along the building's side. 'Look,' said the young man, and then as if by way of introduction, 'the Angel Raphael.'

Surrounded by scaffolding a serene face cut into stone smiled out at her. Whatever did one do when faced with the smile of an angel?

'He's great, isn't he?' The young man spoke with enthusiasm; his earlier antagonism had apparently melted away.

Reassured, Julia Garnet asked, 'How do you know he's a he?'

'It's a convention.' It was the young woman, Sarah she had called herself, who had swung her own way up and had now joined them on the platform. 'They're sexless, angels. Look, see the face is quite androgynous.' And inwardly Julia Garnet observed that the young woman herself, and her brother, were, like the angels, also somewhat androgynous in their appearance.

It was a strange encounter, she thought a little later, as she left the twins eating ciabatta with tomatoes and the elongated rubinous onions she had seen on the street market stalls. Their legs had dangled over the edge of the platform. But a feeling like the warmth of Nicco's cousin's brandy crept through her: she was pleased with herself. She had made another acquaintance.

'Two, really,' she said that evening. 'Though somehow one thinks of twins as one.'

Carlo and she were eating near the Arsenale. Julia's previous diet had consisted of the plainest fare. On the rare occasions they had entertained, Harriet had cooked a chicken using a spoonful of dry sherry in the gravy. After Harriet's death Julia had shopped at Marks and Spencer — dinners for one, compartmented as to meat or vegetables and encased in cardboard and foil. The experience of coming to Venice had not only opened her eyes — it had challenged her appetite. She was learning to enjoy food — especially with Carlo.

'And they are restorers? I must go and look.' A jug of prosecco was smacked down on the table. 'Some prosecco? They serve it quite flat here without the sparkle, but very refreshing.'

Later, after they had eaten tiny clams and slabs of polenta cooked in sage and garlic, she asked, 'It's a chapel they are restoring?'

Carlo had taken a silver toothpick from his wallet. Watching him Julia thought, How funny that I am not revolted!

As if he had read her thoughts Carlo put the toothpick away. 'Yes. It was known as the Chapel-of-the-Plague because it was built for a child — though others say it was for a mistress — dying of the plague.'

'Is that why the angel is there?' She remembered from the leaflet in the church his name in Greek meant 'God's healing'.

'I guess so — he is around Venice.'

'I like him.' How odd that she was already so sure of this.

'Oh, yes — he is nicer, with the smile, than the fierce Michael or the virtuous Gabriel!' He pulled a long face, then laughed. Julia who could not quite rid herself of the belief that it was bad form to laugh at one's own utterances, laughed too, a trifle uneasily. 'But you know, they must be exceptional at their craft, your twins, to be employed on this project. It is unusual for the *Soprintendenti* to employ foreigners. I must visit — poke my nose in! Now, there are crayfish or there is lobster. Which shall we try?'

A few days later Julia Garnet, walking her habitual route down the Calle Lunga, remembered the short cut. She felt, in making a detour past the little brick edifice which bristled with scaffold poles, she was doing something slightly eccentric, if not intrusive, but in fact there was no sign of the twins.

That the twins were not there made Julia Garnet aware that she was disappointed. Without acknowledging it she had been looking forward to renewing acquaintance with the androgynous pair. There was something about the way they swung with easy confidence among the scaffolding (rather like the gibbons she had once seen in a tree at Whipsnade Zoo) which stirred her. And they had trounced her experience with the Stevens twins by being unexpectedly friendly – letting her up there to see the face of the Archangel. Perhaps, she thought, becoming fanciful, it was some form of 'angelic' communication that had prompted Toby's suggestion? For it was he and not the more approachable girl who had made the offer which had led to her meeting with the smiling Raphael.

On the way home she passed two small girls taking something from a basket which hung suspended by a rope from an upper storey. *'Grazie, Nana!'* the girls called, and looking up Julia Garnet saw the face of an elderly woman at an open window. The woman blew a kiss at the girls and, with elaborate pantomime, they returned the blessing.

The episode left Julia Garnet rather low. The elderly woman had grandchildren – to whom she could send down sweets or pocket money in a basket – who loved her. Whatever other drawbacks age had brought the old Venetian lady, she had a family to be attached to – a reflection which contributed, back at the apartment, to a general feeling of being at a loose end. There were letters to write and books she had brought to read but these activities felt uninviting: it was company she wanted and she was grateful when Signora Mignelli called by with an enamel teapot.

'For to make tea in!' said the Signora, pointing at the teapot. 'Sorry, I forget it.'

Julia herself had forgotten that she had ever felt the lack of such a thing. Signora Mignelli stayed and talked, resting her behind on the arm of the sofa. Her husband had had an operation for a ruptured hernia and dramatically the Signora enacted how he had been carried off in the ambulance boat in the dead of night to the hospital. She refused tea but stayed to recount a war between the fishmonger and the local priest. The fishmonger, Julia inferred, had a reputation for favouring other men's wives and the priest had attempted to discuss the matter with him. 'He is a Communist – so he not like,' the Signora explained. 'He say he go to another church.'

'But if he is a Communist why is he going to church at all?'

'Of course he go to church,' the Signora said, dismissive at the suggestion of other possibilities.

Concerned lest she had affronted her landlady Julia diverted the conversation. 'Do you know the Chapel-of-the-Plague?'

Signora Mignelli nodded approvingly. 'Very old,' she said, 'and very holy. Much miracles there once. Now, no more.' She shrugged. 'It is the TV, I think.'

Nicco was not making much progress with his English. Carlo, who had called to tell her he had been as good as his word, and been by the chapel and spoken with the twins, narrowly missed one of the English lessons.

'Do excuse me.' Julia Garnet hastily cleared away a pile of books. One of them, *The Tale of Jemima Puddle-duck*, made her feel embarrassed: it betrayed the fact that she had bothered to bring it with her from England. She had not quite got over her tendency to become unnerved by Carlo's presence and the children's book added to the feeling of immaturity. 'It's the boy I give lessons to.' She shoved *Jemima Puddle-duck* under a copy of *Hello* magazine donated by the Signora.

Carlo's manners were exemplary. If he had spotted the story about the credulous duck and the predatory fox, which Julia had preserved since childhood, he gave no sign. He seemed to want to ask questions about Nicco but she was more interested in hearing what he had to say about the restoration.

'So, I have met your friends.'

But this she felt she must correct. 'Hardly friends!'

'It is fascinating,' ignoring her protests. 'As always the problem is the salt. Venice has its feet for ever in water, you see, and they must refashion the floor. The boy is doing this, on his knees, while the girl is perched above him, working as stone mason. Modern youth, eh? They were most charming, I should say. They allowed me to look.'

'Did they show you Himself?' Julia felt slightly jealous. It had felt free up on the scaffolding.

'Himself?' Carlo looked puzzled.

'The Archangel. Raphael.' More than the humans she had met at the chapel, the angel seemed her friend.

'Oh indeed. This is where the restoration must be most delicate. The girl is trained by a most marvellous man from your V & A who came over in '66 after the great floods. I know him a little. There is nothing to match you English with the chisel.'

'Such a beatific smile.' Julia was thinking of the angel.

'Indeed. She is most charming, your young friend,' said Carlo, politely misunderstanding.

Julia Garnet, calling to collect a parcel of linen, met Sarah outside the launderers. Sarah was not wearing her goggles or her woolly hat – but she still wore the blue overalls.

'Hi! Isn't it absolutely glorious?'

And indeed the day had turned into a painting of apricot and blue. Brilliant pillars of light were almost tangibly striking the enclosed corner where they stood.

'Glorious.' Julia Garnet agreed, weighing the brown parcel. (She wanted to offer some reciprocal hospitality and was simultaneously weighing in her mind how to accomplish this.) 'I don't suppose you would like a cup of tea?'

'That's sweet of you. I get dry with the stone dust and if you breathe near a café here it costs an arm and a leg.'

'Don't you take a flask?'

'Too lazy!'

The girl had a seductive giggle. Julia, as the two of them made their way towards Signora Mignelli's, speculated that with a laugh like that one might get away with murder. So it turned out to be quite easy, she reflected further, Sarah chattering away at her side: you asked someone to tea and they answered; as simple as that. She thought of the years through which she had asked no one (except occasionally Harriet – whom, she now saw, she had tended too much to consider in the light of 'only' Harriet) anything at all. Fearful of rejection she had presented to the world a face of independence which was a sham. Had she been capable of formulating the words to herself during those dull years she would probably have opined that she was too unattractive for anyone to want to be friends with her. Yet nothing in her appearance had, in fact, altered: any difference in Julia Garnet's demeanour was a consequence of other changes.

In honour of the apricot-fingered sun Julia served tea on the balcony. Although the temperature was within a hair's-breadth of being too cold she took a pride in being equal to it. The blue enamel teapot which had superseded the saucepan was brought out and christened. Julia, in fact, rather missed the saucepan which had given substance to her own sense of a daring relaxation of standards. Her father could have made no objection to the teapot which burned her hand and was hard to pour from.

'Sugar? Milk?' she asked, and was pleased when her guest requested lemon for it provided just that slight extra trouble with which to prove herself the part of hostess. They sat looking over towards the church.

'So that's the Angelo Raffaele. D'you know, it's awful, but although I can see the towers from the scaffolding this is the first time I've seen it properly. By the end of the day I'm pretty sick of churches – say it not in Gath!'

'Tell it not . . .'

'Eh?' Sarah had screwed up her eyes, which made her look less attractive. What is it, Julia wondered, which makes one woman attractive, another not? Sarah's face when you analysed it was rather weasel-like, yet one knew for certain she was attractive to men.

'Oh, I'm so sorry, it's being a teacher!' Julia, blushing at the unthinking correction, hurried to explain. 'I was brought up, unfortunately, on the Bible, which sticks when all kinds of other things don't. I believe the quotation is *Tell it not in Gath* . . . Most people get it wrong.' This would never do – it was socially inept, as well as impolite, to correct one's guest. Trying to bring the conversation to safer ground she said, returning to the subject of the Angelo Raffaele, 'It has some rather lovely Guardis,' then felt abashed at her own cheek, for until lately she had never even heard the name 'Guardi'.

If Sarah had minded being corrected she did not show it. 'Oh yes, the disputed organ panels. I should really look at those.'

Frustrated in a chance to show off her freshly acquired knowledge Julia tried to think of some new topic but her visitor, perhaps picking up her hostess's disappointment, said, 'Remind me what's on the Guardis. I ought to know . . .'

'It's an Old Testament story. There I go again – you'll be imagining I'm an expert on the Bible but actually I'm stupidly ignorant. (Would you like some more tea?) My friend calls the story "Tobiolo". I think we call it "Tobias and the Angel".'

'No more tea, thanks. Your friend?' Sarah shaded her eyes. Her funny hostess appeared to be blushing.

'You met him. He's called Carlo. He came to see your work.'

'Oh yes! The art historian with the moustache' – peering

a little too hard at Julia's face; and then, as her hostess seemed really very engrossed with the teapot, 'Go on about Thingy and the angel. I expect I should know the story but if I ever did I've forgotten.'

Julia disliked Tobias being referred to as 'Thingy'. 'I'm afraid I don't really know it myself.' Confusion made her bend further over the teapot. 'My friend told it to me. But you can work most of the narrative out from the paintings. There's a dog.'

Sarah helped again. 'A dog?'

'Yes. That's what caught my attention – rather a contrast, it seemed to me, a dog and an angel. It's a Dalmatian dog.'

'We had a Dalmatian at home.' The girl's face – and really it was quite changeable – looked almost sad.

'At home?'

'Yes – it was my father's dog. Hey, talking of angels, I must fly!' looking at her watch, 'Listen, it's so nice of you to invite me.'

'You must come again.' How odd that the thought of the girl's departure felt like a loss.

'Course I will. May I use your bathroom?' She was up and inside the apartment before Julia had answered.

Coming out again rubbing her hands together Sarah said, 'I used your hand-cream, my hands get like sandpaper, I hope you don't mind?'

Julia, who had bought the scented hand-cream for Carlo, struggled to suppress a sense of invasion. She was thrown by such familiarity so soon. But this must be the modern way and she wanted to be friends with the girl. 'I got it in the *farmacia* by the launderers – it wasn't expensive.' For goodness' sake, though, why was she apologising? Trying to recover she said, 'Bring your brother, next time.' And then, suddenly minding that the boy came, 'Bring Toby to tea, won't you?'

'I will if he'll come.'

Two at a time the girl jumped down the stairs. There was something engagingly childish in her exuberance. From the balcony Julia Garnet watched her wave and walk across the *campo* (quite as if she owned the world) until the boyish shape turned across the bridge and out of sight.

No doubt it was the partial success of this foray into socialising that prompted Julia Garnet to take an evening stroll towards the quarter of the city where the Hotel Gritti Palace was located. She did not go with any fully formed purpose – but the invitation of the departing Americans, issued from the bows of the water taxi, remained guiltily at the back of her mind. She had been remiss in not responding sooner; and besides, she owed them still for the taxi fare.

Maybe it was the opulence of the interior of the hotel, or the subconscious wish not to be reminded of anything which connected her with what she increasingly was coming to regard as her old life, but at the reception desk she found that her memory had played her false: by no wise was she able to recall the Americans' name.

'They are friends, no?' asked the porter. He was bald and not much interested.

'Not friends, no,' said Julia Garnet, flustered.

The porter evinced a lazy surprise. 'So if not friends, please, what is it?' His expression verged on the insolent.

'Acquaintances,' said Julia Garnet, annoyed that her efforts at social intercourse were being thwarted. 'I met them on my way here. In a taxi,' she added unnecessarily.

'A taxi?' The man lifted his eyebrows as if hinting at an impropriety peculiar to foreigners. But as he spoke the situation was remedied for the voice of Cynthia Cutforth came distinctly down the stairway.

Julia Garnet, turning from the porter's disbelief prepared for blank looks, was pleasantly surprised when Cynthia cried out, 'Why hello! We saw you in St Mark's but you know we didn't like to . . .'

Julia explained, rather sheepishly, about the fare she had come to repay but the tall pair wouldn't hear of it.

'We took your place,' Charles said. 'It was so rude of us. We have hoped to meet with you again and apologise.'

'Do let us make up for it now,' his wife said. 'Please won't you dine with us? The food here is quite reasonable. And how is your leg? I was horrified when I saw how you had hurt it.'

The dining room of the Gritti was all marble grandeur. Soundless waiters pulled back chairs and whisked linen napkins dramatically from table to lap. But Julia Garnet, in spite of being unprepared for the occasion, found that something had changed within her. She had ceased to be inhibited — at least in these present surroundings. Maybe it was because she did not mind what these people thought of her. Rich and groomed as they were they had no power to disturb her. In any event she became something of the life and soul for the evening.

'No, really!' she exclaimed as the waiter brought silver-domed dishes under which lay inky cuttlefish, stout portions of turbot and serried ranks of tiny exotic vegetables, 'I had to resort to walloping. It was him or me!'

She was describing her relationship with Michael Morrell, a pupil whose naughtiness had so plagued her that one day — driven to distraction by his refusal to sit still in class — she had chased him into the corridor and whacked him hard on the behind.

The Cutforths listened apparently fascinated to this piece of British anthropology. Cynthia vaguely indicated that in Philadelphia they had other ways of doing things, but their demeanour was respectful, even deferential. And Charles ventured, 'I was whacked good and often as a kid. I can't say it did me harm. I wonder sometimes if we are too liberal in our educational policies?'

Julia Garnet no longer knew if hers was a behaviour she herself could now endorse. Michael Morrell, it is true, had responded to the episode with surly respect. And he had ceased to be so disruptive a force in the classroom. Maybe she had done the boy no harm? She couldn't tell. What was apparent was that she had made a hit with the Americans. He, she learned, was an academic whose subject was Venetian trade with the Levant. He described a house with a picture of a camel raised in relief on the outside. A twelfth-century merchant from the Levant travelled to Venice to set up a trading business. His fortunes having prospered he built a house and sent for his young wife to join him. Through a scribe she wrote: *But how shall I find you when I arrive in Venice? — I cannot read.* Her husband wrote back to her: *When you arrive in Venice ask for the camel — everyone will know it and therefore where our house is.*

'Not very liberated,' Cynthia laughed.

'Or perhaps very?' Julia countered, thinking it might have been fun to be the Levantine merchant's wife and have a camel waiting for her, a landmark of home, as she set out on her own to a strange environment.

In return for the camel she told them about the Chapel-of-the-Plague. Charles, who had lighted a series of little cheroots ('I'm afraid I've given up trying to get him to stop!' his wife interjected as he lit the second), was intrigued. 'I don't know it but I must look it up. That would be the Black Death, I guess, which wiped out half of Europe. Giuseppe will know all about it, I'll ask him.'

'Charles has made terrific friends with a dubious Catholic priest,' Cynthia laughed.

Listening to their banter Julia realised that prejudice had led her to an assumption that the rich were stupid. The Cutforths were, in fact, highly cultivated. They told her where to find the camel in the region of Tintoretto's parish church. 'That has also been restored by your Venice in Peril people.' Charles was enthusiastic. 'They've done a fabulous job. You should go. Tintoretto's buried there and there was a Bellini once. An early one but a beaut nonetheless. Some hooligan stole it. I'd sentence those guys to the electric chair!'

The Cutforths were amused — delighted, even? — to discover that their guest was a Communist sympathiser. ('And there I was,' cried Cynthia, 'imagining you were a duchess. I was going to write to all my friends!' 'Didn't I always say it — scratch a Democrat and you get to find a snob!' her husband had remarked, rubbing his wife's knee affectionately.)

'Which only goes to show,' Julia said to herself on leaving the hotel to walk home, 'that it is possible to have spent a lifetime being wrong.'

Politely, she had declined Charles's offer to go with her. 'No, no it is quite safe and I enjoy the walk!' — for it was her private luxury that there was only one tall man she wished to have accompany her.

Walking home, she actually laughed aloud, recalling her faithlessness to the Reverend Crystal. Before coming to Venice she could never have imagined such an evening.

The next day Signora Mignelli said something incomprehensible and when it became apparent she had not been understood went and fetched a tall bees-wax candle and pointed to the Angelo Raffaele. 'For Our Lady,' she said, working her lips in an effort to make herself understood. 'It is to clean?'

Some ritual to cleanse the church, perhaps? The ochre candle looked enticing, and later that afternoon Julia walked round to the *fondamenta* where the Archangel had first smiled down upon her. Looking up at him again, on his shelf above the *chiesa* door, she saw the sculptor had given him wrinkled stockings. What a comforting sort Raphael was! Somehow the stockings made her think of the Levantine merchant's wife travelling across the seas to find her husband.

The dark green water-weathered doors lay open back. Stepping through the vestibule she made out a procession of candles punctuating the fine gloom with little swaying hollows of light. As she stood the notes of a chant started up. What a world she had entered coming to Venice; a world of strange ritual, penumbras, rapture. Timidity crept over her, the old insidious sense of not belonging, and she stepped back out of the wax-laden smell into the harshness of the foggy air.

Outside Nicco was dribbling a football across the *campo*.

'*Ciao*, Giulia!'

'*Ciao*, Nicco. Nicco, the *chiesa*. What is happening? What are the candles for?'

Nicco frowned. His father's promise to send him to London was proving an inadequate spur to his mastery of English. 'For Maria,' he explained.

'But the candles . . . ?'

Nicco smiled. 'I visit tomorrow.' He scuffed at the football, too polite actually to run off.

Sensing his impatience she let him go. 'All right, Nicco. I'll see you tomorrow.'

It was Carlo when he called by who enlightened her. 'It is the feast of the purification of the Blessed Virgin,' he explained. 'Candlemas, if you prefer.'

Julia did prefer. 'Why ever does she need purifying? Isn't she dripping with holiness already?'

'It was the custom after childbirth. Six weeks after the birth the woman must undergo the rites of purification. How is the boy you are teaching? I never see him here. You see him often?' For the first time in their acquaintance Carlo's face seemed to her to have an unfriendly aspect.

'How very chauvinist,' said Julia, more tartly than she felt, worried that she had maybe shocked him. 'Nicco is extremely lazy, thank you for asking. I'm wondering whether I should really bother to go on teaching him.' She began to tell him of her visit to the Cutforths but the evening which had gone so swingingly became boring in the recounting. For some reason there was none of the usual flow between them and he left more abruptly than usual.

I suppose they're all touchy about their faith, even if they don't make a song and dance about it, she thought, undressing for her bath. Waiting for it to fill (you could not hurry Signora Mignelli's bath – the water pressure was low and the water arrived in trickles) she examined herself in the wardrobe looking-glass. Her body stared out at her, stringy, like a plucked fowl.

The water when she climbed in was hot and watching the heat turn her skin red she felt more than ever like 'an old boiler'. Observing the limbs floating before her – almost as if they did not belong to her at all – she pondered on the unpredictability of human relationship.

She had spent her life avoiding people, afraid, as she now

saw, of their dislike or disapproval. With her firm mind and her astringent views she had provided herself with the means to confound intimacy. If people had wanted to know her — and really she couldn't tell whether they had or not — she had found ways of ensuring that they never approached too far. Carlo had been an exception — a delightful one — for if he had noticed any attempt at 'confounding' he had given no sign but had simply advanced, with long-legged aplomb, into relationship with her. And in so doing he had made out a way for others to follow.

And it was the case she had begun to take his good opinion for granted. Surprise at his seeming to want to go on seeing her — even to see more of her — had given way to the pleasures of anticipating his next appearance and the planning of their next expedition. And yet, today, something had, if not exactly gone wrong, certainly not been right between them. As if by some invisible and malignant presence she felt pulled down. The superstitious part of her related the small reversal in her relationship with Carlo to her pride in it the evening she spent with the Cutforths. Even to yourself, she thought, it wasn't safe to boast.

Lying in the small bathroom the peeling yellow walls suddenly appeared drab and ugly. The book — she had made such slow progress with it, a book on Garibaldi about whom she found she did not much care — which she had taken to read while bathing, had got wet and she laid it down and began to think about her pupil, Michael Morrell. Where was he now? Had he become a crook or a bank manager? (Either seemed equally possible.) If he had not prospered no doubt it was in part due to her: she had been an indifferent teacher. It was evident that Nicco, polite as he was, found her so. And she had been so cocky about teaching him. After a while she nodded off and woke, knees bent, to feel her mouth beneath cold water.

Now that was unwise, she said to herself as, half covered in a towel, she poured some of the brandy from the square bottle which she had purchased after her lunch at Nicco's cousin's. The experience of sliding so easily towards death frightened her. Somehow she associated it with Carlo and her unclear sense of his possible displeasure with her.

 Let us speak of exile. There are two ways with exile: you can fit in, lie low, 'do as the Chaldeans do', as we say — or you can stick out like a lone crow. No prizes for guessing which my renegade kinsfolk chose!

But I must own in the early days of exile I was glad enough to be in Nineveh once the shame of conquest was over. I missed the rolling hills and the pleasant pastures of Galilee. But I had a piece of luck early on in my time in Nineveh: the king took a fancy to me and made me his Purveyor of Goods, so that in those first years of exile I got to travel far over the mountains to the country of Media, bartering and purchasing for the king of Assyria, and often

I met the children of Israel there. We are a shrewd people and our swift reasoning and inventive minds proved useful to our captors. Therefore, many found themselves, as I did, well settled in the new life into positions which commanded respect.

But the king of Assyria died, as kings do, and not long after I lost my place at the old court. The old king had had a great new palace built by many slaves with gardens of sweet herbs and tulip trees and broad, high walls built around the city by the River Tigris. In the old days I had lived within these walls with my wife and had walked in the gardens with my son among the monkeys and the peacocks. When the old king died the tribes of Judah made wars against the new king so that when he returned from battle, defeated, he took his rage out on those of us who had been settled in Nineveh. One day, in his chariot, he drove past me walking in the gardens and lashed at me with his whip. It had become dangerous to be one of the chosen people.

Brutal purges began, with the bodies of our people left unburied to stink on the city walls for scavenging dogs to devour. I hated those dogs. I still recall a certain yellow brute; head of a pack he was and I called him Khan after one of the devils in these regions who is reputed to relish dead flesh. This yellow canine devil got scent of what I did and would follow me around snuffing out corpses. Then it was often a struggle between him and me — whether I would get to bury the body or he would grab it for his pack. He bit me once and the Rib had me bound up with flax and crocodile dung for a month against the foaming sickness. She was a follower of the local medicine man's magic — I couldn't have stopped her consulting him even if I'd wanted to. But I didn't want to; she needed every prop she could find.

With the death of the old king my heart began to dwell on Jerusalem and the days I had travelled there to offer tithes. It came to my mind then that we had been punished by the Lord God for our failure to do as He had commanded: we had not kept faith with the law, the rituals and the rites — therefore we had been taken into exile. Yet all around me I watched our people forgetting the law of the book, the prayers, the observances, the dietary requirements, alms-giving, the warning words of the prophets. And for us the observances of death are strict; it is sacrilegious that one of our own should lie breeding maggot-flies in the sun. There-fore, when I came across one of my kin murdered by the king or his officers, I would make it my business to take the corpse into our own house until sundown, away from the mouths of the yellow dog pack. When the sun dropped, lone-handed I would bury the body.

It is a business, digging the ground in these parts. The dragging and the heaving are enough to tire you out. And then the flies, and the vile stink if the corpse has been exposed long. No, it was not a task to take on lightly, especially since the royal guard were on alert to catch the corpse-snatcher. And in the end a certain one of our tribe in Nineveh, doubtless seeking advancement or immunity for his own family, went and informed on me. With the news that I was a wanted man and that I would be hunted to be put to death I left the city in haste and went into hiding. My house was entered, my possessions stripped from me, all that we had worked to acquire, the chased silverware I had bought from the Aramaean traders, the linen from Egypt, the bolts of dyed cloth from Tyre, the carved boxes and furniture of sandal- and cedar-wood from the caravan traders, even the worked crimson slippers my wife wore on feast days, were all seized; there was nothing which was not taken off to the Royal Treasury; only the lives of my wife, Anna, and my son were spared.

But before long this king got himself killed by two of his sons — I praise the Lord for my own son, Tobias, for surely there can be no worse sorrow than to have a son turn against his father, as Absalom did against his father David. There came a time when I recalled the words of King David as he wept for his son. 'O my son Absalom, O Absalom my son, my son!'

3

The Wednesday after her alarming slide into the bath Julia met Nicco on his way home from school. He smiled appeasingly and the thought came to her: He has been trying to find some excuse for not visiting me.

'I go for my cousin to glass . . .' he flapped his hands, 'to make the glass fit.'

After the disaster Julia Garnet had replaced the red-robed Virgin Mary back on the bedroom wall. 'The glass-cutters, Nicco?' Julia made the consonants explicit for him. 'Cut-ters.'

'I see you later?' Nicco was looking anxious.

Thinking of her words about him to Carlo, Julia felt remorse. She should reassure the boy – she did not want him to feel that to study English with her was so horrible. Their visit to the man with the red hat and the lunch afterwards rested warmly in her thoughts. Nicco had helped her then. 'May I come with you?' she volunteered.

'Please,' Nicco gave one of his smiles. Not for the first time it reminded her of Carlo and her heart jumped. And there, as if on cue, was Carlo, all smiles too and waving at her.

'*Ciao!*' she called across the *rio*, relief flooding through her that she had not, after all, alienated him. And what if Nicco were there? She was not ashamed of her friendship with the boy. 'We're off for a walk, come and join us!' And he came across the bridge with his long stride.

Gravely, Carlo bowed at the pair of them, the slight grey-haired woman and the gold-skinned youth at her side.

'This is my friend Nicco,' Julia Garnet explained, proud that she was the one whose position demanded introductions, 'and this,' she turned towards the tall, silver-haired man, 'is my friend Carlo.'

Julia Garnet's natural diffidence had not fostered in her habits of perspicacity but now, looking at Nicco. she saw that he had an awkward look on his face. And looking back at Carlo she observed that he also looked different.

'The glass-cutters,' she explained brightly, 'we are off to the glass-cutters, Nicco and I,' and not knowing why she flushed.

But Nicco surprised her. 'No,' he said firmly, 'I go later,' and pushing behind her, rather rudely she couldn't help feeling, he ran off along the water-side.

'Well, whatever was that about?' Julia Garnet turned to her friend, ready to share an adult's humorous incomprehension at the doings of a quixotic child; but Carlo was watching the boy intently as he ran over the bridge.

When intuition finally strikes the unintuitive it can be blinding: Julia Garnet had been taken, during one of her visits to the Accademia, by a painting from one of the many minor masters whose works fill the art collections of Italy. The painting was of St Paul on the road to Damascus and what had forced itself onto her newly awakened sensibilities was the look of puzzlement and fear on the savagely enlightened face of the tentmaker. Had she been in a position to observe herself, she might have seen just such a look on her own face now. But only the Angel Raphael, looking down from his position on the *chiesa*, could have seen the corresponding flash of terror across her heart.

Intuition is also a prompt of memory. Out of her memory, clear and unprocessed, came the recollection of the day she had gone with Nicco to the glass-cutters. A man. A man had come out as she had been worrying about paying for the picture, fussing with the Italian currency. The man and Nicco had collided and there had been a moment when Nicco had spoken with agitation, as she heard it now in memory, before the man had walked away. The man, tall and silver-haired, she suddenly perceived was Carlo, and in a moment of painful understanding she saw, watching his hungry, yearning look after the retreating Nicco, that she had been the unwitting dupe of his wish to find the boy who had accompanied her that day. It was not her whom Carlo had wanted to befriend – it was Nicco.

She stood, dumbly unprepared by anything in her previous life for the awful moment of negative intimacy which the recognition brought. And Carlo stood too, aware, as the high red spots on his cheekbones signalled, that something momentous had occurred to his companion. But they were civilised people, Carlo and Julia Garnet, and the sharp rent which had appeared in the fabric of their acquaintance was left unremarked between them.

Carlo spoke first. 'A concert tonight . . . they are playing Albinoni?' His eyes did not look at her directly.

'Thanks, I think I'll stay in. I'm a bit tired.' So lame the words came out; it was all she could do to refrain from crying aloud.

He walked back with her to the apartment, full of the usual courtesies. But his smile was strained. At the door of the apartment he dropped her with a pleasantry – his eyes cold and repelling; she had to stop herself from calling after him.

She did not, however, call after him. Instead she sat at the kitchen table until it grew dark.

Many years ago Julia Garnet, who was blessed with a retentive memory, read somewhere these lines.

Remember this: those who give you life may take it back, and in the taking take from you more than they gave.

She did not recall the source but she recalled, quite distinctly, the sensation with which she read the words. She had known that she did not understand them but, obscurely, they had frightened her.

During the days after what she termed to herself 'the discovery' the forgotten author's words came back to her, relentlessly keeping pace with her steps as she walked the streets of Venice.

She had lived most of her life alone. Her mother had borne her late in life and Julia believed that that, and the strain of trying to please her tyrannical father, had probably contributed to her mother's early death. When her mother died, a few weeks after her sixtieth birthday, Julia was not quite fifteen.

She had escaped from her father as soon as she could, going to Girton College, Cambridge on a scholarship. Although he had tried to make her departure from the family home as unpleasant as possible, there was not much he could do to prevent it and once away from him a part of her had felt she could never again face living with another man. There had been female friends, such as Vera, and there had been Harriet whom, she now concluded, pounding the streets, she had not treated as well as she could have done. Harriet had been more than a friend; but, blindly, she had taken Harriet for granted. Yet she had loved Harriet, she now knew, and she knew it because she had learned to love someone else.

If you spend most of your life alone often you do not know that you are lonely. It was not until 'the discovery' that Julia Garnet knew that she was lonely and that she had been so for most of her life. She had known Carlo for less than five weeks and yet it was as if he acted as a major artery to her heart.

It was the mystery of this which partly forced her out onto the streets as if the puzzle of her swift and intense involvement with this man might be solved by the most thoroughgoing of external explorations. She woke early and walked, avoiding any area where she might encounter anyone she knew, until she found some anonymous-seeming bar, where she drank coffee amid men in woollen hats who reminded her of the glass-cutter, the man with the red hat who, like a figure in some child's tale, seemed to be gate-keeper to new experience.

The reminder of the first meeting with Carlo did not bother her; even, she found, she began to hanker after it. She strained to recover what he had been wearing. Was it his dark grey coat? (She could almost swear to his red scarf — or had the red of the glass-cutter's hat become transposed in her mind?) Driven by a hungry desire to garner every scrap of time spent with him, she combed her memory for forgotten moments: the time he bought her an ice cream; the aspirin he had offered her when she had complained of a mild headache; the water-taxi home when she was tired. Had all the trouble then been merely towards establishing a connection with Nicco? For the discovery that her friend's proclivities were not for women had not detracted one jot from her own feelings.

At first she had been horrified, revolted even. 'Disgusting!' she had spat angrily when finally she had dully shifted her weight off to bed that first night. And she had lain, fully clothed, in the dark holding her sides. But love is notorious for its refusal to observe prejudice and gradually the eyes of Carlo, as she had last seen him, reinstated themselves. They no longer seemed cold. Sad, yes, she was sure that what she had seen was sadness, sadness and dismay. Did he miss her at all? Her heart hurt when she thought of him and she thought of him most minutes of most hours of most days.

Once on her wanderings she had caught sight of the Cutforths, arm in arm, Cynthia looking in a furrier's window — he comfortably lighting one of his perpetual little cheroots — and she had drawn back into the shadow of an alley. To witness such linked and homely familiarity (for the strongest impression she had carried with her from the Gritti was of the Cutforths' close and, somehow, practical intimacy) was starkly painful. Seeing them so unquestioningly together, it was as if the polite pair had put their hands on their spare hips and jeered at her uncoupled state.

In an effort to avoid all known contacts she roamed far from her usual patch. One day, penetrating to the Arsenale, the fortified area where Venice built its ships, forgetting that this is where she and Carlo had drunk the flat prosecco, she encountered a middle-aged woman sitting beside one of the lions which guard the entrance of the old archway. Caught by something in the woman's expression Julia stopped by the lion. 'Do you speak English?'

The woman turned and Julia saw that tears were in her eyes. 'If I speak anything.'

Love — even for what we cannot have — can make us brave. 'Have you lost somebody?' Julia Garnet asked.

But the woman only gave a half-groan and Julia, observing the body of a cat floating in the canal, was reminded of Stella and walked on.

Once, in another quarter of the city, she fetched up in the bar where the gondoliers meet, to which Carlo had joked about bringing her. Maybe he would be there? The lurch in her heart made her dizzy and she ordered a brandy. It was half-ten in the morning and the bartender spoke admiringly. 'Brandy for the Signora?' After that she walked with a lift in her step for an hour or so until the black pit opened again and she and all she ever possessed fell once more into it.

Many days passed like this and at night she hardly slept. I suppose I am having what is known as a nervous breakdown, thought Julia Garnet.

During all this time she heard nothing from Carlo or from Nicco. Poor Nicco! For she found she had no wish to see him, was indeed violently angry with the boy who had done no more than attract the desire, unasked, of the man she had so foolishly come to love. More than love, she adored him. With no other witness to her grief she spoke aloud one day to the red-robed Madonna with the grave child whose picture she had reinstated on her bedroom wall. 'I adore you, I adore you.'

She was conscious of a feeling of shame that these ardent words had as their object not the so-called mother of God but an ageing Italian paedophile. But the Virgin's almond eyes looked back unreproving and a fugitive notion entered Julia

Garnet's thoughts. Maybe, she formed the words to herself, maybe she doesn't mind? — and the idea was curiously reassuring.

Perhaps it was this reassurance which determined Julia to do what she had so far avoided and return to the glimmering domes of St Mark's.

There was a cold wind as she marched back down the Calle Lunga and she pulled down the veil of Harriet's hat. Its fine mesh made a protection against the blast on her face and she found there was a further comfort in it: for behind her veil she could look out at passers-by without herself being scrutinised. Harriet! What would Harriet have made of her friend falling so passionately and, it must be said, so unsuitably in love at this time in her life? It was ironic when you thought how it was she who had always been charging Harriet with unsuitability. Had Harriet ever been in love? she wondered, crossing the bridge where the view of the Salute's bubble domes held out the promise of the basilica's domes to come. She would not now be surprised to learn that there had been a secret lover in Harriet's life. There was the question over the dyed hair and her companion had displayed certain other signs: a tendency to drink too much sherry; a penchant for unusual hats and handbags; a taste for romantic fiction. She had mocked Harriet's Mills and Boon library books. The bitterness of the wind off the Alps made tangible for her now the bitterness of her own remorse. Under the guise of 'common sense' she had cut Harriet 'down to size', a hideous turn of phrase, as she now saw it. Shuddering at her own deficiencies, as much as at the February winds, she came once more to the edge of the Piazza.

And there it was – more powerful than in memory – the big-bellied roofs the colour of opaque crystal, the wings of the angels gleaming as they mounted ever upwards to the cloud-packed sky.

'Why, this is love too,' thought Julia Garnet.

Inside, she felt suddenly as if the hugeness of the interior had abated, transmuted rather, into a great cave of golden kindness in which she was no longer alien but an accepted presence. The door to the little side chapel was closed and it was with a sense of relief that she turned to the transept beside it. A notice read 'For Confessions only' and really not meaning to, she stepped up to the altar intending only to look.

But what a shock! There in a wooden box sat a little, shrunken figure in purple. Only a priest waiting for confession after all, but she fell back, startled, into the main body of the basilica.

The crowd was processing slowly round between roped corridors. Carpets were laid over the marble floors, whose whirled geometric shapes plunged and swooped, revealing centuries of subsidence. The chairs on which she had sat for Vespers were all packed away.

Julia Garnet stopped by the sign to the treasury and sat down on the base of a column beneath a long, curved mosaic of a bald saint. The unlooked-for encounter with the priest had disturbed her gingerly recovering equilibrium. Thoughts of all her past petty spitefulnesses to Harriet came flooding back. It might be a relief to confess her faults but she certainly did not want to confess them to an ugly puppety man in a coffin-like box. She sat on the column base in the golden gloom amid the hushed shuffle and the sense of her despair and loss and her own ultimate irrelevance.

A movement at the edge of her peripheral vision made her turn. High up and towards a roped-off area — for parts of the cathedral were closed off to the shuffling visitors — a small bird had somehow penetrated the interior and was flitting from carved ledge to ledge.

Julia, watching its speckled brownness, felt a schoolmarmish urge to reprove the bird for its unauthorised entry into the famous church. But on the heels of the schoolmarmishness followed another impulse: a kind of respectful admiration for the audacity of the thing.

As she watched, the sparrow landed on a carved figure in the marble. A face, the Madonna's face, and in her arms a child. An intense desire to approach closer to the face beset Julia Garnet and she did a thing she had never before done in her life: she defied an implicit order and ducked under the prohibiting rope.

No one was about. It was towards the end of the day and the cathedral was preparing to close. The long silver lamps were slowly being switched off. Julia's eyes, grown accustomed to the dimness, made out a low stool at the feet of the carving. Removing her shoes she stepped upon it in stockinged feet and stretching up she kissed the marble Madonna's hand.

That night Julia Garnet slept without pursuant dreams. When she woke sun had made its way through the edges of the shutters and was painting oblique bars upon the walls. Going out onto the balcony she felt it warm her shoulders. Although only February the air carried traces of Spring.

She set a pan of water to boil while she went down to look for post. And yes, there was a package on the radiator-shelf. Signora Mignelli must have been in already. Julia took it upstairs before making her tea in the enamel pot.

There was no milk but the scalding tea was reviving and there was a piece of stale almond cake too, which she took pleasure in dunking in the golden liquid. Her father would have disapproved.

'Bloody old bastard!' Julia Garnet spoke aloud. She tidied up her breakfast things, sprinkling the crumbs over the balcony for the birds, before opening the package.

Vera Kessel had not been too surprised when her friend had written asking if she would be good enough to purchase and send on to her a King James Bible. The tone of the letter had been sufficiently like what Vera had known of her old friend not to be too alarmed at the content. *It must be the 1611 translation*, the letter had specified. *No other version will do. And I absolutely do not want* (this last had been underlined) *one of those editions which sickly everything over with a pale cast of modernity. Definitely no New English rubbish, please!*

Vera, who followed the vaguest indication of another's needs as if carrying out a legal instruction, had spent her day off searching out an Authorised Bible. Dyed-in-the-wool Socialist that she was, an acute observer might have detected that there was a kind of *frisson* attached to this enterprise. It was not a thought which Vera herself would have recognised but it was rather as if her old friend had suddenly requested she search out for her seamy or pornographic literature.

I am sending you The Apocrypha as well, she had written. *I thought I might as well send you the whole damn boiling — since you seem to be immersed in Holy writs*. This last was Vera's idea of a joke, and out of gratitude for her friend's efforts Julia afforded it an indulgent smile. It had been generous of Vera to give up her day, although, Julia noted, she had been unable to resist mentioning the fact in her letter.

It is such a trial, these days, getting about in Central London but luckily I had a day off and was able to combine your book search with a visit to the National Gallery.

A picture postcard accompanied the letter. A Titian portrait: the man with a blue sleeve. He stared out, across the slashed, billowing blue silk, with unblinking confidence at Julia. How funny! Vera, ardent Socialist that she was, had clearly responded to the aristocratic hauteur of the man. People, she was beginning to see, were made up of different bits. The portrait reminded Julia of the 'foxy-whiskered gentleman', Jemima Puddle-duck's attentive suitor who, she recognised suddenly, she had, as a child, found sexually attractive. Maybe it was some dim awareness of this that had made

her hide the book from Carlo the day he called and just missed Nicco — when he had seemed so angry with her. Of course she knew now why.

Her stomach plunged and she pushed her mind back to Vera. On the back of the card Vera had written, *To remind you of the real world*. 'Real' was underlined with three stripes of Biro.

Oh dear, thought Julia pouring herself another cup of straw-coloured tea. What is, after all, the *real* world? I wish I knew.

The padded envelope yielded a dense black-bound book with gold-blocked letters: The Holy Bible. The fly leaf announced that it was *Translated out of the original tongues and with the former translations diligently compared and revised by His Majesty's special command*. Good old Vera. She was 'diligent' too. She really shouldn't mock a friend who carried out one's wishes with such exemplary exactitude.

Turning the rice-paper thin page to *The names and order of all the books of the Old and New Testament* Julia scanned the fine-printed list. Genesis, Exodus, Leviticus, Numbers . . . these, of course she knew. But there were others, half registered, less familiar, Joshua, Esther, Ezra, and some she had never heard of, Nahum, Habakkuk, Zephaniah. But of Tobit there was no sign.

There! She knew she had been right. The Book of Tobit was some Catholic extravagance. It didn't even feature in the Protestant Bible!

The discovery made her excited. It fed a partial wish,

emerging out of her increasingly complex feelings about Carlo, to think – while at the same time dreading to think – the worst of him. He had, after all, charmed her with the tale of the old man and his son and the angel, assuring her of its sacred provenance. And she had been suspicious. Rightly so, she reminded herself now as she leaned back in her chair on the balcony, sipping the milkless tea. For Carlo had bamboozled her, that was it (almost she savoured the word). Bamboozled and seduced her with his religion and its cheap trumpery.

It had been Julia Garnet's habit, during her years of teaching history at St Barnabas and St James, to intersperse her lessons with occasional stories whose purpose, she would have asserted if asked, was to point up to the children some useful life principle. That it was probable that no single part of any of the intended moral content of her anecdotes stuck in the minds of her listeners was not a consideration which had deterred her, having little interest in what did or did not attach to the minds of those she taught. Very likely, if the truth be told, she introduced the stories to relieve her own boredom – although that was not an explanation she would have naturally accepted either.

One of her favourite stories of this kind she had used to bring out during her teaching of nineteenth-century social reform. It concerned the MP Samuel Plimsoll who, discovering that hapless sailors were, to increase profits, being carried in ships that sank dangerously beneath the water line, enacted a violent rage out of a cool awareness of the facts the better to ensure adequate safety measures be passed through parliament. 'You see,' Miss Garnet had explained to her indifferent pupils, 'everything is capable of being made objective. Plimsoll's "anger" gave us the Plimsoll Line!' At which point she would herself enact a kind of indulgent beam around the classroom.

She might have added that, generally, anger has a slenderer connection with objectivity; for even in those days she was dimly aware that human beings tend to shy away from self-scrutiny. Perhaps it was this story, for which she had formed, over the years, an affection, or the years of teaching history which had given her a taste for truth. In any case it enabled her now, privately on her balcony overlooking the back of the Chiesa dell'Angelo Raffaele, to own that it wasn't fair to suggest that Carlo had 'bamboozled' her. If there was any 'bamboozling' it had been done to and by herself. Nor was it true that she believed his was a religion of trumpery. There was the marble Virgin she had kissed, and the honeycombed silence of St Mark's to say otherwise; and there was the Archangel, the smiling and enigmatic Raphael.

The package contained another book, a slight, red volume. She picked it up and read, *Apocrypha: Authorised (King James) Version*. Inside, the same inscription as she had read in the black Bible. *Translated out of the original tongues . . .* The inscription finished, *Appointed to be read in Churches.*

She looked further inside. Esdras I. Esdras II, Tobit. So it was there. An Apocryphal book! But what did that mean? Surely 'apocryphal' meant something false? The inscription

declared it 'appointed to be read in churches' so in the seven-
teenth century it was considered a holy book. Or at least
not, she surmised, an unholy one.

Despite the sun her shoulders had become cold on the
balcony and the teapot was empty. She carried her tray of
things inside.

As a child Julia had been taught to keep the most desirable
of her few treats back until all duties had been discharged.
It was a habit she had seen no point in unlearning and she
succumbed to it now as she washed up her cup and plate,
drying them on the cloth, on which the Statue of Liberty was
depicted, brought by one of Signora Mignelli's tenants as a
gift from New York.

This tea towel always induced in her a slight sensation of
guilt. Where she had arrived in Venice empty-handed, the
unknown American had had the foresight — like the scarlet-
robed Magi she had encountered on her own arrival — to
come bearing gifts.

Her own deficiency made her now ashamed. It was an
awful arrogance she now saw, polishing the spoon and knife
with a thoroughness as if to make up for other defects, imagining that somehow being English was honour enough to bring
to another's household. How absurd, how absurd we humans
are, she thought, settling herself on the sofa with her spec-
tacles.

It was many years since Julia Garnet had so much as opened
a Bible. As part of her life-long rebellion against her father,

even at St Barnabas and St James she had refused to take assembly on grounds of 'principle'. But now her 'principles' had begun to take on for her an altogether different aspect – like old photographs, in which the subjects posed and squinted, oblivious to the embarrassing picture they were recording for posterity.

What would her old Party friends think, she wondered as she began to find her way through the small print and numbered verses of the red-covered book to 'Tobit'. It amused her to notice that what she was engaged on felt very like sacrilege.

The names of the places were what struck her first: Thisbe; Nineveh; Raghes; Media; Assyria. Mysterious names, redolent of flamboyant arcaneries. *The laws of the Medes and the Persians.* Were these the same Assyrians who *came down like a wolf on the fold*? Barbaric people, obviously. But there was a brio about them: according to the poet, weren't their cohorts *gleaming with purple and gold*?

And the story: *I, Tobit, have walked all the days of my life in the ways of truth and justice and I did many thousand alms deeds to my brethren . . .*

But, thought Julia Garnet, surely there is some mistake? For the man sounded, well, so full of his own rectitude – too full, surely, to be quite as holy as his words seemed to claim. The pale sun shone through the window, lighting up the tiny print as she read on.

It was the same story she had gleaned from the organ-loft panels. But the bare account in the church pamphlet gave little sense of the strange poetry of the tale of Tobit, the Jewish exile, taken forcibly out of Israel by the Assyrians in spite of his extreme righteousness; and his son, Tobias, who is accompanied on a journey to restore the family fortunes by none other than the Angel Raphael, one of the *seven holy angels who go in and out before the Lord.*

Michael, Gabriel, Raphael — who, then, are the other four? wondered Julia, putting down the book for her eyes had grown tired from the small print.

During the days of her prowlings she had entered one of the many small shops which specialise in Venetian paper and had bought a notebook with a blue-marbled cover. Her original intention had been to note down historical details of Venice, hoping to restore some of her shattered equanimity with the subject which had sustained her for so many years. But the staple of her professional life, her historical mind, seemed also to have suffered from the trauma of Carlo: the memory of the Reverend Crystal, lying abandoned on the floor of the chapel where she and Carlo had first met, acted as a recurrent block to her intentions. So far then, the thick cream pages had remained blank. But now, seeing the blue-marbled book to hand, she picked up a pencil, opened the book and wrote, *Who are the seven angels? Michael, Gabriel, Raphael.* After a while she remembered Uriel from *Paradise Lost* and added his name. *Find out names of other three.*

'The architect in charge of the works is Venetian, of course,' Sarah said, 'and everything, absolutely everything must be referred to the two *Soprintendenti*: one for monuments and one for painting. It's a pain!'

Julia had been disconcerted to hear from Signora Mignelli that while she was out at the post office, mailing a present to Vera (a brown-marbled notebook as a 'thank you' for the Bible and Apocrypha), a 'young lady' had called asking for her. Julia's nerve for socialising had been blasted. But she had made a point before of suggesting Sarah bring her brother to tea. It was impolite not to follow up the invitation. In any case they very likely wouldn't come.

To her dismay, however, the twins had come the very next afternoon as she was sitting on her balcony, and now they were sitting there too, with the enamel teapot doing service.

The conversation had been stilted. Julia had asked rather tentatively about the restoration, but only Sarah had answered. Julia, trying to include the mute twin, asked, 'So, Toby, you're the mosaicist? It's the floor then, that's your depart-ment?' She did not want to mention that it was Carlo who had told her.

But Toby only said, 'Yeah. I need some cigarettes,' and got up and abruptly left the two of them on the balcony.

'Sorry about that,' his sister said, watching him cross the *campo*. 'He's terribly moody. Love does that.'

'Oh dear!' Julia felt perturbed. Over the past days she had found her mind returning to the angel whose name means 'God's healing'. She had wanted to thank Toby for the intro-duction to the stone effigy which presided so beatifically over the chapel. A young man in love was outside her imaginative reach and yet her own condition made her tender towards another sufferer. A sudden image of Carlo's hand, across the table at the restaurant by the Arsenale, made her ask, 'Is it a local girl?'

'No. He expected to hear from her on Valentine's Day and didn't. He's like a bear with a sore head.'

'I'm sorry.' Almost Julia felt it was her fault that Toby's girl had not written to him. She had forgotten about valentines: she had had little cause in her life to remember them.

'He'll get over it. Did you know they used to celebrate Candlemas on Valentine's Day here?'

'I'm afraid I'm very ignorant about the Church.' Julia, casting about for conversational topics, had told the twins about the service she had funked in the Angelo Raffaele. 'I'd never heard of Candlemas.' It was from Carlo she had learned about it – Carlo who had taught her so much – the day she had idiotically read Nicco *The Tale of Jemima Puddle-duck*. The day that, like a fool, she had thought to interest Carlo with her pathetic account of her evening with the Cutforths!

'We were made to go to church at home,' said Sarah, pulling a face. 'Listen, weren't you going to tell me the story of the Guardis?'

Afterwards, Julia could never be sure whether she had already decided not to tell the girl the story of Tobit and his son's journey with the disguised angel, or whether it was in response to what, looking out over the roofs of the *chiesa*, she suddenly saw there, that she all at once stood up saying, 'Is it me or is it getting cold?' and ushered her guest, quite urgently, inside.

⟡

My nephew had got himself preferment, Cup-bearer and Signatory to the new king, a valu-able position and one which breeds trust. So when my nephew spoke for me the king listened; he was a bookish man and his chief fancy was to build a library to house his tablets of clay and to set up his royal observatory to plot the planets and the stars. And perhaps, too, he wished to play 'new broom' and define his differences from the war-loving Sennacherib.

'I told him you were a little crazy, Uncle,' my nephew obligingly explained. 'You can return to your home but you must undertake to live by Assyrian law. When in Assyria, remember . . . ?' and he smiled in that provoking way the young have when they are in a position to patronise one who has once played the taws on their backside.

Our home had nothing left in it but the bare stone it was made of but it seemed to me a haven after the cave I had been sharing with the ravens and the vermin. It was the feast of Pentecost when I returned. The Rib had got together a great spread to celebrate, which she was anxious my sister's boy share with us. But the lad was chary of being seen to be too thick with a subversive like me – I didn't blame him for that: we each have our own field to harrow – and claimed some prior engagement. So I said to my son, Tobias, 'Go out and find some poor person and bring him here in your cousin's place – we should share our good fortune with those less fortunate.'

I caught the Rib casting her eyes up to the sky at this but she held her tongue, out of deference to my recent homecoming. She was about to light the candles in preparation for the feast when my son ran in to say that he had seen the dead body of one of our tribe laid out on the city walls.

His mother made a kind of noise at the back of her mouth and then sat saying nothing, but looking the way women do when they have an opinion they are not going to express openly. I don't know what they think those pointed stares are if not opinions deprived of words? But the Rib knew she wasn't going to be able to stop me because when I got up ready to go out she dropped at once to her knees. To some it might have looked like piety; only I knew it was her way of making a reproach!

The man had been strangled. I remember the body now as if it were yesterday: a thin man, in a dirty striped tunic, with a face like a wolf – the long features purple and grey from suffocation. I dragged him by his two scrawny arms through the streets and lugged the body up to our upper room, which didn't find favour with the Rib either – she was proud of that room where the few remaining bits of her dowry-linen were stored and the use of it to house a corpse was about as far from her wishes as you could reach to.

After sundown I carried the corpse to a spot by the city wall which is rarely visited, which is why the wild dogs like it.

The corpse was stiffening and the limbs would not go easily into the grave I had scraped out of the ground so I was afraid I would have to break one of the arms. It comes to me in dreams at times, that unyielding arm. The clay was so hard and unforgiving a part of me longed to leave the wretched thing there to the dogs and the broad-winged carrion birds which hover over the city for carnage. But I thought of the exile and how my tribe had neglected the ways of the Lord: I had determined to dedicate my life to doing what was right.

When I returned home the neighbours had got wind of what I had been up to and made it apparent that they wanted nothing to do with me. My person was a reproach to them and, worried they might pick up my dangerous taint and get into trouble with the authorities, they had to ensure their own safety with distance. I was polluted from corpse-handling anyway, so I sat out by myself awhile.

To tell you the truth it wasn't merely the grave-pollution which kept me away from the house: I didn't want to go in and face the Rib. I knew she feared the neighbours' talk — after all it had led before to the threat of death — and I knew it would be tears — and after the tears the accusations. This wasn't what she was born to, not what her father and mother had meant for her — and so forth in the way of women. But I did not blame her; it was not an easy life I had given her.

I must have fallen asleep by our courtyard wall for the next thing I knew I heard the birds start up with their dawn chorus. I opened my eyes, gummed with sleep, and saw some sparrows twittering in the purple creeper which half-holds our wall together. Pretty things, I thought. And then one of the little devils shat on me: shat right into my eye!

The birdshit was warm and sticky and stung like ant's gall. I cried out and the Rib, who had been out searching for me, came running. She took me indoors and rinsed my eyes and put warm cloths over them. But although the pain abated the dung had formed a white film over my eyes. From that day onwards I was blind.

4

*I*t was weeks since Julia had seen the twins. A cough, picked up during the directionless roaming in the February fogs, had first become persistent and then turned to bronchitis until pneumonia had threatened.

Signora Mignelli, noticing that her tenant's tall friend had ceased to appear, had at first been tactful. Ignorant of the theories of modern psychology the Signora nevertheless came from a tradition which accepted a connection between emotional and physical health. 'It is the heart which suffers,' she had murmured to her sister, who had been interested in the progress of the elderly spinster's *relazione amorosa*. Only when the Signora had begun to hear the cough across the *campo* had she intervened and a young man in a leather jacket with a stethoscope had been summoned.

Julia Garnet had been too unwell to more than register how youthful the Signora's *dottore* seemed. The cough had first annoyed and then fatigued her, and on his orders she took, with something like relief, to the bed with the high, carved bed-head.

The days in bed, during which Signora Mignelli had insisted on taking over the shopping and cooking, had permitted many reveries. Julia read a little, slept a great deal, and woke to meandering daydreams in which the intricate carvings on the bed-head played a part. The medicine the leather-jacketed *dottore* had prescribed to soothe the cough perhaps contained some opiate. Certainly it was the case that weird shapes detached themselves from the carvings and undulated dragon-like through her mind. The dragons reminded her of the paintings she had seen with Carlo – in particular one by Carpaccio, of the shock-haired, youthful St George, became interchanged with the face of the young doctor.

It was brooding on St George and the look of unswerving dedication with which the painter had endowed him as the boyish saint prepares to slay his dragon, that Julia Garnet – her fever-crowded consciousness becoming still – came up with a thought.

When the body is delicate ideas, resisted by the robuster conditions of health, gain ingress and lay down invisible foundations. The notion which had come to Julia Garnet, as she lay looking at her fingers twisting the fringe of the pearl-white coverlet (which, she had learned, during the course of the Signora Mignelli's care of her, was a survivor of the Signora's once extensive dowry), was that there existed in life two kinds of people: those who tangled with their fate, who took issue with what life brought them, who made, in short, waves, and those who bore their circumstance, taking life's meaning from what came to them, rather than what they wrested from it.

It seemed to her, lying watching the bars of the sun cross the white walls and making them jump from side to side as she tried the child's experiment of winking alternate eyes, that from her limited knowledge St George, Florence Nightingale and Old Tobit fell into the first class, while Socrates, Jane Austen and Tobias fell into the second. Jesus of Nazareth, she decided after further contemplation, belonged to both categories – and so possibly did Karl Marx.

But for such as herself there could be only one category and (this was the conclusion of her thought in the days during which, like a ship coming in to port after a storm, she made her way towards tentative recovery) it was not possible to alter the category you had been born into. The children at school, she knew, had found her repelling and fierce. And Harriet, too – rueful as the thought made her now – had been misled by her brusque manner. But the truth was, for her it had always been a matter of taking what she was given: she would never defy injunctions or make waves. And Carlo, who had seemed to ply her with every affectionate attention, had done so, as she now most nakedly saw, in order to further desires over which he himself possibly had no control. Who was to say that Carlo was not also one of those who suffered at the hands of his own fate? The trick was – and Julia Garnet, by now sufficiently recovered to be reclining on the sofa in the living room, tried for words to express the simplicity of it – yes, the trick was to assume that all one's experiences were somehow necessary.

And tribulation had brought compensations. Adrift as she was among emotions she did not really understand, life – she had to admit it – had nevertheless become more enthralling.

It was the influence of this idea which, when she had improved enough to be able at last to dismiss Signora Mignelli's care, took Julia out in search of the twins again. It did not matter that she had, stupidly, suffered – that was no reason to avoid things. Obscurely, too, she wished to seal up the slight gap in her consciousness which was the relic of the peculiar experience which had occurred on the twins' last visit – an experience she had held off, even in the days of her recovery, from yet examining. Her time in bed had blotted out many recollections – she could not be sure that she had not been rude to the girl when, that day when Toby had left so abruptly, she had hustled his sister, almost violently, inside. And she found, as a consequence maybe also of the illness, that she had become curious about the boy who had the unsatisfactory love-life.

But it was his sister who hailed her outside the little chapel. 'Hi, how are you? We heard you've been sick.'

Julia made short shrift of this. 'I was silly, I'm afraid. I caught a cough and neglected it and made a nuisance of myself. My landlady has been most patient.'

'I expect she enjoyed it. Give her a chance to behave like an Italian momma!'

Toby coming out of the open door frowning said, without any greeting, 'D'you want to see a painting of an angel?'

That made a second time he had offered to introduce her to an angel. Perhaps, unknowingly, Toby had found out a connection between them — for wasn't he also a casualty of unrequited love? Comrades in misfortune! Julia's heightened sense of the workings of distress made her try for a warmer tone than usual. 'I'd love to, Toby.'

'Toby!' Sarah sounded reproving. 'Julia's not been well. We mustn't keep her in the cold!'

Toby gave no sign of having heard his sister. His pale blue eyes stared into Julia's as if trying to make some urgent communication. 'There's a dog in it.'

'Toby!' Sarah's tone was really severe — quite different from the charming child she had seemed on previous meetings. Maybe, Julia guessed, she is the older twin and is in the habit of bossing him about.

Wanting to reassure Toby she asked, 'Like in the Raffaele?' In her notebook she had written: *Why the dog? I have never liked dogs.* Cats, because of Stella, she had developed an affection for. But there was something boisterous and nakedly animal about dogs which ruffled her. Yet for Tobias's dog she had acquired a fondness: he was part of the welcoming party which had greeted her arrival in Venice, the group of stone figures which fronted the Chiesa dell'Angelo Raffaele.

Toby simply said, 'Come and see!' and ducked back inside.

Julia, still a little stooped after her illness, stepped awkwardly into darkness and paused to let her eyes adjust to the suddenly reduced light. It was hard to imagine the humble, bare-bricked space as a sumptuous Venetian interior. Falling back on her history she asked, 'It's Romanesque, isn't it? What date?' There was something almost biblical about the atmosphere inside the chapel.

'Probably about 1350.' Sarah, who had come in from outside, still sounded out of sorts. 'Even though the Gothic style was well under way by then they still occasionally used the Byzantine model.'

Julia gestured at the scaffolding with a barred working lamp on the side. 'Is this part of your restoration too?'

Sarah still sounded impatient. 'Yup – I'm just about to move on to these.'

The grey-whorled columns with their leafy capitals shone faintly iridescent in the fragmented light. They formed a kind of protective arc, like a semi-circle of grained-silk trees, around what was obviously the altar, and above them she could see a narrow window set high up, through which sunlight was stippling and dappling the remnants of a mosaic floor.

'So it's just the two of you? You on high and Toby down on the floor?' Julia felt a pang; what the twins were doing here touched real history – her own lessons at St Barnabas seemed milk and water by comparison.

'When Tobes finishes the floor there'll be others coming. It's too small for many of us to work together so for the moment we have it to ourselves.' A yellow mackintosh and a sleeping bag were laid out on some wooden planks. Noticing the direction of her visitor's glance Sarah said, 'Tobes sleeps there sometimes,' then dismissively, 'with the bats — but of course he *is* bats himself!' and laughed unhumorously.

There was something uncomfortable in all this. Julia, who did not feel she was yet up to bats, changed the subject back again. Smelling the musty air she asked, '1350 must be round about the end the Black Death, isn't it?' She knew the answer to this in fact: Charles Cutforth had spoken of it in the lavish grandeur of the Gritti Palace, in those last days of her innocence.

But Sarah had apparently had enough of questions, specious or real. 'Look, it's bloody crazy you being in here, Julia. Sorry, but damp's fatal for chests.'

If only it were, Julia thought. Aloud she said, withdrawing her elbow on which the girl had taken too tight a grip, 'Please, it's all right, I'm fine.' Out of the darkness Toby appeared suddenly with something cradled in his arms. 'Oh, the painting — is it him, d'you think?' Sarah's mood was making Julia feel inhibited: she found she did not like to speak the archangel's name.

Toby was carefully unwrapping a grey blanket to reveal an oblong panel of wood. 'I guess so. Raphael was popular with the sailors. He's s'posed to have visited this area.'

The blanket revealed a panel, about two foot by three and

two or three inches thick, giving it for all its obvious fragility a substantial look. Around the splintered edge an arch effect was visible, as if the scene depicted were also inside the chapel. But what drew the eye inexorably was the figure within.

The artist had painted the angel with an enquiring look, the great wings folded behind, the darkly lustrous blue of a peacock's tail. Long ago, as a child, Julia had been taken to a stately home into the grounds of which peacocks had been introduced. One had opened its tail before her with a violent rattle, and in fear and wonder she had cried out, her mother rushing to comfort her.

It was the only occasion she could firmly recall on which comfort had been offered, although she supposed, if only by the law of averages, there must have been other such moments available to her. And yet the irony was that, on that particular occasion, it was not comfort she had needed – any more than she needed it now.

'I didn't know he was a visitor here?' Her suggestion sounded faintly absurd as if the angelic being had been a customer on a Thomson City Break.

'The sailors mostly stayed round here. Raphael's their totem – I don't know why. He's good, isn't he?'

Better than 'good', Julia thought. 'Who was the artist?'

Even in the semi-dark she saw the flush and thought, 'Damn, I've made him feel ignorant.'

'Probably some unknown.' Toby sounded embarrassed, then, changing the subject, 'Look, see the dog?'

He indicated with his finger a smudge of black and white

at the feet of the figure. The feet were elegant and long, pointing out beneath the gold and white pleated gown. Julia, looking, wanted to reach out and touch them but Sarah almost pushed her aside.

'Toby, don't you need that new blade?'

'Yeah, OK, OK. I was going to get Francesco to sharpen this one.'

Francesco, it turned out, was the name of the red-capped glass-cutter. Waiting outside the chapel while the twins exchanged words Julia reflected that it was not biological bacteria you needed a cure from, it was the emotional kind: fear, humiliation, loss. For a brief moment, looking at the angel-painting, a promise of some alternative had hovered over the crater in her heart.

'Will you come to tea afterwards?' she asked Toby, not wanting him to go, and was disappointed when his sister spoke across him. 'Tobes has to get home but I'll come if you'd like.'

Toby had gone off with an expression on his face which Harriet would have described as 'taking the hump'. Clearly the twins were engaged in some kind of row. Watching his bent shoulders Julia wanted to call after him, 'There's brandy, if you'd prefer!' (Brandy, she knew from her own experience, being more tempting than tea to the love-lorn.)

Since her thoughts followed Toby to the red-hatted Francesco it wasn't surprising, perhaps, that they should meet Nicco on the way across the *campo*. It was not the first time she had seen the boy since the day they, too, had set out together on the aborted visit to the glass-cutter's. But always since, she had contrived their paths should not cross. Of Carlo she had seen nothing – he had vanished out of her life. Like a thief into the night, she thought, and then felt contempt for herself at the triteness of the cliché.

About Nicco she no longer felt angry – merely ashamed. She had dropped him; and, sensitive as herself, she was aware now that the boy was conscious of having been dropped. And she was aware, too, that the friendliness with which she was addressing Nicco was partly dictated by a wish to impress Sarah with her easy style with the locals.

'*Ciao*, Nicco! How's the football? Are Venezia winning?'

Too polite to allude, even internally, to the fickleness of his elderly friend, Nicco was unable not to respond. '*Si!* They play Hamburg team last week.'

'That's wonderful, Nicco. How did they do?'

'I not know yet. Later I tell you.'

Realising the error Julia said, 'It's *next* week the boy means,' and she called after him as he ran on, '*Next* week, Nicco, not *last* week. Next . . .' And then, not quite as an afterthought, 'Nicco, come and see me soon, won't you?'

'Once a teacher always a teacher, I guess!' said Sarah later on the balcony. 'Here, can I help?'

Julia, feeling the need for activity, had begun to shell some broad beans she had spotted on a stall that morning. Harriet had liked broad beans. Remembering this Julia had bought half a kilo and planned to eat them with lemon juice and olive oil for supper.

'Not a very good one I fear.' Her teaching, Julia had concluded, during the weeks of illness, had been barren, barbarous even. Ever before 'the discovery' Nicco had felt it; she must try to make that up to him.

The girl's mood seemed to have cleared with the departure of her difficult twin. 'Really? I should think you were great! He's lucky to have you, that kid. But kids are ungrateful, aren't they?'

Julia Garnet, slipping the tender green pulses out of their fleece-lined pods, knew otherwise. Nicco was not 'lucky' in being the recipient of her pedagogic attentions. With a natural courtesy he had endured what was very likely a torture for him. Among other things, the discovery of Carlo's true intentions had taught her that it was not desirable to imagine you were better than you actually were. But she had been thinking, too, that there was something not right either in a single policy of plain speaking. To contradict this new young friend, whose intentions were no doubt of the best, would be a version of that impulse to criticise from which Nicco had obviously longed to escape. 'Let's say I wasn't as good as I thought I was,' she after a time offered.

'I gave my teachers hell!' Sarah laughed. Under the evening sun her changeable features had become pretty again and had lost the weaselish look they had taken on in the chapel. It had been somewhat shocking coming across the twins bickering like that – but maybe it wasn't so rare for people to quarrel? She and Harriet certainly had done so – though this was one of those things she might have denied to herself before.

'Did you go to boarding-school?' That easy confidence suggested Roedean or Cheltenham Ladies.

Sarah shook her head. 'Nope. I wouldn't. My . . .,' for a second she hesitated as if not sure what, quite, she wanted to say, '. . . my parents wanted me to go though – typical!'

'Why didn't you want to?'

'I did when it was too late.' The girl's mood seemed to have darkened again. Maybe it wasn't only her brother who was tricky? 'When things got unbearable at home.'

Julia Garnet was surprised. The girl seemed too poised to have come from a difficult home background. 'Oh,' she said, 'I'm sorry.' She found herself flushing again. Such an abomination, shyness!

Sarah, if she noticed, made no acknowledgement of the other's discomfort. Instead she said rather too brightly, 'Doesn't matter. It's true for lots of people, isn't it, frightful skeletons in the home cupboard? How about you? What was yours like?'

Julia Garnet had never, until recently, thought about upbringing in a general sense. Only vaguely had she been aware of deficiencies in her own and that, for her, had been a matter for concealment rather than conversation. 'Upbringing' was not a topic she had been 'brought up to consider,' she had once (rather wittily, she had thought at the time) declared. 'I've never thought about it much.'

She must have conveyed some disapproval at the question for what the girl now said had an edge of admonishment. 'Well, I was sexually abused. No one believed me, of course, but there's masses of evidence now. Hundreds of cases of it are turning up everywhere.'

'Oh dear!' Uncrossing her legs in alarm Julia Garnet knocked an ankle against the enamel teapot, sending it rolling. 'Damn! I'm so sorry!' She didn't know whether it was the subject matter or her own clumsiness she was apologising for.

'Here, let me fetch a cloth.' Sarah had sprung up and was off into the kitchen and back again in a moment. 'Did you burn yourself? Are you all right?'

'No damage done.' She wished the girl would not fuss. Her startling admission had made her more alien just as they had seemed about to be friends. Did every well-intended action come to this? The savageness of the old mood flickered up again. For that brief moment in the chapel it had abated; but the prowling despair was waiting to leap back and destroy all that promised well. Tea had seeped from the tray over the balcony and the tea-things looked dismal in their disarray. Dust and ashes. Dust and ashes. Profoundly she wanted the girl to go away.

'Don't worry.' Sarah mopped at the tea-tray. 'It's not a subject I like to talk about. Tobes and I never discuss it. I'd rather you didn't tell him I said anything, by the way.'

As if I would, thought Julia Garnet in indignation. 'Naturally not,' she said, uncomfortable. She wished she was back in the cold, shadowy interior of the chapel with the boy showing her the angel and the dog. He had nice hands — square and capable. A picture came into her mind of him lying there alone in the dark in his sleeping-bag thinking of his recalcitrant lover. 'How is your brother's girlfriend?' She hoped the change of subject was not too obviously nosy. It was his sister who had mentioned him after all.

Sarah raked an open pod clean of beans with an efficient thumb. 'Oh, that! That's why he goes walkabout all over the place.'

Julia's half-conceived sense of identification with Toby quickened. The walking-cure; she had behaved that very way herself. 'Do you know her, the girl?'

But her guest didn't answer. Maybe she had put her foot in it again? She was so unversed in the etiquette of modern relationship. Perhaps although it was all right to mention sexual abuse it wasn't acceptable to probe the nature of a young man's grief? Well, she understood that – most emphatically, she would not like it done of her own.

But Sarah had apparently only been lost in thought. 'Nothing special, but that's often what we think of other people's lovers, isn't it?'

'Is it? I wouldn't know, I'm afraid.' Julia, who had just had a fleeting vision of the gold-skinned Nicco fleeing from Carlo across the Ponte de Cristo, bent her head toward the last beans. 'What a tiny amount these dwindle down to. I was going to ask if you'd care to stay and eat them with me but they hardly seem worth –'

'I can't, anyway.'

Although she didn't really want the girl to stay Julia felt rebuffed by her rapid response. But she was a girl who did things fast. Julia remembered watching her walk across the *campo* the first time she had come for tea. 'More haste less speed' she might have said to Sarah had she been a pupil, in the days when she had some belief in her own precepts. Sarah now explained she was off to see the architect in charge of the Chapel project. 'Luckily he's a bit gone on me – mainly because the man who trained me is a kind of legend which is useful for managing the *Soprintendente*. She's not in favour – against if anything – especially me. She's not exactly an oil painting – ugly old cow!' Sarah's face, oblivious to the possible sensitivities of a less attractive woman, looked almost cruel in its youthful radiance.

Julia, however, preferred not to join in a conspiracy against the plain *Soprintendente*. 'Maybe she's just unused to a pretty young woman being good at her job. It's rather bold, doing what you do. Do you mind being so high up?'

Sarah stood up. 'I like being "high up" as you call it.' She laughed again and Julia saw how the ugly *Soprintendente* might envy that fair hair and slight form. 'Tobes says I must have been a goat in another life.' Sarah crooked two fingers over her head to imitate horns. 'Look, I must be off and change!'

Before she left Julia said, 'Does he know anything about the panel, your architect?'

But this for some reason appeared to annoy the girl for her voice became sharp again. 'Not at all. It's nothing to do with him – not his department!'

Eating broad beans on the balcony alone Julia thought about the visit. Sarah was quite unlike the children she had taught (and really one thought of her as a child!) but, then, what did she know about it? Her life had been spent in a rigid method of dealing out dead fictions to children who would hardly care if she herself were dead! How could she claim to know what they were like? In that split second which would live in her memory for ever, when she had seen another kind of fiction die and had stared in the face of a living truth (the truth about Carlo), she had descended into hell. But, like the stars which, it is said, can be seen from the deepest pits even at noon, she had seen something else from that 'hell': the faintest light which illuminated something beyond her own pain. Dimly now, by that light, she had a fleet vision of why Carlo was as he was: Nicco was beautiful to him for Nicco was life. No doubt it was wrong of Carlo to desire to use the boy's beauty for his own perverse ends but at least he saw and responded to it. Whereas she . . . shutting her eyes to the naturalness of children she had pressed on with her formulaic sense of what was right and wrong – very like old Tobit religiously burying his dead, eternally insisting on his own righteousness. Opening her notebook she wrote: *Dogs lead the blind. Old Tobit is 'blind' because he doesn't see the limitations of his own values. (Look how he treats his wife when she is working her fingers to the bone for him. He doesn't 'see' her!)*

She had taken her dish inside and rinsed and wiped it dry before going back out onto the balcony, with a glass of brandy, to add: *All that burying of the dead – tunnel vision!*

*

'Aldo knows your friend,' Sarah called down a few days later from her place on the scaffolding platform and even before she spoke the name the crunch in Julia's chest presaged who it would be. 'Carlo Antonini! He was there. Said to say "*Ciao*" to you. He called by here once. He seems to know all about the chapel.'

'Yes,' Julia called up. 'He would.' But her voice was too faint to reach the girl on the roof.

'Come up if you like!'

But Julia did not like. The thought of the scaffolding was no longer tempting. She wanted to return to the chapel's still interior – the haunt of Sarah's brother, Toby, and the bats. The enigmatic wooden panel was there too – wrapped in a blanket like those in the school sick-room. An image of a sleeping child floated into her mind.

The door of the chapel opened and Toby, squinting into the sun, came out.

'Hi!' He looked worried. The girl still, she guessed.

Compassion made her return in kind. 'Oh, hi Toby! Are you working?'

'Yeah. Fancy a look?' She had hoped he might ask.

He held the door for her and passing him she smelled sweat from his armpit. It was a novel sensation, mildly erotic, she realised, and she did not even flush at the thought.

Inside the chapel was lit with the lamp she had seen before but now two additional halogen beams were directed from the scaffolding behind the altar onto the damaged floor. Toby beside her, oddly intimate in the strange light, pointed out the tessarae-less patches of floor like gaping gums void of teeth, the effect of the years of subsidence and the water's repeated depredations. How restful it must be to love stone and glass like that. But she was forgetting, he loved flesh and blood too. From the tiny intact areas of the mosaic she could just make out the same sweeping geometric patterns she had seen at St Mark's — but on the section where he was working there were leaves and what looked like an animal's shape.

'It's a bit of a jigsaw at the moment,' Toby said, 'but if you can see — ' pointing — 'that part's a fish.' *Also, why the fish?* she had written in her notebook. *Fish, dog, man, angel — these seem to be different levels of evolution?*

'There's a fish in the Tobias story, as well as the dog.'

'Oh yeah, right! I'd wondered about Jonah's whale.'

Jonah, the wandering prophet, reminded her too much of her father. 'He was a bit of a misery, wasn't he?' But then, fair's fair, living in the belly of a whale must give one a different point of view. In the beginning, according to the Bible, the world was parcelled out — sea, earth and air — and above the air the ethereal firmament, the element of the angels.

'What do you think of the angel on the panel?' she asked turning to him suddenly, and long afterwards she remembered his reply — almost as if he had meant to say something else.

'I think . . . he must be the nearest thing to heaven I'll ever see on earth!'

ༀ

 I, Tobit, who walked from the shores of Lake Galilee to Jerusalem, from Kedesh to Nineveh, from Nineveh to Raghes in Media, I who had always been proud of my body's strength, was now thrown into impotent inaction. After I became blind I could no longer provide for our family and the Rib had to take on manual work — laundering, sewing and the like — for us to live. For me that was worse than the blindness.

She could not hide from me her disgruntlement. Not that she minded work — she was born with her sleeves rolled up. But women can be cats and the other women made her feel our fall — we who had once been part of the king's household.

It made difficulties between us, who had before known only the usual grumbles and discontents of married couples; I became suspicious-minded and she quarrelsome. I resented her having to work and she resented my resentment. But in time she became quite a noted laundress in the locality and began to take pride in her work.

One day a wealthy widow gave her a kid-goat over and above what she was owed as wages. I heard the creature bleating and not knowing how we had come by such wealth leaped to the conclusion that she or the boy had stolen it. I wasn't tactful in my enquiries but accused her of theft straight out — that is what happens when bad feeling builds between a couple: reproaches stick like burrs. That was the lowest ebb in the tide of our life together.

In spite of my blindness she shook me by the shoulders and screamed, 'It was a gift – a gift from a customer, for my work – because I work hard, believe it or not! What do you think of me, accusing your own wife of theft? Who do you think you are? Don't you think I can see through you? What price your famous alms-giving and good works now, you self-pitying, self-important, self-righteous fool?'

Night after night that terrible list of names played in my head until I began to suppose I would be better off dead. I spent the night by the courtyard wall again, and this time my wife did not come to find me. This decided me: I who had done so much, had given alms in abundance and kept faithfully the ways of the Lord, when all around me had been backsliders and renegades, yet I was treated to nothing but ignominy and slight and now, in my own household, contempt. What point was there in following the path of righteousness? I would be better off dead. But before I took leave of the world I would do my best to put my house in order – leave my family well provided, for all they thought so little of me.

As the first sparrows began to call in the purple creeper (I still liked to hear them in spite of what they had done to me) I remembered something.

I don't know if you have noticed how odd a thing memory is. All those years this matter which now came into my mind had lain there unredeemed. But now, when I most needed it, an image arose before my sightless eyes of my cousin and I recalled that long ago when I was young and vigorous I had visited him in the city of Raghes and finding him in need of it had loaned him money – for in those days, when I had the king's favour, I was a wealthy man. Raghes lies beyond the Zagros mountains in Media. In the days when I travelled as Purveyor to the king there was peace between Assyria and Media, and a hardy man could travel there and back again within a moon.

When the birds were well abroad and I felt the first warmth on my face, I made my way back into the house and called my son.

Of course, when she heard my plan, the Rib was up in arms. I think she was feeling remorse for her retort over the kid and, unhappy at my night under the dew, she was fussing about getting me hot drinks and whatevers, so at first she did not take in what I was saying. When she did I could tell, eyes or no eyes, she had paled – as she used to when I would insist on going off to bury the dead.

But the boy was full of the plan. I see now he had been chafing, wanting to but not knowing how to help the family. When he heard that I proposed he go to Raghes to recover the debt from our relative there, he was ready to be off, getting his baggage together before you could say 'Moses!'

'Whatever are you about now, you foolish old man?' the Rib said. (At the time I was in fact a mere fifty-eight years but I suppose it was true to say I was no spring partridge.) 'Don't you know he's our only son and the way is wild and filled with robbers and Media and Assyria are no friend to one another these days. What if he never returns? You will be the death of me,' and she began to wail and moan.

Now I, too, was not altogether at peace at the prospect of the boy making the journey alone. True enough, at his age I had travelled across the mountains to the city by the far sea, but the times were rougher and anyway one never believes one's son as capable as oneself. So although I told the Rib to stop her noise I began to think of how to safeguard the boy.

'Look here,' I said to him. 'Your mother is beside herself. It would be no bad idea to take a man along with you. Let's walk on the safe side – then she'll be less afraid.' (I didn't mention to him my own mind: it's not helpful for boys to learn fear of their fathers.)

Now my son is a good boy, as I said, and not proud, and he went at once to the market-place where men who would be taken for hire stand to offer their services. For many days he looked, but the men he tried were too rough for his mother or too paltry for me. I wanted a strong man to accompany my boy – there were bandit packs in the high passes which he must cross into Media. Wild men who would slit your throat soon as look at you.

Then one day he came home with a man at his side, a tall young man, thickset and fair-headed, the boy told me when I asked my usual list of questions to discover what manner of man he was. It is unusual in this country to be fair-headed. Maybe it was this but I swear to this day I guessed there was some special thing about him. Some things you 'know' ahead of understanding; it was that way for me that morning.

They came together into the courtyard. I had been sitting there – it was one of my bad days when I wasn't even in the mood for preparing for my own departure and the boy's mother was off seeing about some embroidery she had been commissioned to do for a local wedding. What intrigues me now is that I was not afraid. I was not even afraid of the dog, I who had so often chased off the yellow monster and his pack as I was going about my wretched business, I who had the best reasons to know how a dog will generally seek out a dead thing, did not flinch when that dog pushed his nose into my lap. Without thinking I put out my hand and stroked him. Blind as I was I could see him in my mind's eye (and this is how I began to learn that eyes are not merely for outward affairs): a lean, neat hound with a smooth coat and intelligent ears. I don't know what you think of dogs, but if you think about them at all you will know what I mean by 'intelligent' ears. Ones that communicate.

Maybe it was the dog who put the idea of reversal into my head. The dogs I had known before had always looked towards death; it was a race between them and me and when my mishap occurred we were about quits, me and the yellow monster. This dog was the first intimation I had of a reversal – a going-about in another direction. Yes, that dog who came into our life that day with the young man whom my son had found, was a sign that things were about to turn. In your language if you spell dog backwards ... well, you are not stupid, I guess, or you would not be reading this. No need, then, for me to spell it out.

つ

When Julia Garnet came out of the chapel she looked up. Sarah had come down off the scaffolding platform and she and her brother were inside discussing the application of a chemical compound for shifting algae. Feeling redundant, Julia had come outside again. Gulls were wheeling round the sky, and looking up she saw him again, as she had known she would.

He was not at all obvious. There were no clear signs but up on the roof you could see, if you had a mind to it, that this was not an ordinary man. For a start he stood, without visible support, on the roof's spine, balancing weightlessly against the air like a sail. Except that the apparition did not sway as he stood: he stood poised as if anchored by the finest gold thread to an infinite sky.

Julia Garnet when she glimpsed him first, that day she had invited the twins to tea and had so suddenly ushered Sarah inside, had been struck by something she could not at first pin down. Later, when the girl had gone, and her hostess was washing the tea-things with the inconvenient and definitely unhygienic sponge mop (which she had intended to replace on her first day and had somehow never got around to) she received an impression of what it was that was peculiar: the figure had the transparency of the ordinary. Like a bird's nest concealed in the flourish of a tree, he had stood against the red-tiled roof with the outlines of a man, and yet so easily passed over.

Did the birds notice him? she had wondered that evening, stacking the saucers carefully (they were, Signora Mignelli had let her know, also relics of the wedding dowry). She had not thought to observe whether the starlings had evaded the presence she had so swiftly averted her eye from (why, then she could not quite fathom) as they roamed past the red roofs in their cloudy gangs. But seeing him again her impression now, as she watched the gulls circle the cerulean sky, was that they might fly straight through him – so silently and – what *was* it about him? – so *unassumingly* he stood there. And she understood better why on the first sighting she had felt that strange need to look away. There was something about the extremity of his self-containment which was on the edge of being terrifying. And yet it was not terror she felt now (for, all in an instant, she saw that she had spent her life keeping terror at bay). It was more like the sudden detaching, from inside her body, of a huge and cumbersome weight, which she had carried around unawares. A lightness. An acute lightness seemed to issue from where the presence rested, just above the statue of the angel, as though laughing at his own reflection in stone. It was a lightness which transmitted itself to Julia Garnet and searched through her, down to her toes. (Later she supposed that the feeling was probably somewhat akin to orgasm, were she in a position to make such a comparison.)

And although it was inside only the splinter of a second she observed him, in that moment she knew he had been there for ever.

II
PASSOVER

1

My father is very old now and sits most of his days beneath the camphor trees scribbling at his papyrus. He does not know I have seen him at it, for when he catches me coming he slides the scroll inside the sleeve of his gown and sits plucking at his beard, waiting for me to go away. But his hearing is not as sharp as it once was – though I notice he can still hear my mother's footfall – and there have been times I have stood right behind him at his secret writing, then turned on my heel and gone away, him none the wiser.

But recently, when I was tiptoeing off, he heard me and asked me to stay. He was writing, he told me, the story of my journey to Media – the story which turned around our fortunes. If he died before he finished it . . . but here I interrupted him and told him he was not to speak like that, he was good for another ten years yet.

I lie, of course, but he likes me to lie – with him lies are a form of respect. Very soon my father will leave us and I will grieve, for I love my father. But the news that he is writing about those events so long ago, before I met and married my wife, started a train of remembrance in me too. Funny how even the most extraordinary happenings can fade from your foremost mind, like dew before the noontime sun.

It was the dog – Kish, as I called him – first gave my father pause. He was unlike, my father said, any dog he had known before – so quick in his ways and obliging. I remember Father asked me where Kish had come from and I told him the truth, he had been with Azarias when I met him in the marketplace.

I had been three times to choose a man who would guide me through the high plains and over the mountains to Media. Some told me they knew the way but I could tell they spun a fancy; some had honest faces, but were no better able than I was to find out such a route; and some were no-hopers, fellows who couldn't find their way to their own graves! Again, there were the sort I liked (raffish and cheerful) but my father rejected, the ones he liked (middle-aged and sombre) but my mother found fault with and as time went by I was beginning to wonder how I was going to break it to my father that there was no way I was going to get to Raghes. Then I met Azarias.

Azarias was standing at the edge of the marketplace by a low wall; his foot was resting on it, his arm across his knee, and he was looking. Just looking. But his look seemed to compass the distant mountains and yet take in the smallest stirring round about him. And right away he noticed me and smiled.

There hadn't been much smiling in our household. I am my parents' only child and although they have always cared for me (perhaps too much?) the care has been somewhat careworn, if you take my meaning? Time has been, if you held our household's view, the world has seemed too weary and fraught a place to bear much living in. So when I saw this smile of Azarias's, a place deep down in me woke up and took notice. My mother has a shoulder which aches from her laundry work and when she can she will sit in the sun to ease it. Azarias's smile was like the sun on an aching muscle in my heart: all things became possible suddenly, so that when I approached him to make my proposition I did not think, as before I might have done, He surely will not want to go with me; instead I said, 'Could you guide me to Media perhaps?' and he answered simply, 'Yes.'

And there was another thing: he had a dog with him. Among our people dogs are disdained: *A dog will return to his vomit*, my mother used to say when a person she disapproved of persisted in bad ways. Yet from the start it was different with this dog of Azarias's.

For one thing he had a spotted coat — quite unlike the rough yellow dogs which roamed in packs on the edges of Nineveh. The coat on this dog was smooth and dappled — like sunlight through foliage. Queerer still, he had two spots over his eyes, which gave him the appearance of having four — 'Four-eyes' I found myself calling him affectionately, and patted his flank. And he seemed to enjoy the joke in his doggish way, for there and then, in the marketplace, the dog seemed to choose to go with me, and Azarias never gave any sign that he minded this piece of canine dereliction. You soon learned that Azarias was not a man who 'minded'.

When I took him and Kish home there was a great to-do about Azarias's provenance at first. (I think my father felt he must make up for the ease with which he accepted Kish — and, you know, it is a fact that Kish seemed to know where any difficulty in his being accepted might lie, for his first act on entering our courtyard was to make for my father's seat beneath the wall and put his long nose into my father's hand.) Father wanted to know what tribe Azarias was from. You must understand that, with our people so scattered in exile, the tribes were of the greatest importance — especially to my father! But Azarias smiled again, that smile he had smiled at me in the marketplace, and although there was no way my father could see him smile it was as if his cares became piffle before the wind.

'So, is it a tribe you seek, or merely a hired man to go with your son?' Azarias asked. (And although his tone was respectful, yet somehow you understood the question made a humorous comment on my father.) Then he seemed to relent and told my father who his own father was.

My father, for the first time since I remember him, dropped his high tone. 'I knew Ananias,' he said, referring to the name Azarias had mentioned. 'We sacrificed together at the Temple, long ago,' and his eyes became rheumy and I was afraid he might begin to weep. (I was also curious because it was the first time I had heard of anyone else going with him to the great Temple of the Wise – from the way he had always been telling us he had made that journey alone.)

It was my mother who was most suspicious of Azarias. For some reason she took against him but she was too respectful of my father to make any open opposition. I heard her muttering as she prepared our food for travel: ox-blood sausage, white sheep's cheese wrapped in bay leaves, and goatskins to fill with water. 'Blessed fellow, who does he think he is? Thinks he's above us all, I dare say!'

When we made to depart, though, it was not my mother who was the first to weep. My father stood with tears running from his sightless eyes, grasping the sleeve of Azarias's gown (which I never saw him take off – as if he wished to hide something within its wide folds). Azarias just stood with my father clutching like a child at his sleeve, resting his gaze so lightly upon my father, and a fugitive thought entered my mind: in all the days since he came from his own land this is the first man whom my father has ever let help him (other than my cousin who did it so that his own name should escape tarnish). At that thought I began weeping too, which got my mother going, until soon all three of us were wailing like goats going to slaughter.

ॐ

Vera's letter was a shock.

Ted died suddenly last week. We were all so upset. No flowers (needless to say!) but there was a collection for cancer. I sent a contribution in your name. Hope you don't mind?

Julia looked at the pot of marigolds she had carried out onto the balcony, along with the post, on the tray of tea-things. She had bought the flowers as a gesture of defiance against the withered remembrance of Carlo, which still lay enshrined in the drawer beside her bed. She had not yet brought herself to throw it away. 'Needless to say' indeed! She did 'mind'. She was not at all sure that she wished to contribute to a 'collection for cancer' which when you thought about it might as well, from Vera's representation of it, be a fund for promoting the illness. Julia's father had died of cancer. Who was to say that cancer was not sometimes a necessary end? And in any case, why should Vera take it on herself to offer a contribution on another's behalf? Had she, Julia, wanted to remember Ted in that way the collection would have been no poorer for waiting for a genuine contribution from her own pocket. There was something deplorably controlling about Vera's generosity.

She put aside the letter, using it to mark the place in her notebook, and thought about Ted. A red-faced man with an acute mind, he should have lectured in politics at the LSE. Instead he had spent his working life fighting the cause of the unions and Communism. Where was he now? Julia wondered, for she no longer felt certain that the complex interrelationship which makes up a man could pass out of life and come to nothing. She wished she had been there to defy the injunction on flowers. Ted might have liked flowers — he was a man who responded to colour (hadn't he once paid her a compliment on a scarlet scarf of Harriet's she had borrowed for a march?). Maybe the marigolds would do?

Looking at the letter again she saw she had missed a PTO. Turning the page she read — *P.S. Inspired by your example I am coming to Venice over the bank holiday weekend. With a WEA party.*

Julia Garnet was no stranger to rage — she was aware that it had made up too much of her final dealings with her father — but she was unused to experiencing it with such immediacy. How dare Vera! How dare she track her down, copy her even (for the idea of visiting Venice would never have occurred to Vera without her own example), and with so little sensibility, too, to appreciate the place. Julia had not forgotten that she herself had once possessed a limited sensibility. But the idea that Vera might undergo an alteration like her own in the same environment did not cross her mind and had it done so she would have found no relief in the thought. Indeed the idea of Vera sharing her experiences in Venice appalled her. She stared again at the postscript as if by way of frowning concentration she could erase the offending words.

There was some comfort to be found in the fact it was a WEA affair. That would at least mean Vera would be in a group and somewhat corralled by the timetable of the organisers. And her stay would be thankfully short. But how in the name of all that was serious was she going to deal with Vera's relentless expression of her 'common sense'?

Harriet, who taught infant school, had once remarked that she noticed 'her children' were least tolerant of the stage they had just grown out of. Girls who had barely learned to read scorned as 'babyish' those of their peers who were still fumbling confusedly with their letters. 'I expect we're no different, either,' Harriet had characteristically suggested, and Julia, who enjoyed her own indifference to such matters as 'child development', had made dismissive noises.

Had Harriet been around, she might, in turn, have enjoyed the observation that the prospect of Vera's atheism, formerly such a bulwark of her relationship with Julia and their occasional visits to various cheap Eastern European resorts, now filled Julia Garnet with something like alarm.

What could possibly be done about the proposed invasion? She supposed by 'the bank holiday' Vera intended the first weekend in May. The beginning of the final third of her tenancy in Signora Mignelli's apartment. What Julia was to do when the month of June had expired was a matter she had held off contemplating. She was aware that the cost of the rental soared once the high season arrived. Signora Mignelli had hinted at the special terms she was enjoying, a consequence of her six-month tenancy. And now here was Vera, with her heavy-footed, all-too-common sense, forcing her to consider the future betimes. She began to wonder if she dared to go away for the period of Vera's proposed visit — claiming a pre-arranged trip of her own, say, to the mountains? But there was no guarantee Vera would not follow her there! (For she felt certain that the WEA expedition was a mere cover for Vera's curiosity.)

And in any case, she thought, abandoning the idea, I do not want to miss a minute of my remaining stay. 'I do not want to miss a minute,' she repeated aloud, fiercely to the marigolds.

The post had brought two other items: a letter from her solicitors and a postcard. Not recognising the writing she turned over to see a picture of Vermont. It was from the Cutforths.

Sorry to miss you before we left. But this is to say we are back in Venice at the end of May and are following your example and taking an apartment again for the summer. Hope very much to see you then — Cynthia and Charles

The Cutforths too! She had become almost a trailblazer. The idea amused her and drew something of the sting of Vera's proposed visit. Unlike Vera it would be pleasant to see Cynthia and Charles again. They had called, she had learned, while she was ill and had been sent away by Signora Mignelli. Later a basket of fruit and some flowers had arrived. The flowers had been the source of some distress, for at first she had believed they had come from Carlo — they were just the magnificent kind he would send, tall, pink curvaceous lilies and abundant white roses. When she saw she had misread the name, she had thrust the ribboned bouquet from her — and had manufactured an allergy to the lilies' scent. Signora Mignelli had taken the flowers finally to her own home. Nor, Julia now remembered to her shame, had she even written to the Gritti to thank the Cutforths.

Opening the blue-marbled notebook she had brought out with the post she wrote: *Hurt makes us self-centred.*

The insight made her feel more charitable towards Vera. Maybe Vera was lonely? Her friends were probably few and no doubt she could ill spare the loss of even one. Maybe, too, some use might be made of Vera's arrival. There were things she wanted: a book, in particular, on the Apocrypha. Vera would enjoy the opportunity of being put to trouble.

It was a fine April day; the sky was the improbable blue of a Tiepolo ceiling and the brickwork of the Chiesa dell'Angelo Raffaele glowed coral in the late morning sun. Across the *campo* a slight, boyish shape approached and Julia called out, 'Sarah! Sarah! Hello!'

'Can I come up?' But the girl was with her before Julia could answer.

'What's wrong?' For Sarah was looking agitated. Her long fair hair had escaped its pony-tail and she was raking her fingers wildly through it.

'Julia, oh my God, Julia!'

'What is it? Is it Toby?' Had the unpromising lover caused some further harm?

'He's gone!'

'But where, Sarah? Won't he return?' Surely this was a little melodramatic.

'It's the panel. He's taken the panel, I think. It's gone too! Oh, Julia, Julia.' Noisily, Sarah began to weep.

'Sarah, calm down!'

Inside the kitchen Julia Garnet poured brandy and brought it onto the balcony. She was concerned to see a collection of children, eager to learn the cause of the noise, gathering below. 'Look, hadn't we better come inside?' Sarah allowed herself to be led into the living room. 'There. It's more private here. Now, tell me.'

From the sofa, intermittently weeping, Sarah explained she had woken the previous day to find Toby gone. Julia, who had not considered the twins' living arrangements, found herself wondering about them. She had never asked which part of Venice they were staying in. 'He wasn't there, but that isn't unusual. He often sleeps in the chapel.'

Julia nodded. With the bats. An image of the boy, his long, fair eyelashes drawn like fringed curtains, formed in her mind. 'And he's not there?'

Sarah told how she had gone to the chapel and not finding

Toby had at first assumed some whim or errand. She had worked, increasingly worried, until evening and had returned to their apartment hoping to find him there.

'And the painting?'

'I didn't realise it was gone until this morning. It was only when I was looking and saw Tobe had taken his tools. Then I saw the panel was gone too.'

'I wondered before if it was quite safe.' And it was true she had been bothered at the casual way the painting had been left in the damp chapel with nothing but its grey blanket to protect it.

'There's always one of us there — or the chapel's locked,' Sarah explained. 'Only one of us can get in there.' She clenched her forehead. 'Shit! (Sorry, Julia) I blame myself. I should have guessed something was going to happen. He's been so weird lately!'

Julia saw the pale blue eyes of Toby staring at her the day he showed her the angel. 'Perhaps he's gone to England. Taken the panel with him. Could he be going to get an expert opinion on it?' The boy did not seem to her like a thief. But how was she to tell? She had mistaken a paedophile's affection for a young boy, taking it to herself for her own.

'I thought of that, too. I've left messages on his mobile but he's not answering. I don't know what to do. I should tell someone but then that'll mean the police.'

'But you say only the two of you can get inside the chapel?

Was there any sign of a break-in?' Instinctively, Julia rejected the notion of the police.

Sarah shook her head; she had on her forlorn-child look which meant Julia had to fight exasperation.

'Where does the girl live? Can you ring her?'

But Sarah didn't know the address of Toby's unresponsive lover. She sat on Signora Mignelli's sofa, cradling the brandy.

Julia said, as gently as she could manage, 'I wouldn't bring the police in, you know. Not for family. Wait a bit, I would, and see. You can always say you didn't notice the painting was gone.'

'Only you know about it, actually.' Sarah's voice brightened.

'Only me? Surely not!' Julia felt a stab of anxiety for the fragile wooden piece with its blue-winged angel. The Cutforths' card had brought the story of the missing Bellini to her mind.

'We'd only come across it the day you visited us. It's not listed with all the stuff which got stored years ago before any restoration work started. I checked.'

Julia wondering, Did Carlo know about it – he visited the chapel? said aloud, 'I can't believe I am the only other person who knew it was there. But if I am, then surely there is no need to inform the authorities – at least until you have a better idea of what has happened.' She couldn't bring herself to ask Sarah if she had ever mentioned the panel to Carlo.

Dear Vera, Julia wrote, *I wonder if I might trouble you to bring over a book I need.* She crossed out 'need' and substituted 'want'. *It is not in print but I have telephoned the London Library so if you could manage to collect it for me I will write and reserve it with them. I enclose a note to say you have my permission to collect. You will need this, I think, as they have begun to be particular.* After reading this through she added, *It will be very good to see you and to catch up.* She found this last sentence difficult to write and hesitated, wondering if she could cross out the 'very'. But it was not all untrue. She was fond of Vera. Unable to find anything else to say she concluded the letter abruptly, *Love Julia.*

At least she had managed 'love' — even if, she suspected, it was not wholly sincere.

But what 'love' *is* wholly sincere? she pondered to herself, simmering tomatoes for her supper. Was it 'love' which had driven the boy Toby from his sister and the bat-filled chapel to his unknown destination? And had he taken with him, for companion, the long-footed angel? Nothing had been heard of either of them. Did Toby 'love' his girl and had, perhaps, that love deranged him? Certainly she herself had suffered such a derangement. And was it this, she wondered — chopping basil into the simmering sauce, to which she had added (learning from Signora Mignelli's instruction) just a dash of vinegar, a pinch of sugar — that had brought about the acute and astonishing experience as she had walked out of the chapel that day into the sunlight? The sight itself — of this she was wholly sure — was not the stuff of madness. But maybe a kind of madness had been necessary to pull apart her faculties of perception.

To let the light in, she concluded, pouring steaming scarlet sauce over green ribbons of pasta.

2

 I never asked how Azarias came by Kish. The first stage of our journey was along the eastern bank of the Tigris – the great grey-green river which flows from Nimrod down to Nineveh and thence to the far coast where traders come who bring the dyes. (My mother loved those dyes in the days when she could afford fine cloth.) Kish liked to run on ahead, sniffing out water rats, but when Azarias decided we should stop for the night Kish always met us round the next bend, panting. So it was he, often, who chose finally the place we should halt. They were like-minded, Azarias and Kish.

The first night we set up the tent and Azarias looked at

my feet which had swelled up and sent me off to the river to bathe them (I was unused to walking and felt laggardly besides his swift strides). The water was reedy but quite clear and I was lowering myself in when a great perturbation set up and something grabbed at my foot. Whatever it was was sharp-toothed and I was about to yell out when I felt myself slipping under the water. I was struggling for breath and I must have lost consciousness because all at once there was a blazing light in my head and I half thought, half felt, 'I must not die!'

I came up thrashing, and Azarias was there hauling me onto the bank with Kish yapping beside him. I lay on the bank for a bit gasping and when I got up Azarias was above me, a huge grin on his face. Feeling a fool I said, 'What's there to grin about?' and he pointed and said, 'You've caught us our dinner, I see!' And there at my feet lay the biggest fish I had ever seen!

We roasted and ate the fish — I say 'we' but I never saw Azarias eat a thing: strong as he was, it was as if he lived on desert wind — by the fire which we lit to keep the wild dogs at bay. Azarias salted the remainder down. (I think had my mother seen the skill with which he did it, she might have softened in her distrust.) And then Azarias did a strange thing: he did not throw out the belly-guts of the fish: the liver, or the heart or the gall. We must keep these, he told me: they are medicaments, powerful cures; and he wrapped them in leaves and made me stow them away in the leather pouch I carried at my belt. Although he was the hired hand

and I the master, I did as he instructed. He had a way with him which made you do as he said. But I began to wonder, as I drifted off to sleep, Kish beside me, Azarias keeping silent watch, who he was, and why he had undertaken this journey with me.

༄

Vera wrote back: *It is fine about the London Library and there was no need for you to write — I have telephoned and they are reserving the book for me.* (This prompting an exasperated sigh from Julia.) *Our hotel is the Bellini. I am pleased to say my friend, Peggy, who lost her husband last June, is my roommate — I don't think I should have liked to share with a stranger!*

Signora Mignelli had news of the fishmonger's war — 'He leave fish outside the priest's house. Big fish, big smell!' Here the Signora held her nose. 'Then —' amid laughter — 'he say the father go with prostitute! Because of smell!' More laughter.

She told Julia where the Hotel Bellini was situated — over near the Strada Nuova, near the gondoliers' bar. Julia, who had gathered that the reference to fish was intended to be lewd, was flattered to be included in the bawdy. She amused herself as the Signora talked on — about her cousin's son who had shocked the family by leaving his fiancée for a man, but was now making a success of his shoe shop on the Strada — imagining Vera's reactions to the conversation. Vera, she felt sure, would treat the Signora with all the condescension of her democratic 'principles'. As she no doubt would once have done herself.

What a time it seemed since she had first entered the apartment, Nicco and his friends carrying her case. There had been dark pink anemones in a blue vase. Thinking of the flowers she remembered the Cutforths' lilies. They had been kind. Suddenly she remembered she had never looked for Charles's camel. Now there was a site she might 'do' with Vera, for it was exercising her how she was to keep Vera away from those places in Venice which had become associated in her mind with — well, with what she did not feel able to bear being treated to a dose of Vera's 'common sense'.

'Peggy is lying down. She gets tired since Bob died.' Vera, Julia couldn't help noticing, had a knack of making concern sound like disapproval.

'Has he been dead long?' Despite her resolutions to try to make the best of the visit, Julia was feeling desperate. Conversation was flagging already and Vera had only been in the apartment ten minutes.

'Last June. I told you in my letter.' Vera's disapproval became visible. 'It was very sudden. A stroke.' She had a frown which Julia had not remembered.

'Oh yes,' said Julia meekly. She had met Peggy and wondered if maybe her husband had died to escape his wife's constant talking.

But Vera was rootling in her bag and hauling out a massive tome. 'Your book,' she said. 'I must say it weighs a ton.'

'Vera, you never carried it here? I had no idea!' Guilt displaced speculation about the departed Bob. The book she had requested Vera bring over must have weighed half a stone.

Unexpectedly, Vera gave a guffaw of laughter. 'No one's taken it out since 1952. I told them I thought you had gone a bit potty.' For once she sounded almost cheerful.

'And what did "they" say?' Julia wasn't really listening but had opened and was flicking through the pages of the book to the section on Tobit. Hungrily her eye lit upon tantalising terms and phrases: *Magi – rites of death – consanguineous marriages.* If only Vera would go away so that she could read it. And how ungrateful after her visitor had gone to such trouble! Reluctantly she put the volume down and said with what she hoped sounded like brightness, 'Now lunch. Where shall I take you?'

'There's Tintoretto's parish church nearby. Would you like to see that?'

They had lunched near the Fondamenta Nuova, across the water from the invisible cloud-shaped Dolomites. The meal had not been a success. Vera had argued with the waiter over the cost of a soft drink. 'It doesn't matter,' Julia had said. 'Please don't worry – I'm paying.' But Vera had talked of the 'principle of the thing' in a manner which, for Julia, was too reminiscent of her own former self. Casually she had attempted, 'Principles are not infallible guides . . .' but the effort had fallen away. Why should she disturb Vera's morality after all? Who could tell what else it bolstered up?

Afterwards they had walked in search of Charles Cutforth's camel. This had turned out more successful. Vera enjoyed the story which gave her something to take back to Peggy and the other WEA students. 'My friend knows a historian from Princeton,' Julia guessed she would have declared, with more than a tinge of the boastful. Here was proof of the historicism! A portrait of a Levantine camel offered the right degree of scholarship and political correctness. And Tintoretto – the Dyer – was sufficiently renowned as a painter to excuse a visit to his church.

'I see no reason not to,' Vera said when Julia proposed they visit, and again Julia had to suppress irritation. Why did Vera have to speak in that ridiculous, roundabout way?

The church lay within its own sequestered courtyard. It stood, sculpted by shadows, its high brick façade overlooked by a domed campanile. The two women halted outside as bells rang. Even Vera seemed a little daunted by the magisterial peacefulness of the atmosphere.

Inside, over the high altar, there was a vast canvas on which Ruskin had apparently lavished praise. Grim, twisted bodies writhed under the spell of infernal damnation. Vera who had been consulting her guide became energetic. 'His wife couldn't take it,' she announced with relish. 'It's *The Last Judgement*, you know!'

Julia discarded the impulse to ask Vera what she imagined a 'last judgement' might consist of. What did it mean to be weighed in a balance and found wanting? And was it your deeds or your thoughts which counted, because, if little else, her study of history had shown her that intentions counted for next to nothing when it came to improving things. Wasn't the way to Hell paved with them, anyway? But intentions must, surely, count for something?

'It says here she ran out screaming. She was virgin, you know, his wife.'

Julia, wandered off to investigate the rest of the interior. Was Vera, then, not a virgin? Possibly not, judging by the note of superiority in her tone over the unfortunate Mrs Ruskin. Maybe the dig also constituted some slight revenge on Julia? She imagined Vera rolling robustly naked in a field, – or perhaps on a hillside? – with one of the comrades. At least Vera would know what sex was like.

Turning from a pellucidly-coloured Cima Julia halted. Across the church, at an altar opposite, she recognised, like a friend spotted in an unexpected environ, Signora Mignelli's Bellini with the almond eyes. But why ever was it on an easel? Then she saw. It was not the painting but a reproduction; a print of the original which had, so the inscription told as she came closer, been stolen. She remembered again the Cutforths had mentioned it the day she dined with them at the Gritti. Recalling her first response to the picture she experienced renewed remorse. How sad now the notice of its disappearance made her feel – like those police pictures of missing children. It made her think of Toby, of whom there was still no word.

But now Vera had returned, stimulated by her encounter with damnation, and thankfully it was time for her to make her way back to meet her party. Apparently, they were to visit the Doge's Palace. Julia, who had never ventured inside the great Palazzo Ducale which adjoins St Mark's, found herself, by inference, lying. 'Oh you mustn't miss it. It's quite superb. Let me come with you to the *vaporetto*.'

But Vera wouldn't hear of it. 'No, no. I am absolutely fine. I can quite easily find the stop. I shall call you tomorrow and let you know our plans.'

Julia walked back into the courtyard with her and watched her over the rail-less bridge beetle off up the narrow *calle*.

And the blessed relief of being alone! Feeling she might now look less inhibitedly around the cool interior, Julia wandered back inside the church to inspect Tintoretto's tomb. A notice beside described how the painter had flown into a rage over the execution of a portrait. The row which broke out had been so violent that Tintoretto had been obliged to hole up in the church as a consequence. How tremendous to have the courage of one's emotions! But the Venetian nobleman, object of the painter's displeasure, could no doubt take it. One couldn't really howl and throw things about, like Tintoretto, at Vera, as she had wanted to do.

The door to the right opened and a priest came out; another part of the church! Pushing against the heavy doors she entered a side chapel.

Before rows of candles sat an effigy of a woman, a solid-looking baby on her capacious stone lap. Of course! The

Madonna dell'Orto — the eponymous Madonna who was found in a local's garden, of which Sarah had spoken.

Julia approached the broad-beamed Virgin and as she did so a figure, crouched at the statue's foot, started up from behind the row of burning candles and was by the door through which she had entered before she registered who it was.

'Sarah, where is your apartment? I've always been meaning to ask.'

Julia, returning from the Madonna dell'Orto, had gone by the chapel and had found Sarah packing up her things.

'In the Ghetto. Why?'

The Ghetto, once the province of the Jewish settlement in Venice, was close by the area she had just come from. 'I was up near you, then, today.'

The girl's fair hair made a halo of the early evening sun. With her androgynous shape and face she might be described as 'angelic'. But something held Julia back from the revelation she had come to make. If it was Toby (and she did not seriously doubt that it was Sarah's twin she had seen praying by the stone Madonna) evidently he did not want his presence in Venice to be known. Inexplicably, Julia felt she should protect his obvious desire for anonymity.

'You must come and call.' Sarah smiled and for a second Julia felt guilty that she had not divulged her impression of the figure she had watched hurrying from the side chapel. She had followed, as swiftly and discreetly as she could, through the body of the church. But when she had emerged into the courtyard there was no sign of him. For a while she had stood, shading her eyes from the sun, searching along the *fondamenta* after a hurrying shape. She was as certain as she could be that it was Toby; there was something in the way he held his neck.

But if so, for whatever reason, it was information she found now she was reluctant to share. 'How nice, I should be delighted. You can give me tea for a change!'

'How was your friend?'

'Tiresome.' Julia stopped herself from grimacing. 'She's gone off to see the Doge's Palace with her WEA party. But I took her to see *The Last Judgement* in the Madonna dell'Orto and she liked that!'

'Oh yes. The scary Tintoretto. Tobes likes it too.'

So it probably was him in the church. The coincidence was too great for error. But for some reason still Julia did not feel like imparting the news to Sarah that her brother was still about in Venice. Instead she said, 'He's in good company then. According to my friend, Ruskin thought it was the bee's knees!'

At home, sitting on her balcony, she wrote: *Death draws the line under the account i.e. the 'sum' of one's life when all that can be has been. This must be why it is the moment of 'judgement'. What does my life really amount to?*

3

We followed the barley-growing valleys of the Tigris down for many miles, Kish running before us, and then struck east along a tributary which ran through undulating hills. The valley was narrow and the hills dusty, quite unlike the fertile green country we had left behind. It was a comfort to have Azarias at my side. He told me stories along the way which helped lighten the journey. One in particular, he called 'The Grateful Dead', was about a man who buries a corpse he finds by the wayside and is later brought good fortune by the kind offices of the corpse-spirit, which reminded me of my father. I had never been from home before and the thought of my father and my

mother often made me home-sick. But this I never let on to Azarias.

After a while we left the tributary and struck upwards to a new terrain. Here on the high plains we passed caravans of travelling nomad people, with their strings of camels and donkeys. Sometimes they would stop and offer us dates or the soured asses' milk they drank laced with honey. On such occasions Azarias left me to do the talking with the chief — stepping back into his position of hired hand. Once, one of the mules in the caravan had developed fits and I heard from one of their muleteers that Azarias had run his hand along the creature's back and over his flanks. After a while the mule opened its mouth with a great 'hee-haw'-ing and then stumbled to its feet cured.

But mostly we saw no one. It was a peculiar time and often when we had walked many miles in silence I saw strange sights. At this date I do not know still whether they were phantasms, born of the harsh sun and lonely conditions. Once I thought I saw a bush burning in the distance. It was at a time when Azarias had gone ahead, seeking water. When he returned, the goatskins full to the neck, I could no longer see any trace of fire — so I had no witness of the sight. Another time a cloud, no bigger than a man's hand, hovered over us, seeming to follow us as we walked. But Azarias appeared unaware of anything unusual, and merely strode on with his long gait. Fearful of having him diagnose sickness and enforce a stop (as he had once before when I had visions of water and date palms) I kept the vision to myself.

Once I woke in the night with a dream in which Azarias had left me. I cried out — as I cried when I woke as a child and found my mother missing — and getting up to look by the fire found Azarias gone and only Kish guarding it. Although I was ashamed of it at the time, I can say now that a desolation fell upon me then the like of which I have never felt before or since. I cried out again, this time in real fear — and in a lightning second, as if a hawk had dropped out of the sky, Azarias appeared out of the darkness and was with me again. That night he sang me to sleep — a sweet, high sound. I had heard from the herdsman that Azarias had sung such a song to the sick mule — like a bird's song it was; but such a bird I have never heard in this mortal life.

༄

'There is really no need,' Vera said.

'But I would like to come,' said Julia, on the whole meaning it.

They were arguing over Vera's departure. Julia had suggested she should see them off at Marco Polo. Now that her friend was leaving she felt compunction at her own unfriendliness.

Peggy said, 'It would be a help with the bags,' which made Julia wish she had not volunteered to go at all. But still, she rather fancied the long water journey past the Cimitero, the burial island on which the bones of dead Venetians were permitted to rest for ten years before being transported to the more permanent ossuaries; out past the small, bobbing, diving birds which patrol the roped-off avenues of water leading to the airport.

The WEA party were travelling in the hotel boat. 'I am sure we can squeeze you in,' Peggy had suggested; but Julia, preferring not to be 'squeezed', took the public service.

At the airport she met Vera and Peggy, short-temperedly shunting baggage in a line for the check-in. Feeling rather useless she drifted off in search of coffee to bring back to them.

There was a queue at the coffee bar as well. While waiting, she amused herself observing the reflections mirrored in the window-glass of the surrounding shops: a man with a shaved head and a plait down his neck; a woman with green hair in shorts and high-heeled sandals; a businessman with a silver case — and Toby!

But where was he? Confused, she twisted around trying to locate his position in relation to the shaven-headed man. There was the green-haired girl and there, just ahead, was Toby, walking from her. Extricating herself from the queue Julia pursued his disappearing form across the hall and round a corner. He was walking rapidly and, half-running after, she saw, in her mind's eye, his sister's retreating back, walking away from her across the Campo Angelo Raffaele.

Ahead of her Toby crossed the hall. To her horror she saw the sign 'Departures' and Toby placing — she was almost sure of it — a long flat package under the X-ray machine.

'Toby!' she called out, desperate at the prospect of losing him. And again 'Toby!' But her voice sounded thin in her own ears and he never looked back.

For the second time in two days she was left staring in dismay after the retreating figure of the missing twin.

4

When you walk you have time for thinking. The journey was tough-going, the more so when we reached the spine of mountains which lies between Assyria and Media. But with each day climbing made me stronger, and perhaps it was because of this that a sense of something else also grew stronger within me.

I have not spoken of the great God Yahweh for whose sake my father would anger my mother and bury the bodies of our dead. My father was strict: as a child he would teach me the Torah, the books of law, and tell how the tribes had offended our God by worshipping the bull-god Baal and that because of this we had been taken as punishment out of our own land, which had been promised us, to serve under the yoke of the Assyrians.

I had taken this idea in with my mother's milk and felt pity for the boys of other families whom my father said had forgotten the land of their fathers and were growing up godless heathens. And yet here, high on the mountain passes, climbing with Azarias and Kish, and the camels we had bought for the journey, I felt a new freedom: a relaxing of my spirits, as if away from my father and his austere God I had a chance to be someone else. My mother used to tell stories to me of the hills round Lake Galilee where she grew up; there was a light, she said, which dances on the waters there and she spoke of her grandmother Deborah, who had the gift of foresight and told how a day would come when a man would walk on that water and by that it would be known he was the Messiah. My mother spoke, too, of the high, green places and leafy sanctuaries which were shrines to the old country gods where our people had gone secretly to sacrifice. The old gods perhaps were kinder than our Only one, who (I dared to think as we walked further and further from home) was somewhat demanding. I had so often heard he was a jealous God and how his name was 'Jealous'. It seemed to me that perhaps I understood why our God Yahweh had been forsaken: He was a hard taskmaster; maybe other gods asked less of their worshippers?

One day, these thoughts running through my head, I asked, 'Do you worship, Azarias?' and then felt awkward for a man's god is his own affair.

But Azarias was not the kind who made you feel awkward. 'Indeed,' he said. 'You might say worship is my business!'

That was rather too enigmatic for me; Azarias was a hired hand who gave his labour in the marketplace. 'How so?' I asked.

But to this he gave no reply. He was having trouble with one of the camels, a bad-tempered beast at the best of times, and he was talking coaxingly to it. Eventually he said, 'Maybe you will find that out when we get to Ecbatana.' Then he whistled his bird-call whistle at the camel, who sneezed at him.

The mention of Ecbatana drove all god-interest from my brain. 'Ecbatana? Why Ecbatana when we're for Raghes?' The city by the far sea, my father named it.

'No,' said Azarias. 'Not Raghes. Ecbatana.' He whistled some more at the camel.

At this I grew alarmed. 'No, no, Azarias,' I cried out. 'My father demands we go as quickly as possible to Raghes to recover his debt; he will be counting the days to our return. We must do as he desires.'

The camel seemed to have calmed down and was now walking sedately beside Azarias with its high-stepping gait. 'Tobias,' Azarias said, and I realised then that this was the first time he had addressed me by name, 'we shall not go to Raghes tonight. We shall go first to where your kinsman, Raguel, lodges in Ecbatana.'

I had never heard of this Raguel. 'Listen,' I said, 'I think you misunderstand. In the absence of my father I am the master here and you the servant. So let's have no more about Ecbatana, please. We are going to Raghes and that's that!'

When I was a boy the king had a steward, a fat old eunuch who, never having promise of a child himself, took somewhat to me. He told me tales of the fierce Sea People and of terrible creatures from far-off lands. One he told of could look at you and turn you to stone with its glance. Azarias did not look at me like a basilisk, for his glance felt as if it could turn you not to stone but set you on fire – but that is the closest I can come to describing the effect it had upon me. All I know is I cried out, 'Very well, very well, we will do as you say. To Ecbatana, by all means Ecbatana!' and I said nothing for several miles.

After a while we descended to a wide plain and stopped. Azarias wordlessly pointed to a city of high towers lying before us. 'Ecbatana, I suppose?' I said, speaking as coldly as I could, but he just swung on down leading his camel.

At the outskirts of the city Azarias, who was still walking ahead, motioned me to halt. 'I have a thing to tell you,' he said. 'Listen. There is a girl here; she was set apart for you from the beginning.'

At these words I became strangely frightened. I knew that one day I must marry. And I had had thoughts of girls as I lay in my bed. Once, when we were travelling in the desert and had passed the night in the company of one of the bands of nomadic people, I had seen a slave girl with her breasts exposed and felt myself become excited. She had eyed me and inclined her head towards her quarters – but

I was too lily-livered to go after her. In the nights which followed I thought of her often and cursed my shyness. But I had had no marriage thoughts of any particular girl. And now here was Azarias speaking of the beginnings of time.

'But my father . . .' I said, weakly. (There was little point because I already knew that even my father was no match for Azarias.)

'Raguel is of your father's tribe.' Azarias was coaxing the camel again with camelish grunts so that you would swear he was one of the beasts himself. 'He has one daughter, named Sara. I will speak for her that she may be given you for wife.'

Then he added something which I did not understand but my spirit quaked within me as I heard it. He said, 'She is one in whom the dark is equal to the light.'

*

The book about the Apocrypha was heavy but enlightening. Julia, lying on Signora Mignelli's sofa, was re-reading the cautious, scholarly prose a second time. The Book of Tobit, the editor conjectured, although dealing with the events of the eighth century BC, was probably not formally written down until the last quarter of the second century BC by a Jew possibly living in the Jewish colony on the island of Elephantine in Egypt. Persian soldiers may have brought the story to Egypt. The tale almost certainly contained elements of much older legends.

Lying back, Julia closed her eyes and thought again about Tobit who had been carried off into captivity over twenty-eight centuries ago from his own country of Israel. She had looked up the event in the Old Testament. According to the Book of Kings the northern kingdom of Israel (which was distinct from Judah, the separate kingdom in the south), had grown lax in its worship of Yahweh: *They set them up images and groves in every high place and green tree.* But not old Tobit! By his own account he toiled off down south each year with his tithes to the Temple in Jerusalem, which was in quite another country — for the tribes of Israel had quarrelled, split apart and become two kingdoms.

Poor old Tobit, whose insistence on the law lost him his own sight! Opinionated and censorious as he was, she felt for him — as if he might have been a brother or a cousin she had never had. For after all was she herself not somewhat akin to the cantankerous, faintly comical figure who made such heavy weather of always doing the right thing? And then, when things didn't work out for him, such a business about his uselessness and wanting to die! Didn't she just know (as Cynthia Cutforth might have put it) how he had felt?

The phone rang. 'Julia?' She could hardly believe the voice. 'It's Cynthia — I rang to say "Hi!" — we're back in town.' A muffled noise at the other end. 'Charles says you can't call Venice "town" — you see what a pedant he still is! Now, when can we have you come over?'

Julia, a little stunned at the prescience of her own train of thought, asked where they were staying and Cynthia explained they had taken an apartment on the Gindecca, the island which almost faces the entrance to Venice's Grand Canal. 'So you can run across to us easily on the 82,' she said, naming the boat-line which ran from the direction of the Raffaele.

Two afternoons later Julia was sitting on the Cutforths' wide balcony; across the water her eye ranged over buildings painted rose, buildings painted terracotta, blue, ochre, pistachio green. Before them, dipping and criss-crossing, veered boats carrying crates of vegetables, boats carrying buckets, boats carrying sugar, detergent, cornflakes, lavatory paper, boats carrying steel shafts, sand, planks, green garbage boats, blue police boats, one with birds in cages and chickens in coops and others conveying humankind of all nations. Man's ingenuity is the product of difficulty, she thought: the Venetians have made of their watery environment a way of life which is an art form.

Although the three of them had met only once before, the lapse of time, since their first encounter six months earlier, had somehow swelled out the acquaintance. They had been talking – or more accurately, Charles had, with the women listening with varied degrees of concentration – of the Chapel-of-the-Plague.

Lighting one of his cheroots, Charles stretched back in his chair, the smoke curling up in the air before him. 'It's fascinating. I must tell you how grateful I am to you, Julia, for drawing it to my attention.' He had a hint of pomposity and a way of nodding his head while he spoke which Julia, observing it, guessed his wife might find maddening. 'Absolutely fascinating. There was a death – I think you said so, our evening at the Gritti – or a near miss, anyway. A young woman looked like dying of the plague during the Black Death and then when all her relatives believed she was a goner, *bingo*!' he snapped his fingers – his nails, Julia noticed, were pink and carefully cut – 'she recovered. Being the fourteenth century they called it a miracle.'

'Charles is a true man,' said Cynthia comfortably, 'and can't bear to imagine that there is more to life than meets the eye.'

'I'm afraid I was like that once.' Julia, who had in the past objected to the attribution of rationality as the prerogative of the male sex, spoke remorsefully. 'Who was she, the girl? Did you find out?'

'The only stuff I've managed to get hold of is kind of vague. From what I can make out she was the only daughter of one of Venice's numerous minor nobility. It sounds as if there was something wrong about her before she ever got the plague, because they kept trying to marry her off and she came home every time with the marriage unconsummated.'

'Probably psychosomatic.' Cynthia folded her hands across her stomach, confident that here was an area in which she was better versed than her husband.

'But could one recover from the plague? I'm so foggy on my medieval history.' And it was true that her old certainties had been fast vanishing.

'I guess some folk did – but it was rare enough. And then

there's the name – the Chapel-of-the-Plague, although that may have been adopted later – after a series of supposed cures. You know how these superstitions grow?'

'Superstitions?'

'There was supposed to be some icon – reckoned to have healing powers.'

Julia said nothing. Her mind had veered dangerously towards Toby and the missing panel. No word of either had been heard since that day she had watched his departing shoulders at the airport.

'I like angels,' Cynthia said. She did not want the conversation to become too scholastic.

Sometimes Julia woke in the night, and realised it was not herself but the blue angel she was anxious over. She had said nothing further to the girl – but with the passing weeks the time when the authorities must be informed drew closer. And then it would become a matter for the police.

Charles had risen to fetch a book and the smell of his cheroot wafting past her suddenly brought back Carlo. Another who, like Toby, had disappeared into the dark. Perhaps it was her? Maybe, like the girl in the Book of Tobit, she cast a baleful spell upon men?

'We are planning a party,' Cynthia said. 'Just a few people we've gotten to know over the years for drinks. Promise you'll come.'

Charles returned with the book he had been searching for. 'See, here.' He indicated a photograph among the illustrations – the chapel, but desolate, surrounded by what looked like barbed wire. 'That was taken just after the war. Looks a mess, doesn't it?'

Julia, looking, mused, I wonder if he was there then? The Archangel Raphael, who had elected to walk on foot with young Tobias across the mountains from Assyria to Media, had also travelled across the seas with the sailors to Venice. Aloud she said, 'Charles, how did the plague get here? My brain's getting soft; I can't remember any of the things I used to know.'

'Tragically, it came in on the shipping routes, on the trade ships from the east.'

So that was why he had come! She pictured the long feet striding the seas, keeping swift invisible pace over the water alongside the ships which harboured the death-dealing rats.

'Weren't you going to take Julia to visit the Monsignore?' Cynthia asked.

They took the 82 across the water.

'Damn, I can't phone,' said Charles putting away his mobile. 'I've left the blasted number behind.'

A man in blue working-overalls sped by, his dog standing alert on the stern. Looking at the dog Julia said, 'The icon. Did you discover anything about that?'

'No, but Giuseppe may know. Hell, what a nuisance. I should have rung before we left but Cynth was harassing me. She doesn't like the Monsignore.'

'So she's palming me off on him!'

'Yes, but I reckon you'll like him,' said Charles, not understanding the joke. 'He's an authority on the East. But he's an authority on all kinds of things. If anyone knows about your chapel it'll be him.'

With nothing else to do, Julia said she was glad to accompany Charles as the water-bus took them in its zigzag journey back across the water to the island of San Giorgio.

'Look at it, our finest piece of Palladio.' Charles waved his manicured hand as San Giorgio Maggiore's imposing façade slid towards them.

Julia, about to agree, changed her mind. 'I don't like it. I'm probably being philistine but it feels unholy, somehow.' Once she had ventured inside the famous church's marmoreal interior and had crept out again, frozen to the bone. 'It's so cold there. Have you been?' Only the great weather-beaten bronze angel which usually tops the campanile had warmed her interest. It had been brought inside for repair and furtively she had bent and kissed its great angelic foot which peeped from beneath its brazen gown. But this she did not confide to Charles Cutforth.

'I guess I'm not too hot on what is holy.'

He is a nice man, she thought, as he extended his arm to help her onto the landing stage. It was on a waterfront they had first met. How different she had been then. To her surprise she found herself saying so to Charles. 'Oh, I was against everything the least bit "holy" before I came here. Venice has changed me.'

'Well, I guess beauty can do that.'

They strolled by the tethered, bucking gondolas, along the waterfront towards St Mark's. She had not been back since she had seen the sparrow which had led her to the marble Madonna. Thinking of that day she remembered the purple-clad priest who had frightened her in the confessional box. Perhaps he had been the Monsignore. 'Charles, what exactly does the title "Monsignor" mean?'

A crowd of camera-waving tourists was pell-melling round them and he steered her through the chatter and up a narrow *calle*. 'It's a priest without portfolio – an honour given by the Pope for special service. In Giuseppe's case he did sterling work with the Vatican's secretary of state, Ottaviani, which involved him in all kinds of diabolical diplomatic intrigues. I met him, in fact, when he was over in the States on Vatican business. He's been retired now for many years and free to pursue his own interests, which in Giuseppe's case is practically everything. If anyone does, he'll have the dirt on your chapel.'

They had stopped by a stone gateway with a garden behind. Roses, reaching towards the light, reared leggily over wrought-iron gates. On the gates a painted heraldic sign featured a lion and what looked like a palm tree.

Charles looking at it said, 'An ancestor with connections in the East. Giuseppe comes from one of the oldest families in Venice. He's quite a character. Remind me to tell you about his sons.'

'Sons?'

Charles laid a finger on his lips as, in answer to the bell, behind the gate there were sounds of bolts being pulled back and a woman with a visible moustache appeared through a gap in the wrought iron.

Charles produced his card and spoke fluently in Italian and the woman, after a few minutes, returned and opened the gap wide enough for them to enter a leafy courtyard around which ran a green-painted veranda.

Seated beneath the veranda, a pug dog at his feet, was a man in a black gown. Even seated, and at some distance, it was evident he was ugly and very short.

The man in the black gown opened his hands, 'Carlo amico!' Just for a second Julia's heart contracted painfully before she remembered that Carlo was the Italian version of Charles.

'Giuseppe!' Charles was striding towards the veranda. 'How fortunate that you are here. Forgive me for not telephoning. Like a blasted idiot I mislaid your number.'

The Monsignore had got up from his chair and was embracing Charles. He must have been a good foot shorter for his arms seemed to come somewhere only a little above the tall American's waist. Gesturing towards Julia Charles said, 'Giuseppe – this is our English friend Julia Garnet.'

'The garnet is my favourite stone.' The Monsignore had bright brown eyes like a bird's – a blackbird's, perhaps – though his face looked rather more like his dog. The dog, having lost its protection from the clerical gown, had moved under the table and was staring up at Julia with its comical snubby face. 'My mother was convinced I was homosexual when I was a boy because always I loved to wear her jewellery. She was not correct in her fears. But in any case, you see I sublimate any homosexual impulses by wearing rings and a dress.'

He proffered a freckled hand on which gleamed a large garnet ring and Julia shook it, unsure how to respond to this introduction from a dignitary of the church.

'Julia was the first person we met here back in the New Year,' Charles said, sensing his companion's awkwardness.

'Sit down, sit down. Oh, your pardon, Marco!' Inadvertently the priest had trodden on the pug which had given a protesting yelp. 'It is hot for him – he likes the shade of my gown. If nothing else my position gives protection for my dogs! Some prosecco?' and not waiting for an answer the Monsignore called out, 'Constanze, Constanze, prosecco per favore!'

Julia, who had been disconcerted by the reference to homosexuality so close to the reference to Carlo's name, was even more put out at being offered the drink she associated with him. She sat, feeling supernumerary, while the two men exchanged pleasantries.

After a while the priest turned back to her. 'And flowers. Being English you must like flowers, Signora Garnet? I insist you admire my roses. Of these I am most proud.'

'Julia, please,' said Julia as she was propelled towards the blooms which had met them at the gate.

'They are a colour I especially admire. The colour almost of your name.' Cupping a dark red rose with his mottled hand the Monsignore breathed in its scent. 'Of this I never tire – it is even more lovely than the perfume of women. And so, garnet –' tapping his ring – 'it is a propitious name. You are a historian, Charles tells me.'

'Oh hardly. I was a school teacher.'

'But this is the best authority of all. And Charles tells me you are curious about the little chapel near the Raffaele.'

'Yes, the Chapel-of-the-Plague. My friends are restoring it.' She supposed it was all right by now to call the twins 'friends'.

'So?' The Monsignore looked pleased. 'I was a great fan of your Ashley Clarke and the English restorations are the best, in my view. Without such efforts Venice would have lost many of its treasures. And they do not tell you the story of this chapel, your friends?'

'I don't think they know it.'

They had walked back to the veranda where the woman with the moustache was setting down a tray with a jug and some glasses. Charles had disappeared. 'Charles is in my library looking for a book. He pretends it is me he calls to see but I know it is my library he prefers. Still,' the Monsignore giggled, 'it leaves me alone with a pretty woman which he knows I like!'

Julia, uncertain how to respond to this, accepted a glass of prosecco. Perhaps it was the effect of the alcohol, or the reminder of times spent with Carlo, but she found herself saying, 'You are not what I would expect a priest to be like.'

The Monsignore looked smug. 'I am sometimes a worry to my superiors,' he admitted. 'But I am strict with my vows. It is the priests who speak scornfully of sex who are caught with their pants down. I love the women — but I love Our Lady more. And because I love women I know better how to love her. It makes sense?'

'Yes, I suppose it does.' The priest's directness was making her feel exposed so that she brought the conversation, almost defensively, back to the chapel. 'Charles told me it was built for a young woman who survived the plague.'

'But did he tell you that she was a Jewess? No, I see he didn't!' The Monsignore was triumphant.

'How could she be Jewish?' Julia asked. 'If it's a chapel surely it must be Christian. I don't see.'

'But this is the whole point.' The Monsignore's voice took on the tone of a man rubbing his hands. 'It had to be concealed because even though Venice was, in fact, the first Christian state who passed laws making it illegal to harm the Jews, still there were strict controls forbidding the congress of Jews and Christians – even the prostitutes, if they were Christians, were forbidden to the Jew, although it is an interesting thing, you know it is comparatively rare for Jewish men to visit prostitutes as it is even rarer for them to murder.'

Charles, who had emerged with a book, hearing this said, 'Some would say they murdered Jesus Christ.'

The Monsignore held up a hand. 'Of all people I am aware of this. But the death of Christ, lamentable as it was, is not in the ordinary sense murder. The Jews are a legalistic people and they would say the crucifixion took place under due law. For them the sanctity of life is everything. The death of Our Lord aside, it is a matter from which we Christians could learn a thing from the Jews.'

'But the girl who died . . . ?' said Julia, not wanting the story to get lost.

'Forgive me. I am riding on my hobby-horse.' The Monsignore sipped his glass. There was a delicacy in his gestures which suggested the surgeon. 'So although it was us who give the name of Ghetto to the world –'

'From *gettare*,' interrupted Charles, keen to display his knowledge.

'Just so. Charles as ever is right.' The Monsignore made a slight wink in Julia's direction. 'As Charles will tell us, this word has the meaning of casting metal, and originally we put the Jews in an old cannon-foundry – which disturbs me when I think of what Hitler has done later. Of course there is nothing new under the sun, but I wonder sometimes if with our Venetian cannon-foundry we give him the idea for his gas chambers? However, it is not until 1512 that the Jews are shut behind gates at night with Christian guards we make the Jews pay for!' The Monsignore laughed. 'Shylock was right – it is we who were the mercenary ones!'

Julia, thinking of the conversation with Charles, said, rather timidly, 'They were the principal traders here, weren't they?'

The Monsignore smiled as if she were an intelligent child. 'Of course! In fact, as Charles knows better than any of us, the Jews make excellent business for Venice – most of our wealth is born out of their transactions with the East. And this, in fact, is relevant to the story. Listen, Marco, while I tell Signora Garnet!'

The dog, who had been sniffing in the flowerbeds, came back and settled under the black gown. 'The girl's father was a Venetian nobleman who married, in secret, the daughter of a Jewish doctor. (The Jewish doctors have an excellent reputation, by the way. Almost always the Doge's personal physician is a Jew.) The Jewish women were famously beautiful and the god of love is no respecter of human laws!'

'By which I can tell you he means Dan Cupid, not the Holy Trinity,' said Charles, amused.

At this the priest just raised his hands as if in surrender and said, mildly, 'Eros, please. "Cupid" is not a respectful name for such a dangerous god.'

'Oh,' said Julia, 'I agree!' and blushed when the priest turned and looked closely at her before continuing.

'It is said that this nobleman prayed for a son — and when his wife died after giving birth to a daughter, he rejected the child. According to Jewish law a child takes on the mother's race — and so she was brought up, out of his sight, in the upper storey of the family palazzo, a Jewess unknown to herself.'

'This sounds apocryphal, Giuseppe!' said Charles.

'Ah, Carlo, you are a rationalist. Suspend your disbelief, please, or I will not tell you . . .'

'Oh, do, please, go on,' said Julia. She rather hoped Charles would go back inside.

'One day there comes a young man, from the East, from the Levant, in fact where my family also once long ago came from, which is maybe why I like this story. He is a trader in silk and somehow he sees and falls in love with this young woman. How he meets her we must guess. Maybe he calls to do some business with her father? The young silk-trader is, however, also a Jew and her father will have nothing to do with the young man except by way of business. This the daughter knows although she is not aware that she herself is Jewish and this is why her father keeps her out of his sight.'

The Monsignore paused to sip his prosecco. 'I hope this drink suits you?'

Julia, not thinking, said, 'Oh yes, my friend, another Carlo, used to buy it for me.' It was the first time, since 'the discovery', she had mentioned his name.

The priest rested his eyes on her again for a moment before he resumed. 'So the young couple meet in secret. Meantime the father tries to marry off the girl to various of the young nobility. He has great wealth so there is a valuable dowry.'

'This is what I read too,' said Charles suddenly.

'It is good my story is verified!' The blackbird eyes shone rather spitefully. 'Where there is money naturally there are many suitors, as your Jane Austen knew – what an intelligent woman!' He kissed his fingers theatrically. 'Many young men wish to marry the girl but in all cases she is returned after the wedding. Why? The marriage is not consummated.'

Julia wanted to ask what happened to the failed husbands but the Monsignore held up a hand again. 'One day, to the horror of her household, the girl wakens with symptoms of the plague. There are buboes like blackberries breaking out all over her sweet young body.' He paused, looking over at the roses, as if to condole with them for the ruined charms of the long-dead girl. 'Her father is distraught. In fear and guilt he calls upon every known medical resource, for he has come to realise, too late, that he loves the daughter who reminds him of his dead wife. Excuse me,' and here the Monsignore drew out a handkerchief and blew his nose. 'The story is affecting,' he resumed, 'and this I think vouches for its truth.'

'In that case you might as well say that *The Sound of Music* is "true"!'

The Monsignore's eyes, ignoring Charles, addressed Julia's. 'The young man hears of the illness. Knowing that he will not be permitted to see his beloved and that her death is likely within a matter of a few days, he prays outside her window. And here is the marvel.'

He paused dramatically.

'OK, Giuseppe.' Charles was a touch impatient. 'Give us the marvel!'

'It is night and he prays across the water from the noble palazzo. As he prays he is visited by the Archangel Raphael, who tells him how the girl can be cured.'

The Monsignore sat back folding his hands in his lap as if that was all he had to say. 'Come on then,' said Charles. 'You can't stop there. What happens next? How come the chapel?'

'I see you warm to my story, Carlo! Somehow the young man persuades the household to admit him to the girl's chamber — contagion in cases of the plague is almost instantaneous and it is unusual for anyone to choose to go near those affected. The young man, presumably following the advice of his angelic counsellor, performs a medical miracle and the girl survives. Of course there is an alternative version which suggests she is cured by the help of her grandfather, the Jewish doctor, and that later this is turned into a story of the visit by Raphael – see what a good friend to you I am, Carlo, to tell you this rationalist counter to my mumbo-jumbo! In any case the girl recovers and her father gives permission for the couple to marry. But by now the Jews have become scapegoat for the plague – Venice lost two-thirds of her population and the Jews, when they were not dragged into the streets and burned, had most of their property confiscated. The young couple must keep their religious identity secret. So Papa builds the chapel on the site where the visitation occurs, as a thank-offering to the Angel Raphael. A cover, you see! And this I find very amusing for this reason: because the angels are, in fact, Jewish. We Christians have hijacked them, and this is how the father was able to cover up the unfortunate Jewish origin of the miracle. It became a Christian chapel after all. Certainly yes, we are great hijackers,' said the Monsignore, evidently enjoying the word.

'And the young couple. What happened to them?' More than anything she wanted to know.

'They lived happily ever after!' said Charles ironically. 'How much of that is bullshit, Giuseppe?'

'One should never dismiss bullshit, Carlo. The greatest truths lie in improbable stories. Look at the gospels!'

Later, as she and Charles walked back along the *fondamenta* Julia said, 'What an extraordinary man!' The Monsignore exuded an energy which made Charles's company seem almost bland.

'He is,' said Charles. 'During the war, when he was still in his seminary, he helped the Jews to safety through his knowledge of the secret passages which run through Venice. Presumably that's why he's so taken with the fairy story about the chapel!'

'We didn't ask about the icon,' Julia said. She did not want to hear the story criticised.

'So we didn't,' Charles said. 'But Giuseppe will surely come to our party. He loves a bash. You can ask him then.'

5

 I know it is easy to be wise after an event but even before Azarias disclosed what he knew I smelled danger — a hollow feeling below my ribs — as we made our way to the house of this relative Azarias had thrown at me. Everyone we asked seemed to know who he was. 'Raguel?' they said. 'Surely we know Raguel. Go to the house with the tower by the ditch of bulrushes.'

And it was the case that here in Ecbatana were many buildings which zigzagged to the skies.

When we reached a house with such a tower Azarias insisted I go forward to meet my relatives though they had no foreknowledge of our arriving.

I went in and found a man sitting by the door of the courtyard and my heart gave a lurch when I saw him, a broad-shouldered man with just that same squint along his nose, which resembled my father's look before he lost the use of his eyes.

The man gave a greeting – 'Much cheer to you, stranger!' – and he brought me into his house. He introduced me to Edna, the woman of the household who greeted me courteously, a woman with a flat friendly face, not at all like the face of my mother, Anna. My mother's face, my father always said, was like the face of a roe deer.

But it was Edna who recognised me, so that I had no need to say who I was, for the moment she clapped eyes on me she said, 'Raguel, how like he is to your kinsman of Nineveh, Tobit!'

'That is very fit,' I answered, 'for Tobit of Nineveh is my father.'

Then Raguel sprang up and embraced me saying, 'Blessings to you, lad, for you are the son of a good and noble father.' And he ordered a ram of his flock to be killed to receive us.

I was pondering how to broach the question of their daughter but I need not have worried because at that moment a maidservant came down the stairs, wailing and wringing her hands. The girl Azarias had chosen for me to marry was threatening, it seemed, to throw herself from the window of the topmost tower.

*S*ignora Mignelli had referred from time to time to the date when the tenancy came to an end. 'I miss you,' she explained to Julia, regretful. 'But I must let to tourist to make money.'

Julia, who had not yet decided what she was going to do after she had left the Campo Angelo Raffaele, mentioned to Sarah that she might need to find another apartment. She was not at all sure she was ready to return to Ealing. The small flat where she had lived so many years had, in her imagination, become dreary and confined.

Unexpectedly, Sarah had offered a solution. 'I'm going to have to go home myself in early July,' she explained. 'I'll be back but you're welcome to use my apartment while I'm away. In fact it would be great to have someone there to keep an eye on things. D'you want to come by and see?'

The Ghetto was near the Madonna dell'Orto, where Julia had had the oblique encounter with Toby; where the young Levantine might have found quarters, while awaiting the visitation of the Archangel Raphael. Julia found the top bell, above the rows of brass nameplates (one name, Melchiori, made her think of the myrrh-bearing magi) on the side of a tall house near the synagogue.

'They're tall — the houses here — because the only way the Jews could spread in the Ghetto was upwards,' Sarah explained. She had come down to meet Julia and they were climbing the stone stairs to the top of the house. 'Hey, I've just thought, is it going to be too much for you? Walking up all these steps?'

Julia was affronted. 'Certainly not – I'm fit as a fiddle, thank you.'

'Sorry. I didn't mean to be patronising.'

They had reached the upper storey and, entering, Julia found herself in a large wooden-floored room with kitchen facilities in one corner and a double bed in the other. A roll of green baize into which Sarah's long chisels were slotted lay on a pile of magazines by the bed.

'It's a bit primitive, I'm afraid.'

'Is this the only room?' Julia, looking at the bed, couldn't help thinking of Toby. Where had he slept?

Sarah walking to the corner of the room said, 'There's a bathroom – it's a tad poky.' She opened a door in the corner to show a truncated bath with a shower attachment. 'That's a hip-bath. Neat, isn't it?'

Julia, looking, saw bottles and pots. The gold-topped potions and creams reminded her of how Sarah had borrowed her hand-cream. Looking at the girl's features she observed her skin, the kind which is called 'porcelain'. Her own felt papery and old. It's all right for her, Julia thought, following Sarah, with seeming meekness, out of the bathroom.

There was no sign of Toby in either room. Had he slept on the floor? Though, of course, more often, no doubt, he had spent the nights on the floor of the chapel. With the bats.

The apartment was smaller than Signora Mignelli's. Julia tried to envisage herself there. She liked the effect of light from windows on three sides. A balcony led off one of the windows and stepping out she saw the faint grey margin of sea.

'You can see the Dolomites in the winter.' Sarah joined her. 'But not in the summer. I don't know why not.'

Julia, her lunch by the Fondamenta Nuove with Vera in mind, said, 'A friend who was here told me it has to do with refraction of the light.' Her last sight, almost, of Toby. Where was he now? she wondered.

Sarah, as if reading her thoughts, now said, 'I have to go back to see if I can find Tobes.' Frowning she looked older. 'It would be a relief, actually, to have you here.'

'Well, it would suit me.' Definitely she did not wish to return to England. She would telephone Mr Akbar at the first opportunity and see if he would like to continue his tenancy. 'When do you want to leave, Sarah?'

Sarah suggested the first week of July. She offered to lend a hand with moving Julia's things from Signora Mignelli's when the time came. 'I have very little,' Julia said, grateful that she had not had to ask. 'Just a few books and papers; almost no clothes.'

But there was the Cutforths' party, and really she must give some thought to her clothes, she decided as she made her way back to the Fondamenta Nuove where the Dolomites rose invisibly behind the clouds across the water. Ruskin, Vera had informed her, had liked to promenade there when the mountains were not in hiding. Probably he had walked up and down, lecturing the virginal Effie who had run in horror from Tintoretto's *Last Judgement*. But 'virginity' – what did it mean? There was the Virgin Mary (the Bellini with the almond eyes) but Ruskin's virgin wife wasn't, to be sure, like her! What about the beautiful Jewess who nearly died of the plague? – until the fortuitous arrival of the silk-merchant all her 'marriages' remained unconsummated. And there was the girl in the Tobit story whose resident demon strangled her lovers before they could enter her body. Maybe virginity was an unwillingness to allow yourself to be altered? Is it true that we would rather be ruined than changed? she meditated. Perhaps it was not so much a matter of what you did with your body but what you allowed into your mind – a reluctance to admit mortality?

Certainly, until Harriet died, her own mind had remained in much the same state for thirty-five years. It was Harriet's death which had thrust her into new ways, ways in which she had sometimes swum, sometimes floundered, like the fish young Tobias had landed on the banks of the Tigris.

And now the number 52 *vaporetto* was approaching, and joining the queue of people waiting to travel she found herself next to Cynthia Cutforth.

'My dear,' said, Cynthia, smelling of something dry and expensive, 'I have been out to Burano. Charles refuses to go – too touristy he says – but I wanted a lace tablecloth for the party. And it's fun, once in a while, playing hooky from one's husband. I got a beauty, too.' She indicated an elaborately wrapped blue-tissue parcel.

'I was just thinking about your party,' Julia said – which was almost the case, for she had been worrying what she should wear to it. The cream blouse and black skirt were more appropriate for winter. And then she associated them with Carlo. 'What shall I wear?'

Cynthia, who had not forgotten her first impression of Julia at Marco Polo airport said, 'My dear, it's not grand. Wear whatever you feel like.' Which was not helpful, Julia thought.

They disembarked near the Pietà. 'Do you think Vivaldi went in for little girls?' Cynthia asked. 'I mean, what was he doing teaching those young orphans? My guess is he was a pederast!'

Julia, who had been debating whether to tell Cynthia she thought she had seen a kingfisher flash across the bows of the boat as they passed through the deserted boatyards of the Arsenale, found herself saying instead, ' "Pederast" is boys, isn't it? And so what if he was? Isn't it his music that counts?'

Cynthia was not a person who took offence. Perhaps she detected, in her acquaintance's reply, a hint of something personal. In any case she made no rejoinder to the fierce little riposte and they walked without further conversation along the Riva Schiavoni. Soon they would pass the *calle* where Charles had taken her to meet the Monsignore. Julia, conscious of the silence her retort had induced, considered remarking that she had enjoyed meeting the Monsignore; but the comment seemed too banal to describe the curious encounter and besides she remembered that Charles had mentioned Cynthia did not entirely like the priest.

They were approaching the area of the city where fashionable shops cluster and, her mind still on the forthcoming party, Julia made an excuse to part company. Cynthia, she decided, away from her husband, was annoying.

The concert-going blouse and skirt aside, it was many years since Julia had purchased any item of clothing other than for wholly utilitarian purposes. Harriet's death had endowed her with blouses, but Harriet had been wider-hipped and fuller-figured than Julia, and the skirts and dresses had been dispatched to Oxfam. It was a dress – or 'frock', as Julia phrased it to herself – which she felt was wanted. Something 'light and informal', her mother might have said.

The first shop she entered had, as assistant, a young woman wearing a skirt so short and make-up so pronounced that Julia felt herself literally back away.

'Excuse me,' she said, pretending that it was all an error that she was on the premises at all, 'please excuse me,' and she turned and walked away. But in one of the smaller *calli* she found a dimmer, less self-announcing store, and the woman who came to greet her wore skirts of reassuring length, and was plumply middle-aged.

'Signora,' the woman said. 'Please?'

Long ago Julia had given up trying to divine how it was that the Venetians could recognise her Englishness so unerringly. 'I am looking for a dress,' she simply said.

'Good,' the assistant clapped her hands together. 'For a formal occasion?' She indicated a rail of splendidly metallic costumes.

'Oh, no, no!' The metallics glinted alarmingly. She had had thoughts of fine cotton, muslin even.

'Something a little casual perhaps?' A rail of formidable trouser-suits was indicated.

'Not trousers,' said Julia firmly. 'A dress.'

The woman frowned as if attempting to compute a problem of ferocious complexity. Julia, looking through the door, saw another dress shop across the street. 'Thank you,' she said, and made as if to leave but the woman leaped before her, almost barring her exit. 'I have *very* beautiful dress for you,' she announced. 'Wait!'

She disappeared into an interior area and after a few moments emerged with three garments over her arm.

'That one,' cried Julia, pointing at a dress of lilac-coloured material.

Trying it on in the small mirrored dressing room she became ashamed. Her underwear looked incongruous and dingy. Certainly it did not match up to the elegance of the dress she was contemplating. And she had to admit the frock was pretty, with its swathes of material and flowing line. Looking at the reflection in the mirror she heard a cough.

'Signora, perhaps you like try these?'

Discreetly, over the door of the changing room, were placed some silk items — a camisole and a pair of French knickers edged in lace. They were of a kind Julia had occasionally eyed in embarrassment as she passed the exotic underwear shops which were commonplace in Venice. Her first thought on seeing the cobwebby lace and sheen of the material was:

How utterly ridiculous! But then, after holding first the cream-coloured camisole and then the knickers up against her, and looking intently at the reflection in the looking-glass, she stepped out of the lilac dress again.

The assistant, wrapping the lace and satin in elaborate tissue, was triumphant. 'They are so pretty,' she said. 'My husband like me to wear them very much!' She laughed, indulgent of the easy susceptibility of men.

'I regret I have no husband.' Julia, not knowing why she volunteered this, felt that politeness required from her some equivalent contribution to the assistant's confidences. She felt also rather apprehensive. Whatever next? She hoped she was not going to become one of those unseemly old ladies who expose themselves. A vision of her father in the nursing-home bed, masturbating for all to see, flashed disturbingly across her memory.

But the assistant only beamed the more. 'Your lover will adore you in them.' Competently, she pressed black and gold stickers to the tissue parcel. 'And the dress too? This you must have. It is charming on you.'

Leaving the shop with a wide, stiff black and gold bag Julia felt faintly criminal. She had never indulged herself so lavishly. Or so pointlessly, sneered an insidious inner voice. A story — was it about Rita Hayworth? — came back to her. Rita Hayworth's dresser neglected to provide for a shoot the silk underwear which the film star liked to wear. 'No one will know,' the dresser had said, seeking to pacify the disgruntled starlet. 'I will!' was the regal reply. It was a story Harriet had told her. It didn't matter that she had neither husband nor lover to enjoy her new purchase. She would know that, secret and inviting, cream silk lay next to her skin. Thinking of Harriet cheered her up. Harriet, she now knew, would have approved of the frivolous underwear.

But wasn't it queer that you could get to know a person better when they were dead than when they were alive? Perhaps it was because the dead could not reprove you? It was fear that made one hold back from knowing people. She thought of the girl of the Chapel-of-the-Plague, trapped in her high rooms, clinging to her virginity, unaware that passion awaited her in the person of the young merchant who had sailed across the seas from the Levant.

We are closed in and the key is turned on our uncertainty, tolled a voice in her mind, as she threaded her way down the Calle Lunga.

6

 I admit I wanted to run, run for my life! A girl I had never before that day heard of, from a strange and, for all I knew, barbaric land was bad enough. One who threatened to kill herself was not, you may be sure, the dream-wife of my fantasies. It made matters worse that these were kinspeople, for if nothing else courtesy demanded I stay there, at least for a night. And I had the added worry that my poor father would be counting the days fretting about his debt, and my mother counting them for my safe return. I could have knocked Azarias's teeth out for landing me in this.

It was obvious that the parents wanted the maid to hold her peace. But she came bursting out with how her young mistress was upstairs and refusing to come down. 'Seven of them, seven,' the maid kept bleating and when I asked what was the meaning of this everyone went very quiet.

Azarias, who had been feeding Kish, appeared suddenly and took the girl by the elbow and steered her from the room. I was concerned that the parents would see this as a grave piece of interference but they sat there, looking solemn, their gaze fixed to the floor, so I followed Azarias outside.

The maid was sitting on a wall by the well, shaking out her hands as I have seen my mother do when in her eyes my father has gone too far, and Azarias was listening, one foot up on the wall as he had stood that first time I met him in the marketplace. I remember it still, that posture of his — the foot had a sureness in it.

'All dead, all dead,' the maid was crying, 'and now my mistress says she wants to die too!'

Right away I knew I was for it because Azarias didn't take his foot from the wall but he left off looking at the maid and looked at me instead. I realised then that I had never really looked into his eyes before. They were like the 'eyes' on the tail of the great birds that the King in Nineveh had in his palace gardens when I was a child; you couldn't say if they were blue or green for they appeared to shift into many colours as he looked at you.

Azarias looked at me now with his peacock-tail eyes and a kind of terror spread through me and I spoke without thought. 'Azarias, I am afraid.'

This is what Azarias said. 'This is your wife who awaits

you. Go now and tell her father that you came here to marry her.' Then he said again, 'Do not fear – she was set apart for you from the beginning.'

At this I felt a violent rage well up in me, which was as well, as otherwise I might have begun to howl. Instead Kish began to howl for me but Azarias just touched him on the head between the spots above his eyes and he piped down. 'And what if that is not what I want?' I all but yelled at Azarias but he simply went on looking and said not a word in reply.

The next thing I knew I was back in the house and speaking to the parents. 'I have come to marry your daughter,' I said and I still don't know what brought me to say it. At that the flat-faced mother started to weep and cry out, 'No, no, you can't, we can't.'

For some reason this seemed to bring out a resolve in me and I said, quite easily, 'The law says she is mine if I want her.' (From what I had learned Sara and I were cousins and by the law of Moses I had first refusal of her hand. My parents were also each other's cousins and my father was a great advocate for this law though to tell you the truth until that day I had not given it much thought.)

Raguel, who had so far said nothing said, quickly, 'Sister, hold your peace! He is cousin to our daughter. It is lawful that they marry. Go up and fetch our daughter and see she washes her face and tidies herself before she meets her suitor.'

Azarias meantime had entered and was standing behind me. He never shamed me by showing me up in front of others. Although I was angry with him I was still afraid and it was a comfort to feel him there.

After a while Edna came downstairs and behind her was a slight figure wearing a veil. I could not look at her at first and I felt the blood leave my face and my whole body begin to tremble. But Azarias stepped forward and took her hand and led her to me. And then Azarias parted her veil and I saw her face and I thought I might die, so immediate and unavoidable was my desire for her.

࿚

*T*he day of the Cutforths' party was one of those days which are lowering even in late June – with a sultriness which gave off little sense of warmth. A spiteful day, Julia decided, taking off her dressing-gown.

The lilac frock looked somehow wrong and having put it on she took it off again – hurting her ears by dragging the thing over her head and messing her hair. But the silk underwear she kept on – she had promised herself she would wear it.

The change into black skirt and a white cotton blouse she had bought from the man who sold the tablecloths made a delay, so that she almost ignored the phone when it rang. Hurrying back up the stairs to catch it she slipped, wrenching her knee, and had to keep irritation from her voice as she answered.

It was Sarah calling about the proposed move. 'I'm free tomorrow, if you like? – only I'm off the day after next.'

Julia, who was aware that her tenancy expired at the end of the weekend, had nevertheless put off thinking about it. To be reminded of it just now seemed part and parcel of a day which was turning out unsatisfactorily. 'I suppose that's all right . . .'

'Well, not if it's a nuisance, I just —'

'No, no.' Julia pulled herself together. 'I'm sorry, I was trying to organise my thoughts. I'm on my way out.'

'Oh, where to?'

'To my friends the Cutforths' party,' said Julia, not much liking to be asked her movements.

'Oh yes.' Sarah sounded knowing. 'Our architect, Aldo, is going to that. I may tag along with him.'

Julia found she did not welcome this possibility. The Cutforths were her discovery. Technically, they were her oldest friends in Venice and Sarah's suggestion impinged on a sense of what was hers. Tentatively, she said, 'But wouldn't they mind? They're quite grand: it was RSVP on the invitation.'

There was a snort of laughter from Sarah who said, 'Aldo and Charles have known each other yonks! I shouldn't think they'll mind me. But I'll ring and ask, if you like!'

'No, no, please don't if you think it is all right.' Julia, thwarted, back-tracked but Sarah had rung off already and when Julia rang her number back it was engaged.

The small exchange set her on edge. It was muggy walking to the water-bus stop and she had gone no further than Veronese's church with the gaudy ceiling — she could never quite get to like Veronese — before realising that it had been

— 196 —

a mistake to shed the lilac dress. Its cool folds would have been a protection in the clammy heat. Too late to go back now – she walked on, sweat running down her spine.

The Cutforths' apartment boasted a roof-terrace. Cynthia, smelling of her expensive scent and glorious in white linen, kissed Julia and directed her up the wrought-iron stairway. 'I'm not sure if it's better out or in, but Charles is up there doing the honours.'

Julia, climbing the stairs, caught a glimpse of herself in the hall glass. I am old, she thought.

There was already quite a crowd on the roof but Charles, seeing her emerge, came over with a bottle and a glass in his hand. 'Welcome, Julia!' He spoke loudly so that she wondered if he was slightly drunk. 'Would you like a drink or would you prefer a joke? When the Freuds entertained in Vienna they always met people with a joke.'

'Both for choice,' said Julia. 'Who are the Freuds?'

'Sigmund Freud,' said Charles pouring a glass of prosecco, 'the Herr Doktor Freud, discoverer of the unconscious. This OK for you?'

This was better; Julia took a sip of prosecco. 'I don't somehow associate him with jokes.'

'Oh sure, he was mad about them. Wrote a book: *Jokes and the Unconscious.*'

'Is it funny?'

'Dire,' said Charles. He was definitely tipsy. 'Anyway, what shall I tell you to make you laugh?'

Julia felt it was not her place to supply her host with the

material for her own welcome. 'I never remember jokes myself so I can scarcely expect you to.'

Charles laughed uproariously as if she had said something hugely funny and she remembered how confident she had been when she had dined with him and Cynthia at the Gritti Palace. Under the false colours of her relationship with Carlo she had managed to be expansive, almost witty. You gave people an impression of yourself and they held on to it however you may be at other times, like a dog with a bone, she grimly thought and, turning a little aside to stand out of the way of another guest, she saw that it was Carlo. And behind him Sarah.

Sarah was wearing a long, narrow dress of a pale blue material which matched the blue of her eyes. She had done her fair hair up on her head where it was caught, with seeming carelessness, by a silver clip in the shape of a fish. Two more silver fishes hung drolly from her ears, like some portrait of a sea-nymph. Julia, staring at her, thought, I am ludicrous, an old woman in silk underwear.

There was a heartbeat's pause and then Sarah and Carlo both started to speak at once, halted, and Sarah, alone, resumed. 'Julia! You know Carlo, don't you? He is our architect's oldest friend.'

'Our fathers were at school together,' Carlo said. His smile was rigid. 'Aldo and I. And, Julia, how are you? I was going to call you tomorrow and — here you are!'

The sun had emerged and across the water from the Cutforths' balcony the sudden sea-light shone on the forbidding white frontage of the church of the Gesuati. They both knew he was lying.

But the shock was over and Julia found a way to meeting him. 'You might not have found me. Tomorrow I am moving my things.' Sarah had drifted away and was by the railings talking to Charles Cutforth. 'To Sarah's as it happens.' How stuffy she sounded. He raised his eyebrows, and she added, struggling not to be stilted, 'She has to return to England on business. Didn't she say?'

'I hardly know Sarah. We met before, I think when I was in Venice after Christmas.' He did not say that it was when they too had met, but stood gallantly (she couldn't help admiring it) bearing the embarrassment they both were experiencing. After a while Charles drifted back towards her and Carlo made an excuse to get away.

'Pretty thing you've brought with you,' Charles said, nodding towards Sarah. He appeared to have recovered his sobriety. 'Our boys should be here. They'd eat her for breakfast!'

'I didn't bring her. She came with a friend of yours.' Julia hoped she didn't sound defensive. Wanting to change the subject and seeing the Monsignore across the terrace she said, 'You never told me about the Monsignore's' sons.' She hoped Charles wouldn't refer to Carlo.

'Did I tell that to you? Cynthia would kill me! She hates me gossiping!' Charles's demeanour did not suggest he was much trammelled by his wife's disapproval. He leaned confidentially towards Julia. 'He has a son – a pair I should say!

— twins, would you believe, though I've only met one of them. He's a fine historian too in his own right. At Stamford. We get together occasionally at conferences. Nice guy.'

'But he's a priest?'

'It's all kept hush-hush. Giuseppe refers to them as his "nephews",' said Charles, looking across to see the Monsignore himself almost at his elbow.

The Monsignore gave no sign of having heard. 'We meet again. What a pleasure for me,' he said bowing his head at Julia. Down his tonsure-stock was a narrow border of purple silk. Like my lilac dress, she thought, regretful again that she had not worn it. 'Charles, may I fill my glass?' The Monsignore extended a mottled hand. 'One of the many benefits of living in Venice is that one never has to drive and therefore one need never worry about drink. Although I feel sure anger is much more dangerous than alcohol. What do you think?'

'I hadn't thought about it. I don't drive.'

'Neither do I!' said the Monsignore cavalierly. 'I don't know why I mention it!'

He talked on; and as he talked Julia felt her shoulders and spine unclench and settle. It was not the content of his conversation, acute as it was in every detail. It was a quality about him that made the air around him more alive — a power to improve the dispositions of those he encountered.

The day which had begun so inauspiciously became more pleasant. Aldo, a short bald man with intelligent down-turned eyes, came over and she was able to ask about the Chapel. 'We are most fortunate,' he said, picking at a plate of salad.

'A relative of Sarah's puts up the money for this project.'

'I didn't know. Is that why she is doing the work?' Hadn't Sarah mentioned that the architect was keen on her?

'Actually, she is also very good and very well trained with stone. But it helps, of course, that it is money from her family. And with money it is always possible here to pull strings!'

So Sarah's family were wealthy. 'Did whoever it was choose the chapel, then, to restore?'

The architect nodded so that the salad almost fell from his plate. 'Oh yes. It is quite small and therefore possible to do with a limited sum. Of course,' he laughed, 'you know, that is relative!' But he's *gay*, Julia said to herself, not knowing how she knew but feeling rather proud of the observation. 'Did you know where most of the money from England comes?'

'I had supposed donations.' Did Sarah really imagine this man fancied her?

'Pizzas!' A nearby woman wearing silk, flinched as salad from Aldo's fork threatened her clothes. Oblivious he went on. 'It is your Pizza Express. Many years ago the owner comes up with a bright idea. He offers a special pizza, *Veneziana*, and twenty pence of each pizza *Veneziana* sold, goes to the Venice in Peril Fund. It has already restored many, many buildings. A lot of pizza, eh!'

Carlo and Sarah seemed to have drifted away from each other. Occasionally, she snatched a glance across at Sarah, who seemed to have the gift of making everyone laugh. Perhaps it was just an accident that they had arrived together. And Carlo was an old acquaintance of Aldo's; it made sense.

The conversation with the architect gave her a sense of accomplishment. Cynthia, encountering her later, after a hard-going conversation with an American woman who had married a Venetian doctor, was admiring. 'You're a saint. Mina is a tremendous bore. I'm fond of her but she's one of those people one dreads meeting because she talks endlessly about her children. Have you met the mayor? You'd like him — he's a Communist too!'

'I don't know that I'm a Communist myself any more.'

'He's also a professor of philosophy,' said Cynthia. 'Anyway, it's different being a Commie here. He has a cute beard.'

Charles came up behind Cynthia and kissed her on the neck. 'Close thing,' he said to Julia and winked conspiratorially.

Julia, who guessed this referred to his indiscretion over the Monsignore and remembering that Charles had said Cynthia disliked gossip, said, 'Charles was telling me about the Monsignore helping the Jews during the war.'

'Your whiskers are tickling me, Charles! Of course that was admirable.' Cynthia managed to sound polite about the priest but unenthusiastic. 'Excuse me, my dear, if I leave you with my *caro sposo*. I must go and mix.'

'Her ancestors came over on *The Mayflower*,' Charles explained. 'She thinks all Catholics are corrupt. But there's no doubt about Giuseppe's courage during the war. He's on the side of life, I tell Cynth. Hence his fathering a few kids!'

'Charles, why didn't the Catholic Church help the Jews

more in the war? It's shocking isn't it that people like the Monsignore had to do it by stealth?'

'I guess because in their eyes the Jews murdered JC.'

'But what about turning the other cheek? Isn't that what he advocated?' A memory of her father hitting her across the face. She had 'turned' her cheek, certainly – but in fear and shame, not Christian humility.

'It wasn't all bad. The first edition of the Talmud – you know, the compendium of rabbinical wisdom – was published here. And there's a good story, too, about the Inquisition: they wanted Venice to step up her quota of executions which, I guess, were falling behind some of the other city states. Venice sent a message, "No heretics here!" "What about the Jews?" the Inquisition guys flagged back. And the Venetians answered that as the Jews did not believe in Christ they couldn't be classified as heretics! I love that – the "super subtle" Venetians!'

'But they still blamed the Jews for the plague?' She was remembering the Monsignore's story.

'Hell, yes!' Charles, the other side of drink, had now moved to elated sobriety. 'Whole families burned. But that was true everywhere: the "dirty Jew" smear has a history as long as your arm.'

Strangers and sojourners. Away across the water she could see the graceful twin towers of the Angelo Raffaele with the squatter tower of S. Sebastiano between. 'He's right, though, isn't he, the Monsignore? We've stolen from them. I'd no idea the angels were Jewish. I'd always associated them with "gentle Jesus, meek and mild" — rather Pre-Raphaelite and soppy.'

But not the Archangel Raphael. For even in her unrepenting ignorance had he not summoned her from Ealing, to her lodging by his church?

Before she left she asked, 'D'you think the Monsignore heard us talk about his sons?'

'Not at all.' Charles was confident. 'Mind how you go, now — don't slip into the lagoon!'

But Julia, as she waited for the number 82 to take her back, was less sure. There had been a flicker in the Monsignore's eye as he approached, which might have been humorous. Her hip hurt and her leg ached where she had twisted it. She had survived the encounter with Carlo and on the whole the occasion had been a success. But crossing the green water to the Zattere she felt herself drooping with the humidity and the fatigue of unaccustomed socialising.

The evening continued close and later that night, still in her silk underwear, Julia lay on top of the sheets, unable to sleep. The meeting with Carlo, so successfully negotiated at the time, returned to mock her. What did *he* think? she wondered. How did he explain to himself the sudden cessation of intercourse between them? If he thought about it at all, for of course she was just a means to an end for him — a trivial episode in the catalogue of his life.

Her limbs continued restless so that it seemed she had not slept at all as the sky grew first green-grey then yellow, then rose and orange. Watching the light increase from her balcony she was aware of all that the *campo* had come to mean to her: the two stone wellheads; the unpromising-looking trattoria, where the fish was some of the best in Venice, to which the archangel had also kindly donated his name; the balconies with their humble adornments of washing and geraniums. And, presiding over it all, the dignified, crumbling presence of the *chiesa*. It was as if the events of the last six months, the pity and the wonder and the terror of it all (for in her private musings she had begun to permit herself such grand phrases), had imprinted themselves upon the rich, still, old scene which lay before her and now, silently and unexcitedly, reflected back her own emotions, among the accumulated emotion of the centuries.

Suddenly a desire to be out in the early air gripped her and she was dressed and in her shoes before she had any formed plan of where to go. Why not walk to the Ghetto in the cool and see her new habitation? It was a longish walk but her leg felt better and it was feasible while the morning was still fresh.

Because Venice is not one island but many, laced together by a series of bridges, it is rarely possible to walk directly to any one point. The usual method is to travel by water letting the canals act as pathways. But this morning Julia wanted to walk and the facility with which she made her way, first along the familiar route by the Calle Lunga to the Accademia bridge, then through the squares of S. Stefano and past the Goldoni Theatre, where they were playing *Othello*, rewarded her with a sense of pride. 'I know my way!'; in pride she almost spoke the words aloud. It was a short step from there along by the part-covered Rialto (where Antonio spat on Shylock's gabardine), the other principal bridge which provides a crossing of the Grand Canal. Here, at the limit of familiar terrain, she stopped.

The Monsignore had given her some advice the first time she met him. 'Remember how to be lost in Venice – this is something I remind myself of every day!' But this morning she felt that to be lost was not what she needed and avoiding the bridge she swerved and wove, moving quite surely, until she came out at the church of the Apostles, by the beginnings of the Strada Nuova, the only dull street in Venice.

The bells in the Apostoli's tower were tolling. Six o'clock. No one was about except a tramp with a yellow-braided naval cap. During her winter wanderings Julia had seen him often, lying with his brown paper bags in the shelter of the long arcade of the Doge's Palace. An old doge returned to a former stamping ground, she had fantasised, admiring the man's fortitude in the freezing cold. And then, suddenly, he had disappeared, and vaguely she had wondered about him. So these were his summer quarters.

The Strada Nuova, where the Venetians do their shopping, is usually the busiest street in Venice. A solitary man with a brush was out, washing the patch in front of his shoe shop, perhaps Signora Mignelli's second cousin out of the closet? Not a soul otherwise. Past shuttered shops, past churches, arches, pointed Gothic windows, she walked on in the direction of the Ghetto until she came to a place where she halted by the head of a woman over a high, carved, peeling door. Previously she had come to Sarah's by the *vaporetto*; she was lost.

Except for the birds it was utterly quiet. She had not heard such singing before in Venice and looking up to identify a host of agile sparrows, popping in and out of the tangled ivy, she read the old Venetian script: *Calle Gheto Novissimo*. She had found it.

She followed the *calle* down to a wooden bridge. On either side of the narrow canal washing lines stretched between the high buildings and looking down she saw knickers, petticoats, jumpers, overalls, perfectly reflected in the dull green water. Boats covered in tarpaulins, roped and tied across like parcels, were moored along the buildings' weedy sides.

Julia crossed the bridge and ducked to pass under a low wooden lintel and through the dark *sotoportego*. She came out into the *campo*, which had once been the centre of the old Ghetto. Pigeons were bathing in the water of a dripping pump; in the intense quiet, only birdsong.

Why is it as a race they have been so much persecuted? Julia pondered, watching the pigeons preen their feathers in the water. Is it because people are made uncomfortable by their certainty? Counting the trees (nine) which contributed to the peaceful air of the place, she thought again of Old Tobit, brutally uprooted and marched off from his home in Samaria, to Assyria where he and his tribe, and the other nine tribes of Israel, disappeared, along with their kingdom, for all time. That was a holocaust too, though so long ago that no one thought about it any more.

A cat who had been watching the pigeons strolled over, wrapping itself round her legs. Reminded of Stella she bent to caress it. She was still stroking the cat when the door of Sarah's house opened and a man came out.

He was a tall man with a moustache. Sarah was standing in the doorway behind him. Her fair hair fell down her back onto a dressing gown. The man made a discreet farewell with his hand and went quickly through the tunnel of the *sotoportego*. He did not see Julia Garnet who stayed stock still, crouched over the cat, as if, in that position, her very life hung on a thread.

III
VISITATION

1

Julia remained frozen, squatting, while the cat, seeing the open door, padded across to investigate. Sarah standing in the doorway was watching after the vanished Carlo. She had turned to go back inside when she must have half caught sight of Julia and swung round again.

'Julia?'

'Sarah.' She could not say more. Even to say the name seemed as much as her life was worth.

'Julia! What are you doing?'

Julia, still crouching, stared at her. Impossible not to grasp the significance of Carlo's hasty, furtive departure. Her vertebrae felt as if they had fused together in a hoop, leaving her bent in a posture of humiliation.

'Julia. Are you all right? Come and have some coffee.'

It was a long way up to the top of the house. Julia laboured up the stone stairs behind the youthful back, careless in its dressing gown, the fair hair streaming. Had Carlo caressed that pale hair? Don't think about it. Go on climbing.

At the top she almost swayed and fell, the climb and her dipping blood sugar making her dizzy.

'Come in, Julia. Coffee? Or you prefer tea, don't you?' Sarah fussed around the sink, making a distraction for both of them.

'Tea, please, if you have it.'

The large bed across the room was a cascade of dishevelled sheets. Sarah, having set a kettle to boil, went over and pulled vaguely at the cover. 'Sorry about the mess. I shouldn't have asked you in to see all this but it was rather a surprise you being there.'

'I felt like a walk.'

'Were you coming to see me? I'm not generally up at this hour.' The pale blue eyes looked dead at her and it was Julia who blushed.

'I wanted to see the house . . .' Dust and ashes.

'I see.' Sarah put tea bags in the teapot. Without turning round she said, 'And you saw your friend.'

'My friend?'

'Carlo. You saw Carlo leaving here. I'm sorry if it embarrassed you.'

'Not at all.' Julia found a vestige of an old tone. 'I was startled, of course, but . . .'

'These things happen. It was the party, I think we both had a bit too much to drink.' Sarah laughed. The laugh fell into the middle of the high room and died. They sat and looked at each other in silence until Sarah said, 'I'd rather you didn't tell anyone.'

'My dear child,' said Julia, pleased to have found a voice, 'who on earth would I tell?'

More silence. Julia sipped her tea. The milk was off – not yet fully sour but tasting buttery. The slight sickly taint on her tongue was gratifying to her mood.

Sarah said, 'You won't mention it to him either, will you, that you saw him? I feel a bit of a twit. He's probably old enough to be my grandfather. I know he's a friend of yours.'

'Hardly.' Julia spoke stiffly. It was abominable having the girl press the matter like this. 'We are slightly acquainted.'

'Oh, but he told me how fond he was of you.'

Julia, her heart lurching painfully, tried to suppress a dart of joy. Not wholly succeeding she couldn't resist asking, 'What did he say?'

'He said he liked going to concerts with you. Julia, do you think I'm mad?'

'Really, I couldn't say.' And then because the girl's eyes were filling with tears she said, 'Sarah, I'm not familiar with the conduct of love affairs. I'm sorry.'

Sarah, who had got up and was staring out of the window, said, 'It's all such a mess.'

Upbringing can be a ruthless god. Although she longed to

rush from the place screaming, Julia's mouth formed words. 'A mess?'

'Yes, me, Tobes, everything.'

'But you have your work.' Always in her mind lay the cool interior of the little chapel: a tranquil oasis – the home of the blue angel. Struggling to be fair she felt her own tears rise. 'And you have done the restoration work so beautifully.'

'Oh that!' Sarah spoke almost contemptuously. 'It's my private life that needs restoring.'

'What is it that you think is wrong?' Extraordinary that she, of all people, should be discussing such a subject with a young woman who had casually spent the night with the man she herself loved.

'I told you. I was a victim of child abuse. You didn't want to hear. People generally don't.'

Julia, summoning up the balcony overlooking the Angelo Raffaele where she and Sarah had sat, thought, I shall not sit there again. Dust and ashes. Dust and ashes. 'I'm sorry if you felt I spurned your confidences.'

She had intended a half-irony but Sarah, taking her at face value, said, 'It doesn't matter. Nothing matters really, does it? The main thing is I can trust you not to talk about any of this. Do you know, sometimes I think of throwing myself out of this window. It's terribly tempting.'

Oh, yes, thought Julia, I know how you feel!

'Shouldn't you see someone? I don't know much about these things – well, nothing at all, in fact – but I seem to have heard there are people one can talk to.'

'I went.' Sarah spoke roughly. 'Five years of therapy. That's how I ended up wanting to top myself.'

'Oh dear! Does anything help?'

'Yes,' said Sarah baldly. 'Sex helps. That's why I do it. Still, it's better than doing drugs, I suppose.'

She jumped up and walked over to the window again. Looking at her long, youthful back Julia thought, I can't blame him. She's lovely!

With her back still turned Sarah spoke; she sounded angry. 'Look, I'm sorry, Julia, this isn't your thing at all. Let's talk about how we get your things over here, shall we?'

And here memory becomes blurred: I do not rightly remember how I spent most of the days in Ecbatana. What I do remember is the sense of difference.

For one thing there was more merriment than I was used to at home. They say their prophet Zarathustra was born into the world laughing, and the need for good cheer among men is part of what he taught. And they despise death which to them is the victory of the Lord of Lies and Darkness – the Adversary they call him. This I remember.

I remember, too, that I began to wonder about my father putting the bodies to rest in the ground. Here they build high towers – the Towers of Silence they call them – where they lay out the bodies of the dead and the wild dogs and vultures come and strip the corpses clean so that their own hands do not touch death. They laughed at me (they are great laughers) when I spoke of the one God, for they have their 'Wise Lord' the Lord of Light, who is tolerant in the ways and the gods of foreigners. It came to my mind, here in Media, he was a more easy-going god than ours whose name I had so often heard is 'Jealous', and I wondered about my father in the days of his youth when he travelled here as the king's Purveyor. Had he too felt his spirits lighten when he came to the city of Zarathustra, the holy city of Raghes?

Sara did not like me and she made it plain. I never knew if it was my face, or my origins (for although we were of the same tribe she had lived all her life in Media). Maybe, I came miserably to think, she is born a hater of men; certainly her tongue was waspish.

I'd hardly been in the company of a young woman before and certainly not one so beautiful as Sara. So it came as a shock to hear her speak. I had supposed from her appearance her voice would be gentle and low but instead it had an edge which set your teeth. She laughed at everything I said but not with joy. I felt she was laughing at me rather than at what I had to say to her. 'So you want to marry me?' she said, and there was something in her way of speaking which diminished me. 'You'd better be careful, I'm not safe, you know!'

Of course there were the stories of the men who had tried to marry her before. Apart from Sara's hints there were sinister mutterings elsewhere: in the town they spoke of a death, seven deaths even, some said; but although they had blended with the local community Sara's family were still foreigners and you know how people love to spread rumour especially about those who do not wholly fit in? I hazarded that Sara had broken the spirits of the men who had courted her, so that they became faint-hearted and weak-kneed, and you might as well kill a man as take his resolution from him. I did not intend to 'die' that way!

Meanwhile Azarias, from whom I expected help, had turned unforthcoming. He spent so much time with Sara's maid that I began to suspect some amorous entanglement and one day challenged him with it. 'Hey!' I said, speaking more sharply than was usual, perhaps because I'd had a particularly sore time of it with Sara. 'You're supposed to be helping me to marry the mistress, not bedding the mistress's maid yourself!' After all this whole enterprise was his idea.

But you couldn't get a word out of Azarias that he didn't want to give. He just grinned at me in a manner which I might have found insolent if it didn't also somehow hurt. I had come to think of Azarias as more of a friend than a servant but now, seeing him grin like that, I was tempted to remind him of his place again. Only this time I couldn't quite bring myself to it.

That evening it was a brilliant sunset. I had not paid much attention to such things in the past but the shock of meeting Sara had altered me. I went for a walk alone outside, to enjoy the cool air after the heat of the day but also, let me admit it, to consider whether I had done the right thing in asking for Sara's hand in marriage. Kish was out with me – oh, and that was another thing. Kish did not like Sara. From his first sight of her he had bared his teeth and growled a low disconcerting growl; it was out of character and I confess it troubled me. That dislike of Kish's was preying on my mind too – though one should not look to one's dog to choose one's wife!

I had thrown Kish a stick and he had come bounding back with it in his mouth and I was preparing to throw it a second time. My hand was poised over my head, ready to throw, and Kish was panting in anticipation, when I happened to look across to Sara's chamber-window in the high tower.

There was an oil-lamp lit within and a figure came to the casement and looked out. For a second I thought it was Sara and was considering whether to risk more rejection and wave to her. Then I saw it was not Sara at all, although certainly it was her chamber. It was Azarias I had seen at the window.

Have you ever had your world turned upside down? I lost my known world in that moment in which it appeared Azarias had played me false. My betrothed wife with my man-servant! Kish came yapping up and I did something which it shames me to tell: I kicked Kish hard in the flank so that he gave a sharp yelp and scurried off with his tail between his legs. I felt a rat. A rat and an ass and a cuckold to boot (if you can be cuckolded before a woman is yet your own). So that is why, I thought, angrily, Azarias wanted me to offer for her in marriage – to beat a path for his own entrance into my property!

Kish's bark must have alerted Azarias because when I looked again across the water he had stayed at the window and was looking out. Suddenly he saw me and I felt my face begin to colour – Noah knows why, but I felt for him, being found out in his master's mistress's chamber. But to my utter astonishment the man seemed not to be discomfited at all. Instead he gave a wave of his long hand and even that distance across the water I swear I could see that blessed smile!

2

J ulia had not walked back to the Campo Angelo Raffaele. The sun was already too warm, she felt wrung out and exhausted and after the talk with Sarah she wanted brandy and a bath. Waiting for the various *vaporetti*, by which she made her way back across the city, she allowed nothing to penetrate her unthoughts.

It was a relief, after the dreadful, unwelcome intimacy, to reach the security of her apartment and she sat on the sofa for a while simply looking out of the window, too tired even to fetch the brandy bottle. It was Saturday and she could hear Nicco and his friends outside playing football. I don't want to go, she thought. This is my home. I don't want to leave here. But her 'home' was where Signora Mignelli's new tenants were arriving on Monday evening. Severely she reproved herself. You can't have whatever you want. Life isn't like that! Not even for Sarah who had had, she presumed, what she wanted with Carlo.

It took only a short time to pack her suitcase. The unworn lilac dress and the silk underwear she wrapped in tissue and laid on top of the black skirt and cream blouse. She had purchased an additional bag, a voluminous navy affair, in one of the cut-price shops near the Rialto, and into this she placed the overflow accumulated during her stay: some winter woollies, shoes, her wash-bag, a spare towel, Harriet's hat, some papers and her books. That left only the book about the Apocrypha and other ancient Jewish writings, too bulky for her luggage, to deal with.

Randomly, now, she opened the large volume which Vera, with unexpected good humour, had lugged all that way from London. There were other books of sacred Jewish writings printed at the back:

And these are the names of the holy angels who watch. **Uriel**, *one of the holy angels who is over the world and over Tartarus.* **Raphael**, *one of the holy angels who is over the spirits of men.* **Raguel**, *one of the holy angels who takes vengeance on the world of the luminaries.* **Michael**, *one of the holy angels, to wit, he that is set over the best part of mankind and over chaos.* **Saraqûel**, *one of the holy angels who is set over the spirits who sin in spirit.* **Gabriel**, *one of the holy angels who is over Paradise and the serpents and the Cherubim.*

Remiel, *one of the holy angels, whom God sets over those who rise.*

The Book of Enoch, she read. So those were the 'seven angels'. Whatever were 'spirits who sin in spirit'? And Raguel 'who takes vengeance on the world of luminaries' (why did the sun and moon and stars need vengeance taken on them?) – wasn't 'Raguel' also the name of the father of the girl who kills off her men in the Book of Tobit? The slight red volume of the Apocrypha was visible on the top of the navy bag and opened readily at the now familiar story:

> *It came to pass the same day, that in Ecbatane a city of Media Sara the daughter of Raguel was also reproached by her father's maids;*
>
> *Because that she had been married to seven husbands, whom Asmodeus the evil spirit had killed, before they had lain with her.*

Those were simpler times, when a girl's malice could be referred to an evil spirit. But in the story the holy angel Raphael came to heal the possessed girl.

The phone rang, making her jump.

'Hello,' said Sarah. 'It's me. Look, when do you have to be out of there? Only I was wondering – would you mind if we moved your stuff tomorrow?'

'As a matter of fact I don't have to be out of here until

Monday.' Julia tried not to sound as if she wanted to drop the phone.

'Oh, that's a relief. Could we do it tomorrow then? Only various things have sort of cropped up.'

Sarah giggled and Julia, who presumed that 'things' meant Carlo, finished the conversation curtly and rang off.

A reprieve! She lay down on the sofa, pushing off her shoes. What were the names of the seven angels? Uriel, Raphael, Raguel, Michael, Saraquel, Gabriel. Damn! She couldn't remember the last one. Trying to, she fell asleep.

A young man with a dog stood on a river bank watching up at a window. 'It's all right,' she said. 'It's not what you think. Nothing ever is.'

The boy was Toby. 'Where have you been?' she asked. 'We've been worried about you.'

'I had to go to Raghes,' he explained. 'For my father.'

'But the angel?' she asked. 'Where is the angel who was to go with you?'

The phone rang again and woke her. This time it was Cynthia. 'We're having a scrap supper,' she said. 'Bits and bobs rescued from the party. Come over if you don't mind left-overs.'

'Thank you,' said Julia, confused with sleep. 'I'm supposed to be packing. But maybe I'll be finished by supper time.'

'If you feel like it then,' said Cynthia, ever hospitable. 'Are you really moving in with that young mermaid?'

'It was a very good party.' Julia did not wish to be drawn on the subject of Sarah. 'Thank you for inviting me.'

'Oh, the pleasure is entirely ours! You were our star guest.' Cynthia was jubilant. 'I heard you discussed Dante with Joyce's boy – he was lyrical about you. You're a miracle. It must be all those years of teaching. The boy is usually autistic in company!'

Julia, who had been genuine in her wish to discover the source of the lines of the Yeats poem which had beaten in her mind, felt annoyed that sincere interest had been perceived as mere social skill. The conversation had been instructive. 'It's a reference to the penultimate circle in Hell,' the young Dante scholar had told her. 'Count Ugolino – he's shut up in a tower with his children and in the end he's forced to eat their dead bodies.' 'But how unfair,' she had said, 'to make him suffer in Hell for merely trying to stay alive.'

There was little, in fact, left to do in the apartment. Julia swept the floors a second time and dusted the furniture. Tomorrow she would put bleach down the lavatory and rinse out the tea towels. But really there was nothing else to attend to. And to sit inside, or even on the balcony, waiting for tomorrow seemed suddenly intolerable. She tried to repack the Apocrypha, then, not managing to get the book to fit, tipped others out onto the floor.

A programme for a Baroque concert fell out of one of the books: a memento of an early outing with Carlo. She was on her knees and, overwhelmingly, 'Oh, my love, my love . . .' she rocked back and forth, missing him as much – no, more bitterly than ever.

Suddenly it entered her mind that she wanted, urgently,

to see the Monsignore. There was something about him which acted as a deterrent to plaguing thoughts. She hardly knew him – could she turn up at his door out of the blue? But, why not? Why not do just that? Why not turn up out of the blue – he could only send her away again!

·

Few people were out in the virulent sun. Tomorrow was the first day of July. Exactly six months since her arrival in Venice the weather had swung to its opposite pole. A crowd of Japanese tourists, in the same position on the bridge near the Monsignore's *calle* as they had been the day Charles brought her there, blocked her way. Indefatigable! Was it the self-same party, endlessly recycling itself?

Near the gate with its crest of roses apprehension clawed her stomach. Maybe the Monsignore was asleep? Very likely he would be on such a hot afternoon. If so her visit would be an intrusion. She had better go away.

As she stood, weighing what to do, the bolt of the gate was pulled back and Constanze was there.

'Oh,' said Julia, 'I am so sorry. I wondered if the Monsignore might perhaps . . . ?'

'*Ingresse, prego!*' Constanze jerked her head towards the courtyard and marched away leaving Julia at the gate.

A hesitation – then she stepped inside. 'Monsignore Giuseppe?'

'Who is this?' A voice called back.

'It's Julia Garnet. I was passing so I . . .'

The Monsignore came forward, holding out his hands. He

was wearing only a black gown and a round straw hat on his head. The pug dog, which had been lying on the veranda, got up and trotted over. 'See, Marco, a visitor! But this is a marvel! Just as I become bored you arrive like one of the holy angels of heaven!'

'Oh,' said Julia, flustered by the extravagant welcome, 'I was just reading about those.'

'Indeed? What is it you read? I am on the angels' side.'

'It was the Book of Enoch.' Whatever else she had expected last January it most certainly was not that she would one day talk of the heavenly host to a Catholic priest.

'Ah, the seven holy angels, you mean.'

'Yes. What are the spirits who sin in spirit, do you know?'

'Perhaps like our Catholic sin against the Holy Ghost? The defiance which denies the good yet knows it is good as it does so. May I pour you a glass of prosecco?'

'Thank you. I wonder why they set an angel in charge of that?'

'To sin in this way is not inconsiderable – maybe the worst? It is an interesting topic; I must think more about it. And you, you are well after the great party? For myself I drank too much – but my excuse is that I knew I would. At least I did not pretend it was by mistake!'

Julia, who had been going to say she was 'fine', said instead, 'I'm not too well, actually.'

'I am sorry to hear this,' said the Monsignore.

He said nothing else and they sat in silence. A pair of doves landed in the courtyard; there was no other movement in the implacable afternoon heat. Julia, who wished she had not come, sat unable to speak or move.

After a while she said, 'I'm sorry – I shouldn't have bothered you,' and got up to go.

'I, too, am sorry you do not feel able to tell me whatever it is,' said the Monsignore.

'I don't know how,' said Julia, miserable.

'Maybe I can guess,' said the Monsignore. 'Mostly when people come to make confession, people who are not used to making confession that is, it is for one of two reasons – either it is about some wrongdoing or it is a matter of the heart.'

'I suppose it is about my heart, then,' said Julia, sitting down again.

'So,' said the Monsignore, pushing the jug of wine towards her. 'I know a little about the heart.'

There was silence again. 'The thing is,' said Julia, 'I don't know where to begin. I'm embarrassed.'

'Of course.' The Monsignore was matter-of-fact. 'The heart is a breeder of embarrassment. But we are all of us imbeciles in that area, that you can rely on. We all at times put up our hands before our cheeks in shame.'

'All right,' said Julia. 'I'll try and tell you.'

There was another silence.

'Say nothing,' advised the Monsignore. 'Let us sit, just. Take some repose.'

They sat. The pug, who had settled himself beneath the skirts of the priest, began to snore. After a bit Julia said,

'When I came to Venice I'd never really seen beauty before. I had, of course, some aesthetic appreciation but I'd never really let it inside me, if you see what I mean? I met someone, a man, who showed me beautiful things — who explained the beautiful things of Venice to me — and I fell in love with him.'

'That is good,' said the Monsignore.

'No — but you see I thought he liked me too. Not loved me, I knew he didn't love me, but I thought he liked me. I thought it was my company he enjoyed.'

'And it wasn't so?'

'No. It was a boy. A young Italian boy I was friendly with he wanted to get to know.'

'Ah!'

'Yes. At least I thought that was the case. I was very angry and very upset and then I became very ill — I was silly about it all, I'm afraid.'

'Perhaps. But I think no love is really "silly", as you call it.'

'Well, anyway I had just about got over it when I met him again.'

'When did you meet him?' Then, answering her silence, 'At the party, was it at the party?'

'Yes. He was awkward and I was awkward and it was quite ghastly.' Such inadequate words to describe that heart-stopping encounter on the Cutforths' terrace. 'But then . . .' How could she explain to this man of God what had happened next. 'There is a girl.'

'Ah! A girl in the picture now.'

'Yes. She was with him at the party. She is someone I had met here too – a restorer in fact at the Chapel-of-the-Plague.'

'Of course, we spoke of it. It is part of your English "Venice in Peril" work.'

'She is going back to England and I have to leave my apartment so we both thought it was a good idea if I took over hers while she was away.'

The Monsignore poured himself more prosecco. 'A hair of the dog!' he said. 'I am sorry. Please, go on.'

'I couldn't sleep well so I got up early. It seemed a good idea to walk over to her house. To look at it. God knows why I thought that! Sorry.'

'Please.' The Monsignore waved his hand. 'God is not so fussy about His name.'

'I was outside the house where her apartment is very early in the morning and I saw them.'

'Them?'

'Him and her. He was leaving. She was in her dressing gown.' That supple young back. She clasped her face in her hands. 'I'm so sorry. I didn't mean to do this.'

He waited, making, to her relief, no move to console her. After a while he said, 'I am not sure that I understand but if it is that you have become resigned to this man being homosexual – and you are certain that your original impression is the right one – but it is difficult for you if now it turns out he sleeps also with this young girl, then I would say to you that I doubt that both things can be true. Sometimes, yes, but it is quite unusual. Mostly if a man likes boys he will prefer more maternal women – if he likes women at all in that way.'

'How do you know all this?'

The Monsignore grinned. 'Oh, my dear! The confessional is a marvellous teacher of life. There are not so many sexual realities that I have not heard of in my little box. And, at times, out of it!'

'But she told me. Sarah told me she had slept with him.' She thought of Sarah's boyish shape. That might have appealed to Carlo. How could a Catholic priest possibly know about such things?

The Monsignore placed a hand on either side of his face as if trying to ward off toothache. After a while he said, 'You see, a statement is like a cheque. Its value depends upon the resources with which it can be met by the person who issues it. If your Richard Branson writes a cheque for a million pounds it is one thing – if I write it –' he raised his hands dramatically – 'it is another! The statement takes the account into overdraft.'

'But I saw them,' Julia said unhappily. 'She asked me not to tell anyone.' She was not much comforted by these financial similes.

'Listen, my friend,' said the Monsignore. 'I will tell you a story about myself. It is a story I have told no one, not even in confession.'

'Oh,' Julia protested, 'then you mustn't tell me.'

'But why not?' The blackbird eyes looked opaquely at her. 'It is a true story and as it happens it contains nothing which is the business of my confessor. And I am old and soon I must die. You have entrusted your tale to me – it is good I entrust this tale to you. But first we must take some more prosecco.' He hailed someone inside the house.

While they were waiting Julia walked across to the dark carmine roses by the gate. 'They are lovely.'

'Unhappily they have blight,' said the Monsignore. 'But I am lazy and I tell myself nature is better than I at sorting these things out. Of course it is a lie to excuse myself – but not a serious one!' A young woman arrived with the tray. 'Will you have some more?'

He chinked her glass, like a crystal tulip. 'So, now I tell you. It is the war. I am a young man, not yet ordained, still at the seminary in Rome. My home is Venice and when I have leave from my studies (which are pretty tough – we must not only write but speak always in Latin!) I return here. All my life when I am away I miss Venice!'

'I have been thinking I would miss it too and I've only been here six months,' Julia said.

'It is rumoured that Hitler plans to make Venice his headquarters and a few of us work to ensure that if this comes unhappily to pass the little corporal does not get his greedy hands upon all our Venetian treasures. This, of course, I do not tell my bosses in Rome. Not all of them share my view of Hitler!'

The Monsignore giggled. Julia, who felt some response required of her, gave a rather awkward laugh. She was nervous of the honour being done her.

'There are ways, forgotten passes, through Venice known to some of us who come from the old families. Now it turns out these are useful for our treasures and also to help our Jewish friends. You understand?'

'Charles told me you used secret passages to help the Jews escape.'

'Exactly. My family knows these places but my elder brother is not so reliable. He is not too sure that he does not quite admire the little corporal and his plans. One night it is proposed that I take a Jewish family to hide, I get a feeling.' The Monsignore tapped his stomach. 'I get this feeling in my insides: a voice says to me, "Giuseppe, don't go!"'

'Did you think your brother might give you away?'

'Perhaps. I don't know. Maybe I am quite wrong and my "feeling" here is because I dislike my brother. I never know the truth because my brother has died before I can ask him.'

Not knowing how to take this Julia said, 'I'm sorry.'

The Monsignore blew his lips. 'It is only death! And I did not like him, God rest his soul. So, I tell this family "not tonight". You will have some more prosecco?'

'Thank you. It's very good.'

He drank with little, rapid gulps. 'You know it is quite peculiar telling this now. Every day of my life it is inside me. To speak it is strange.'

'Please don't, if you don't want to.'

He patted her arm. 'No, no. I want to tell you and, you know, the greatest wisdoms are not those which are written down but those which are passed between human beings who understand each other. There is a girl in the family — very beautiful. She has a figure like Sophia Loren — did I tell you my story about Pope John?'

'I don't think so.'

'OK, I tell you later. Remind me, please, or I will forget. Her mother says to me, "Please take her now. There is a boat. She can get to America but she must go first thing tomorrow." I do not think it is safe but the mother is very insistent and the girl is very beautiful.' He sighed. 'And I am a young man — not yet a priest!' Laughing. 'So I take the girl but I think to myself: Where can we hide that is safe until I know I can get her to the boat?" And then I think: OK. The little chapel.'

'The Chapel-of-the-Plague?'

'Just so! By the way I like your Rudyard Kipling of the *Just So Stories*. "If you can keep your head when all about you, Are losing theirs . . ." It is a fine poem.'

'I like it too!'

'It is to the point, because in fact I used to say it to myself very often in these times. Maybe I said it this particular night? I do not remember!'

Julia, who supposed he had been going to 'remember', felt pleased: the Monsignore was not a man who painted the lily.

'At that time the chapel was used only for certain festivals — baptisms or weddings. But I knew where the key was kept — under the wellhead in the *campo*. And I knew it had a secret.'

'A secret?'

'Indeed. There is a passageway into the wall which once led to an adjoining palazzo. I knew this from the story I told you, when you were kind enough to call on me with Charles. Charles, by the way, does not believe these old stories because he is a rational man. It is one of the better things about the Catholic Church that it is not at all rational.'

Julia did not say that surely all Christianity was irrational. She did not want to interrupt the story.

'But I know for sure, empirically, as Charles would say, that there is a passage because I have spent the night there!'

The Monsignore brought this out with a certain pride. Julia, sensing something, asked, 'With the beautiful girl?'

'With the beautiful girl.' He nodded with satisfaction. 'Isabella, she was called. A wonderful figure!' He carved a fulsome shape near his chest with his hands.

'Goodness!' Julia decided to be impressed. It was apparent that this was what was required of her.

'But here is the point of the tale. We spend the night together in the chapel and maybe I put my arm around her because she is afraid. And I too, I am afraid also. But there is nothing more.' The blackbird eyes were tightly earnest.

'I'm sure there wasn't.'

'I know there was not for I am in fact virgin. I was not yet ordained but I was serious about my vocation and it would not have appeared right to me, in any case, to take advantage of this young woman's terrible experience. This is not to say I did not want it, you understand.'

'I am a virgin too.'

She did not know why she had said this and began to flush but the Monsignore reached across and patted her hand again. 'Good, good, you keep me company. I do not think any longer there are too many of us intact! But you know, I think it is a pity if this is matter of shame to you. For me I am proud that I keep my virginity in spite of all the temptations I am sent! Of course, no one believes me.'

Julia, who was thinking that 'temptations' might make virginity less shameful, only said, rather weakly, 'Oh, I'm sure they do.'

The Monsignore gave one of his high little giggles. 'Let me finish and you will see. After I get this girl to her boat I do not hear again from her, oh, for some time, until one day after the war is ended I receive a letter from America. It is from Isabella. She tells me how she made it to America and now is married to an American GI and I am happy for her. Also she has twins. I am happier still. Then the bombshell. *I have told no one*, she writes, *that the twins are yours.*' The Monsignore sat back like a conjurer who had produced an astonishing rabbit.

'But,' Julia was puzzled, 'I don't understand?'

'Neither did I,' said the Monsignore cheerfully. 'Hey, we are out of prosecco. They are so lazy when Constanze is not here. Oi! Prosecco, *per favore*!'

'Really,' said Julia, confused. 'It's fine. I've had enough.'

'But I have not. Oi!'

When the replenished tray had been brought the Monsignore resumed. 'You could have knocked me down with a feather from the wing of the Holy Ghost! Here I was, a young priest working in the Vatican, on my way to great things, concerned to make my mark, and — presto! — I learn I am a father.'

'But you said . . .' she didn't like to be explicit.

'That I am virgin and so I am. I knew that, and now you know it too. The blessed Signore Himself, I am happy to say, knows it — but the lovely Isabella it seems did not. I have thought about it many, many times,' said the Monsignore pouring himself another glass.

'And . . . ?' It seemed almost impertinent to ask.

'And in the end this is the conclusion I reach. I believe that she herself did not know. Who knows what that night of extreme fear did to her? At any time she might have been handed over to the *fascisti* and for all we knew the concentration camps. She may never see again the family who have chosen her to take the passage of safety to America. In such circumstances the mind plays tricks. And after all, I am flattered she believes she and I had intercourse.'

'But who was the father? The GI?'

'I think no. Maybe an encounter on the boat to America when she is confused? Who knows? Like so many things this is known only to the mind of God.'

'What happened to the children. The twins?'

'Well, this is the point. They grow up. Their mother and her husband get a divorce, as is so unfortunately common nowadays. I never knew what she had told her husband but one day I receive a call. It is during the period I am working for the Secretary of State and we are in some pretty delicate negotiations with the USA about the troubles in Ireland. So, one day a man telephones to say he comes from America and asks if he may visit. When he turns up it is the son of Isabella.'

'And he believed you were his father?'

'Apparently yes. It seems his mother told him and his brother this after her divorce. I think they do not get on so well with her husband and maybe she thinks to help them.'

Julia frowned. 'Tough on you, though, surely?'

The Monsignore gave another squeal of delight. 'Oh yes. Another feather of the Holy Ghost and I am knocked flat! And this, you see, is quite serious. I am in a sensitive position within the Vatican. Any scandal – ' he puffed his cheeks – 'and I am out on my backside.'

'So what did you do?'

'I think about it very hard. Day and night. Shall I tell my boss, Ottaviani? He is a pretty hard taskmaster and would not tolerate anything improper. Maybe I go to the top and tell the Pope – who, in fact, would not be so unsympathetic. In the end I decide to do nothing. The young man's mother has warned him it is a deadly secret. Also, I suspect she had told him that she is the love of my life – a romance which is not entirely untrue because certainly I have no greater experience of human love than the night I have spent with his mother. Maybe even he believes that it is out of this love for his mother that I have become a Catholic priest.'

'Disappointment, you mean?'

'Who knows? I never saw her again after that night and

in any case it does not matter. I guessed he was not going to give me away. Of course, I had not met his brother but twins are alike, and so I felt in my bones I could trust the other brother too.'

Are twins always so alike? wondered Julia, thinking of Sarah and Toby.

'I was wrong, as it happens,' the Monsignore beamed. 'Someone spoke. Maybe Isabella repeated her delusion. In any case there grew up a rumour that I have sons in America whom I refer to as my "nephews" although it is kept always hush-hush. One of them is an academic and that is how Charles comes to know of the story. I heard him tell it to you at his party.'

Julia blushed. 'I thought you had heard! Charles said you couldn't have.'

One blackbird eye winked at her. 'It is sensible sometimes to be deaf. But now, enough of me. I tell you this story for two reasons. One, because I like you and it is good to confess even if one has not, in fact, sinned. Two, because I wish to show you something. Sometimes a woman may say she has slept with a man – even believe she has done so – and still it may not be so. I think you are a person with a brave spirit. If it is the case that your friend sleeps with this girl you will not lie to yourself. You will know. But do not make the mistake of believing bad news just for the reason that it is bad. We live in an age, God forgive us, where bad news is preferred to good. "Vatican Priest Did Not Sleep With Beautiful Jewess" does not make a headline! Also, you know, now that I have met you I think it must also be the case that your friend liked you for yourself too. It is not reason enough that he hangs around only for the young boy – there are other ways . . .'

Julia made a face. 'Yes, but I was giving Nicco lessons. It was a perfect excuse to meet him – with me as chaperone, you see!' And she knew for herself about that ravaging, feverish longing which got into your blood and raced through every mental process. Wise in the ways of humankind as this man was, was he likely to understand that?

The priest gave what might have been a sigh. 'You do not like my suggestion that your friend also liked you because, forgive me, you are intoxicated at present by the prospect of the worst. Believe me, I know that feeling. Luckily nowadays,' he raised a glass at her, 'I am intoxicated only by this!'

They sat again in silence. Julia, who had been annoyed by his words, found herself trying to imagine the ugly little priest as a young, frightened man. What must it have been like hiding there with the distraught girl? 'What was it like then, the chapel?'

'It was place full of sweetness,' said the Monsignore. 'I remember that I thought it was not surprising that the Angel Raphael had visited there.'

'You believe he did?'

'Certainly the artist believed so.'

'The artist?' she said, not knowing why she was near tears.

'Did I not say? There is a diptych painted by an anonymous master which stood always in the chapel: the story of Tobias and Raphael.'

'I know the story.'

'A very old and holy painting which performed many miracles.'

'Yes?' Her breath hurt in her throat.

'The night Isabella and I hid in the crypt, I hid the diptych there too. To hide it from the little corporal.'

'Was there a dog?'

'A dog?'

'Yes. A dog in the painting of the angel.'

In her notebook she had written: *The dog and the angel arrive in the story simultaneously, just at the moment we are told Tobit and Sara are each contemplating death. Perhaps Tobit and Sara are different sides of the same coin — so the dog and the angel could be aspects each lacks, and needs in order to be cured?*

The Monsignore appeared to be concentrating. 'Of course,' he spoke slowly. 'You are right. I had forgotten there was a dog with him — the dog is usually with the boy but in this case Tobiolo was on the other side, with his father.'

So it *was* the same panel. 'What did the angel look like?'

Again the Monsignore paused. His eyes, hooded over, looked more like a dormant reptile's than a bird's. He stayed mute so long that Julia, thinking he had dropped off, had risen from her chair and was about to tiptoe away when he opened his eyes suddenly and said, 'I can see why this artist painted him the colour blue — the colour of heaven. But when I saw him with my own eyes, it was impossible to say what he looked like.'

There was a silence and into it Julia felt pour out of her,

unstoppered, an indescribable emotion. The Monsignore had closed his eyes again and one was twitching slightly as though trying half-heartedly to wink. Like an ineffable stream the feeling flowed from her, into the leafy courtyard, up over the high walls and into the multiple, timeless luminosity, of which Venice is but a version. After a while she sensed the Monsignore had truly fallen sleep and when he began to snore with his dog she got up quietly and left the courtyard.

That night I dreamed. Among the things my father taught me which I still heed was to pay attention to dreams: he told me dreams were messages brought by angels and how our ancestor, Joseph of the Patched Coat, earned fame through telling the meaning of Egyptian Pharaoh's dreams.

I dreamed I was walking by a river and I looked across to Sara's chamber – as I had done, in waking life, the previous evening. But now, with the eye of the dream, I could see right inside the window and into the chamber.

Azarias was there and Sara too. She was lying on the bed with her hands thrown back over her head and she was thrashing about as if she were demented. Azarias was standing there just looking at her – quite still.

Suddenly he moved forward and I saw he had a rope in his hands. He whipped it round and bound her tightly and for a moment I saw her lying there, trussed up like an animal for sacrifice.

I was so enraged by what I saw that I cried out and I must have cried in my sleep for when I woke Azarias was standing by the bed — smiling as he had smiled that first time I ever met him.

3

Julia did not go to the Cutforths' for supper after leaving the Monsignore. Instead she walked round to St Mark's. It seemed a long while since she had first stood beneath the pillared arcade at the edge of the Piazza.

She stood now and looked at the basilica again, trying to be dispassionate. But why bother, she thought crossing the great square and entering through the porch into the atrium. Why bother to be dispassionate? Isn't passion what it is all about? The passion of Christ. She had never thought about the words before. No, that wasn't true: she had thought about the words but had not allowed them meaning. From the Latin — *passio* — suffering. All the jasper and porphyry, all the blue-veined marble and sea-green serpentine, all the refulgent gold – she was standing beneath the mosaic ceilings of the atrium – was there to recall the ardour of one man's passionate sacrifice.

Looking up she saw the creation of the world revealed in the southernmost dome. And after all, she said to herself, it is a revelation. In a spiral unfolded the division of night and day; the creation of the stars; the sun and moon; the seas; the fish; the birds; the beasts, down to the furthest edge of the dome and the hauling of Eve out of Adam's side. From his rib – you could see it (just) like a turkey drumstick in God's hand!

The Japanese were out in force again. A party stopped and aimed a bank of phallic cameras at Adam and Eve. No wonder they felt embarrassed in their nakedness. Julia turned aside in disgust. Really, she thought, it should be made difficult not more easy to get to places of beauty. One ought to be required to pass a test before being permitted to enter St Mark's.

A notice reminded her that in all this time she had never yet climbed up to see the famous bronze horses. It was bound to be crowded inside the basilica. And she was curious to look down on the Piazza from the vantage point above. She set off up steep stone stairs.

Coming out into the upper gallery she saw a body hanging from a tree. Judas Iscariot: the traitor. The mosaicist must have put him up here, away out of sight. Poor Judas! How must it have felt, betraying what you knew to be the best? Maybe that was the job of Saraqûel, the fifth angel? To defend us against self-treachery?

But the horses? She had come to see the horses. It was said they were no longer safe to stand outside where the polluted air might ransack their gilded bronze sides. She had seen one of them once when, dutifully, she had queued in a line at the British Museum. But she had no proper memory of it.

She made her way along the finger-smoothed marble and suddenly, she caught her breath for there, like ancient gods, they were, ears pricked, nostrils flared, each with a hoof delicately raised. Thousands of years old, they had survived magisterially their history as loot and plunder. Whatever were such riches doing in this poky room? Who cared about the pollution? They should surely be outside in the free air! Horses are like dogs, she reflected, hurrying from the room: guardians of our instincts.

Julia went out and onto the roof. It was early evening and down below, with the heat beginning to abate, tourists had begun to fill the Piazza. On the sloping marble surfaces she walked past the replica horses, reaching up to touch one on the hoof. Tough always to be the substitute! She sat down at the corner, feeling the bulk of the basilica at her back, on a level with the blue and gilded clock-tower which strikes with hammers the quarters of each hour for the city of Venice.

The Monsignore's extraordinary story remained to be digested. It occurred to her that he might have been making it up — to console her — to help her through her unhappiness. She could not be sure, but he was the kind of man who might fabricate to assuage distress. But the bizarreness of the story seemed to work against that theory. There was reassurance in its very unlikeliness. And besides there was his other revelation.

So what was the truth of the events of the previous night? She had not been mistaken, of that she was sure, about the nature of Carlo's interest in Nicco. She had first begun to work out, in what she now inwardly referred to as her 'walking cure', that in just the same way as she had conceived an impossible passion for Carlo, he had conceived one for the boy. Sitting with the Monsignore, she had understood better the nature of that cruel hunger and thirst after the thing you could not have; call it 'love', call it 'desire'. The Monsignore's words hung in her ear: '. . . you have become resigned to this man being homosexual . . .' Had she? Perhaps she had. The humiliation of loving Carlo had given way to something deeper — a sense that, like her, Carlo was also vulnerable. No doubt he too was ashamed of his feelings. We cannot commission desire, thought Julia Garnet.

But the girl, Sarah. That was a different kettle of fish. (Here her mind ran distractedly off to Signora Mignelli's story of the war between the priest and the adulterous fishmonger.) It was true what the Monsignore had hinted at: she was jealous of the possibility that Carlo had found Sarah desirable. And yet what right had she to be jealous?

An English couple appeared, wanting to squeeze past her. She got up and moved back along the roof. To the south was the lagoon where the waters waited to swallow Venice up. It was too awful to think about. And yet, she mused (passing further along round to the corner of the Doges' Palace), it is the things we don't think about which do real harm. If Venice was in peril, it was only by being clear-sighted that the peril might be averted.

A group of giggling girls were testing the railings, seeing how far they could lean over, their skimpy skirts riding up over their behinds. Beyond and beneath them, guarding the entrance to the lagoon, the two great granite columns from the Levant reminded her of the Monsignore's other story — of the young man, the silk merchant, whose love, by the grace of the Angel Raphael, had summoned for him the power of life and death. On one of the columns stood the spurious St Theodore beside his crocodile, which Carlo had pointed out to her on their first meeting. Why a crocodile? (Too late to consult the Reverend Crystal!) She had been reading about crocodiles lately. Of course — in Vera's book. The story of the great fish's remedial powers in the Book of Tobit was perhaps attributable to the magical properties of crocodiles. Evidently the Egyptian believed that the dung and gall of the crocodile cured leucoma — the cause of Tobit's blindness.

But her own blindness — if only there were a cure for that! With a shock she remembered Sarah, standing at her balcony which looked across to the invisible mountains. Sarah had talked then of throwing herself down. Up here she saw how easy that would be: there was a kind of thrill attached to the idea. She and Sarah both afflicted unto death by love for Carlo?

But that was silly, she remonstrated, as she returned to

the gallery and made her way down the steep steps (for a whistle had blown to usher them all down). Sarah's motives for throwing herself off her balcony were more serious than any passing fancy she might have had for Carlo. And if the Monsignore was right, and Sarah hadn't slept with Carlo, what had he been doing there so early in the morning in her apartment? And why should Sarah lie about it anyway?

On her own balcony, watching the reflected light of the setting sun colour the clouds over the *campo*, she wrote:
The fishes were the first in the story of the Creation. Old Tobit has got 'above' himself, up on his moral high ground – the girl, too, has to 'come down' from her chamber. They both need to have something fundamental brought to their attention. Maybe the fish 'cures' because it brings them down, not 'to earth' but to an even lower level? (NB Find out about Garum.)

In the end it was Nicco and not Sarah who helped transport her belongings to the Ghetto. Signora Mignelli, she learned when she returned for her last evening at the apartment, had organised it all for the following day. 'We see you here again,' she said, as if the matter were beyond question.

'I don't know when I will be back,' said Julia, slightly melodramatic.

'Of course you visit us,' said the Signora, with her customary command. 'You come to take coffee with me next week! Yes?'

Nicco and Julia travelled across the city almost in silence. Her mood was not one for conversation. But the silence was not uncomfortable and, hoping (after he had hauled both case and holdall up the stairs) it had not been too great an ordeal for the boy, she was pleased to hand him a 50,000 lire note, conscious that this would not have been permitted under the dragon-gaze of Signora Mignelli.

'No, no,' said Nicco, declining fervently.

'Absolutely, Nicco, I insist. You have been so kind.'

'OK.' Graceful as ever, Nicco allowed his resistance to be overcome. 'I help you some more, Giulia?'

'Thanks, Nicco, just put the books over here, would you? Then I'm fine. Now, let me give you my number here. And do please, come and see me.' And then, quickly, 'Not for lessons – I shall be lonely.'

'OK,' said Nicco. And then, with surprising fluency, 'Now you not live so near me, Giulia, I visit you.'

Sarah, who had sounded relieved on the phone not to have to come over, had left a note, with the keys, with a young Irishman in the apartment below.

Dear Julia – I'm leaving first thing tomorrow so am staying at Aldo's so as not to disturb you.

As if you haven't disturbed me already! thought Julia.

Everything fairly self-explanatory. If you get into difficulty Sean downstairs knows all about the apartment. He's a film director and very on the ball! Take care and have fun! Sarah.

There were three xxxs.

Julia, too bone-tired to unpack, looked about for clean sheets to make up the bed. Was this something to ask Sean, the film maker, about? Doubtless there were reasons why he knew 'all about the apartment'. Finding no sheets, she boiled a kettle of water for tea (at least there was a tea-pot) and not wishing to engage with 'Sean downstairs', she balanced her mug on a pile of magazines beside the bed and lay down full stretch on top of the bedspread.

The London Library tome had been placed by Nicco beside the bed and idly she opened it at the first page of the General Preface.

In its earliest use the term 'apocrypha' was applied to writings which were withheld from public knowledge because they were vehicles of mysterious or esoteric wisdom too sacred or profound to be disclosed to any save the initiated.

In Ancient Greek *ἀπόκρυφα* meant hidden. What was it the Monsignore had said to her? 'The greatest wisdoms are not those which are written down but those which are passed between human beings who understand each other.'

She read on. *'Apocryphal' has only latterly come to acquire its meaning of false or heretical.* Charles had called the Monsignore's story of the young Levantine and the building of the Chapel-of-the-Plague 'apocryphal'. And yet all that the Monsignore had spoken of today made her sure of its validity. It all depended on the way you saw things. What was it Blake had said?

I question not my Corporeal Eye . . . I look thro' it and not with it.

༄

'Azarias,' I said, still muddled in my wits. 'Whatever's happening?'

'You were dreaming,' The clear voice drove out sleep.

'Where is Sara?' I asked, for the violent dream was coming back to me. 'Azarias — what is wrong with her? Who are those men the maid talked about? What were you doing in her chamber?'

Azarias tried to settle me down back to sleep but I wasn't having any of it. 'No,' I said. 'I am not a child and you are not my nurse and I am more awake now than I'll ever be. Speak plainly, or I will leave for Raghes tomorrow.' I was becoming agitated about my promise to my father.

Azarias looked me dead in the eye and time held still as I had the sensation of being sucked towards the Vast. Then he lifted his gaze.

'There is an evil spirit possesses her.' He spoke in his sweet, severe tone. 'Seven men who tried to enter her have died. But do not fear. Light for dark, I am his match.'

Lying there, helpless and uncomprehending, I felt my stomach grow cold and all other feeling drained away. All I could think of were my father, my mother and how all this was happening without their knowledge; and I their only child.

'Azarias,' I said, and this time I did not protest or speak angrily. 'I cannot in good conscience risk my life for this woman. For myself it is nothing but I fear lest I die and bring my father and my mother, because of me, to the grave with sorrow; for they have no other son to bury them.'

(I hoped that what I said was true — I know I did at least have some part concern for my parents!)

Azarias looked at me again, and again I felt myself being pulled into those whirlpool eyes.

'Hear me, brother,' he said. 'Make no reckoning of the evil spirit for this same night Sara shall be given to you in marriage. Remember the great fish by the banks of the Tigris which threatened your life? And remember that I counselled you to save the heart and the liver and also the gall? Touching the heart and the liver, if a devil or an evil spirit trouble any man or woman and a smoke is made before them of the heart and liver of this same fish, then they shall no longer be vexed with the evil. When you come this night into your marriage chamber, take the ashes of the perfumed woods and resins which burn there and lay upon them the heart and liver of the fish and make a smoke with it. And the evil spirit shall smell it and flee away and never come any more. Then when you have entered your wife for the first time, you must rise up, both of you, and pray to the Wise Lord who is merciful and will have pity on you and save you.'

Then he repeated the words he had said before to me but

now instead of terror they inspired in me a longing and a wonder: 'She was set apart for you before the world was; and you shall save her and she will go with you.'

4

Julia lay on Sarah's bed rereading the book on the Apocrypha which Vera had brought (such a long time ago it seemed) from England. The cautious, scholarly prose was soothing. It appeared that the author of the Book of Tobit was a Jewish exile too. An exile writing about exile. Maybe that was why she was drawn to the book, drawn to old Tobit whose dedication to the dead lost him his sight? Poor Vera! How mean to her she had been. There were horrible depths of meanness in her character — no wonder she found herself on her own now. But unlike old Tobit, or his anonymous author, she had no Jerusalem to mourn — one would hardly yearn to return to the temple of Ealing!

It had grown dark outside. Conscious that she had not eaten, nor yet located the sheets for the bed, she hauled herself up. Her hip was hurting again and on top of that she seemed to have pulled a muscle in her arm. Lack of food, lack of sleep and the recent trek across the city with Nicco and the luggage brought on further dizziness. She did not want to make a journey down the steep stairs to the shops.

There was some cereal in the cupboard and a carton of milk in the fridge. Not much else apart from an opened tin of anchovies and half a lemon. Wistfully, she remembered her arrival at Signora Mignelli's: the apartment spanking clean, the bed made up with crisp lace-topped linen, fruit and flowers to welcome her.

But this was babyish! She was a grown woman and not a child who needed her mother. The cereal and milk and a cup of tea, nursery foods to be sure, would have to do until the morning. And the night was warm – the coverlet would do without sheets.

Sitting up in bed with the bowl of cornflakes balanced on a magazine, she copied some words from the volume beside her into her notebook: *At a Parsi funeral a dog (with certain spots above the eye) is brought in to gaze at the body and so exorcise the Nasu.*

There had been a Parsi girl at St Barnabas. The family came from Bombay and she remembered the parents had been thrilled when she had awarded their daughter a history prize. The family had invited her to tea and, unusually (for as a rule she did not socialise with her pupils – perhaps because the invitations were few and far between), she had paid a visit to their home in Brentford – a modest, terraced house but cultivated she seemed to think. The father had explained to her how the Parsis were the living inheritors of the ancient Persian religion who had fled to India when the Muslims curtailed their ancient religious practices. They were exiles too, the Parsis. But unlike the Jews they melted into the communities they landed up in. Maybe that was the choice – join in or define your own? Parsi or Jew. Either you fought your god's corner, like old Tobit, or you took the local spirits as you found them, trusting to the universal recurrence of whatever it was that mattered to you in your own version of god.

But who or what were these 'Nasu' – nasty-sounding name? Obviously some sort of evil spirits. Like the demon who inhabits Tobias's future wife. Poor Tobias. Whatever could it have been like, preparing to make love to a girl whom you knew to be filled with a murderous spirit? A spirit you knew, as you attempted intercourse for the first tremulous time, had killed seven lovers before you?

Resting the notebook on her knee she wrote: *Why does the dog have spots 'above the eyes'? An extra pair to 'see' better? Dog as 'seer'?*

Seven men gone to their death. Were there seven devils to match the seven angels? What were their names? Uriel, Michael, Raguel, Gabriel, Saraqûel, Remiel. And Raphael, of course.

*

She woke with her heart jumping. Someone was outside the room. Commanding herself not to move, she lay rigid. There it was again. An awful, muffled fumbling sound and then the door was being opened. Horror of horrors! An interloper! She must not cry out. Stay calm. Don't say a word. Play asleep. Play dead. No, not dead, not yet, she wasn't ready for that!

A man's voice swore softly, 'Shit!' Then the light came flooding on and she had sprung off the bed and was crouched beside it ready to do she knew not what to her assailant.

'Who the fuck . . . ?'

'Toby!'

She had come close to hitting him. They glared at each other. Then, 'Oh, Toby I'm so glad it's you. I'm sorry. I must . . . sorry, the bathroom.' She had nearly wet herself. From the mirror her face stared at her under the greenish bulb. Going out she said again, 'I'm so sorry. It was a shock.'

'Why are *you* sorry? It should be me.'

He sounded belligerent but she didn't care. 'It must have been a shock for you too. Shall I make us some tea?'

'Yeah, thanks. D'you mind if I smoke?'

'No, go on. Please.' How English they were being.

Toby took out a packet of Golden Virginia tobacco and some papers and rolled a spindly cigarette. She watched him, fascinated by his dexterity.

'Do you mind me smoking because, look, I can go onto the balcony?'

'Not a bit. I quite like the smell.' It reminded her of Carlo.

Carlo who had perhaps slept here with Toby's sister. 'Toby, does Sarah know you're back?'

'Of course.'

'Oh!' She felt forlorn that she was not to be the one to break the news: the return of the Prodigal Son. 'Where is she, Toby?' That she had not meant to say.

'Search me! I expected her to be here. What are you doing?'

So the twins hadn't spoken. 'Sarah asked me to stay. She's been beside herself with worry.'

'You're joking!'

'No, Toby, it's true. She had no idea where you were.'

'Sarah?' Now he was staring at her. A gap opened in her mind and she could see there was something she had misconstrued. 'Sar knows exactly where I've been!'

'I don't understand.' Panic began to threaten – her heart was fluttering like a bird – for a moment she struggled to breathe. Was she losing her mind – like her father? 'Toby – have you got the painting?'

'What painting?'

'The angel panel.' She knew he hadn't. Only true sincerity manifests itself in a certain kind of stupidity.

'The angel panel?'

She wanted to shout, 'The angel painting! The one you showed me. The one you found the day I walked under your scaffolding and into your chapel and into the life of you and your bloody sister. The one wrapped like a portion of blue sky in a grey blanket which the two of you – damn your

eyes! – played fast and loose with. The angel, *my* angel, the
Archangel Raphael.' But instead she said, quite gently, 'Yes,
Toby. The angel with the blue wings.'

'Isn't it in the chapel?' He sat down awkwardly on the
bed.

'Toby,' she said, for suddenly an idea was slipping in and
out of the rapid gap in her mind and she needed to speak it
before it became impossible to say. 'Where do you sleep?
When you are not in the chapel – when you are here, where
do you sleep?'

He turned puzzled eyes and she saw how like his sister's
they were: the palest aquamarine, ringed with black. 'Here
of course,' patting the unmade bed. 'I won't tonight but
normally . . .'

'With Sarah?'

'Yeah with Sarah. Hey, this is the late twentieth century,
you know. We're over age – consenting adults. I mean, it's
not illegal.'

'But she's your sister!' Toby got up from the bed and felt
in his pocket for his tobacco. 'Toby, you have a cigarette
already.'

'Oh, sure.' He sat down again. Neither spoke. 'Look, I'm
sorry. I've forgotten your name.'

'Julia.'

'Yeah, of course. I'm sorry.'

'That's all right, said Julia. 'Why should you remember?'

'She's not my sister.'

'What?'

'She's not my sister.'

'But you're twins.' Toby got up, stubbed out his cigarette in the sink and sat down to roll another one. 'You even look alike.'

'Yeah, that's right. We *are* twins. We're cousins – not brother and sister.'

'But Sarah said you were twins?' Now it was she who sounded stupid.

'That's right. We are. Same birthdays. Both on the first of May. My mum and her mum's sisters. My mother came to visit my aunt in hospital and went into labour – two months early. I was born the same day, just before midnight. Sarah always says it was seeing her ugly face did it! My aunt says it was my mum being competitive. Sibling rivalry.' She'd forgotten how when he smiled he became attractive.

'Cousins?'

'Yeah. And, you know, it's all right for cousins to do it.' Embarrassed, he looked at the floor.

'So you do sleep together? I'm so sorry, Toby, this is absolutely not my business.'

'It's all right. I don't mind. Sarah been telling you tales then?'

'Well . . .'

'Bet she has. Did she say she was abused as a child too? That's one of her favourite lines. Her dad worshipped the ground she trod on, but there was never any funny stuff.'

It was fantastic, what he was saying, and yet, dumbly, inexorably, she knew it was the truth. She was not a perceptive person, and yet even she had felt — what could you call it? — the ghost of an intimation of something not quite right in Sarah's story, something, well, out of *true*, was how best to describe it. Yes, Sarah's story of childhood abuse had not touched or angered her — she had put it down to her own limitations of feeling, but now she knew the response was an accurate one — because of how differently this was making her feel.

Toby's voice was still speaking. 'She couldn't do anything wrong so far as he was concerned. Auntie Daisy was a bit tougher — but there wasn't anything sinister in Sarah's childhood apart from the fact that they wouldn't let her learn tap.'

'Tap?'

'Yeah, tap dancing. She created a scene about it when she was six. I still remember her yelling and screaming like they were murdering her or something. I was impressed.' He laughed angrily. 'I never got my way, not like her, anyway — but then my mum and dad were poor. We spent all our holidays together, right up to art school. They always called us "the twins", the family did.'

'But Toby, why has she said these things? Why would she want to make up something so appalling?'

Toby shrugged. 'God knows. Look, she'd been having these headaches. "Migraines", yeah? Then she started to not eat — lost about a stone. Some jerk told her it was psychological — pressure from home — which was bollocks. There was never any pressure put on Sarah. She wouldn't even wear braces to put pressure on her teeth when she was a kid! So,

one day she goes to this therapist –' he made a movement
with his mouth as if to spit – 'near where her folks live down
in Devon – they have this big house, lovely garden, horses,
all that.'

'Did you mind?'

'What?'

'All that. If you were poor. The big house, the horses?'

Toby pulled at his cigarette. 'Nah! Home was OK. And I
could go to Sarah's any time. Uncle Bill and Auntie Daisy
used to be my second mum and dad.'

'So, the therapist?'

'Well, you know the joke, don't you? Take *Therapist* apart
and it spells *The Rapist*. And that's what this one was.'

'No good?'

'Evil! She got Sarah in her clutches and the next thing we
knew Sarah was saying she couldn't stay home any more. She
came to stay with my mum and dad for a bit. Uncle Bill and
Auntie Daisy started out by saying that it was only fair because
up till then I'd always gone down to Devon. They were like,
"She's just balancing things up." You could tell they were
hurt though. I didn't like it because I missed the horses. And
Sarah had gone weird. Funny diets, couldn't touch the things
we ate, raw carrot, no alcohol – which was a laugh 'cos she'd
always put it away – had to have her bed facing north – that
kind of crap. Anyway, after a while she wrote to Uncle Bill
saying she wanted a meeting with him at her therapist's place.'
Toby grimaced. 'Hey,' he said. 'D'you want to hear all this?
It's pretty shit!'

Julia thought – I have been so wrapped up in myself all my life. Aloud she said, 'If you want to tell me, I'd like to hear.'

'Yeah, well, it cuts me up. Sorry. Anyway, Bill and Auntie Daisy rang me up about it and I could tell they were a bit worried so I said not to touch it with a bargepole. Fat chance!'

'He went anyway?'

Toby took a meaningful drag. 'Yup! Old Uncle Billy toddled off, innocent as a new-born babe, to be told by this cow that he'd fucked his only beloved daughter – sorry, I shouldn't have said that.'

Julia passed him her handkerchief. 'It happens to be the correct word for what you describe,' she said. 'Why be sorry? What happened?'

'It killed him,' said Toby, screwing the embroidered square of lace into a ball. HMJ: Harriet's initials. 'He couldn't take it. He adored her. Everyone started this "no smoke without fire" stuff – which is bollocks, by the way, you get smoke from dry ice – even Auntie Daisy started to ask questions. I couldn't stand it – it really did my head in. Is there any more tea?'

Julia got up and went over to the pot. She kept her back deliberately turned while she refilled the mug. 'They're insidious, those expressions. "No smoke without fire" – it gives a false sense of wisdom.' It had been said, she remembered, of Mr Kenton. 'Please go on, if you want to, that is.'

'It was breaking them up. Auntie Daisy was in the middle between Bill and Sarah. Sarah refused to see Uncle Bill, wouldn't come to the house if he was there and so on. He was about to move out. If I ever meet that fucking therapist I'll fucking kill her too.'

'How did he die?' She didn't really want to know but the story was too awful to leave suspended.

'Hanged himself,' said Toby briefly. 'In one of the barns.'

'Oh, Toby,' Julia said.

Her lips had gone numb. In his senile years her father had once torn open her blouse and scrabbled at her breast, trying to suck at it. She had pushed him away, repelled, and buttoned the blouse angrily and left. But later that night, in the bath, she had remembered that once, after her mother died he had pulled her to him and fervently kissed her, his lips wet. Most definitely she had not liked the experience. But suppose he had hanged himself on account of it?

'But this woman. What happened to her? Didn't the family do something?'

'What could they do? Bill was dead. Daisy nearly went round the bend with guilt. And Sarah — how d'you bring yourself to face that? She never has, far as I know.'

'But she doesn't see this dreadful woman any more, does she? She told me it had made her suicidal.' No wonder the girl had spoken of wanting to throw herself from the balcony.

'Nah. She stopped seeing her. But there was no inquiry. Nothing. The mad cow is probably still destroying decent families' lives.'

And according to Toby, Sarah's father had most faithfully and properly loved his daughter.

'So, that's why I stick around. She needs someone to look after her. We don't make love, by the way, since you mention it.'

'Oh, but only because I thought . . .'

'She can't, well, won't anyway. Hardly surprising. I get to cuddle her a bit but we never, you know . . . Sometimes it all gets too much and I need to take off. Sort my own head out.'

'She seems so . . .' What did Sarah seem? She was learning she was no judge of human behaviour. '. . . I always found her so full of confidence.'

'Yeah? She can charm the birds off the trees but underneath . . .' Toby scrubbed at an invisible stain on his jeans with Harriet's hanky, 'she's . . .'

'In hell, I should think. Is that what happened this time? You went away for a break?' What an accomplished liar Sarah must be. The story of Toby's unresponsive lover had been delivered so plausibly.

'Sort of. We had a row. You were there!' The day he had gone to the glass-cutters. Toby hesitated as if to say more and then apparently changed his mind. 'Anyway, I had these drawings I needed to show a guy in London — a job I might move on to. It seemed a good moment to blow — cool things for a while. But Sarah knew where I was. She always does.'

'She told me you had a girl.' On Valentine's Day, out on the balcony, the Feast of the Purification of the Virgin Mary, which had once been celebrated as Candlemas.

'There was never any girl for me but Sarah.'

So it was all a tissue of lies. Well, that was, in its way, a comfort. 'And you love her?'

'Yeah, I love her. She's a mess but I couldn't ever love anyone else.'

'For she is appointed unto thee from the beginning?'

'Yeah,' said Toby. 'You've got it. Something like that!'

I slept no more that night. The mating frogs were ak-akking to each other in the bulrushes in the ditch below and I watched the sun rise over the distant mountains where Azarias and I had camped together in the days before I knew Sara. Even now after all this time I miss them still, those high, lonely days, with just the two of us and the camels and all my life before me. A chain of black cranes flew along the green bands of the sky, their legs trailing. The world seemed suddenly a marvellous place; I did not want to leave it.

Sara's maid called me and laid upon the bed garments made of silk, wedding-robes embroidered in blue and purple. How many before me, I wondered, had worn them? The maidservant, poor soul, was distraught, weeping and urging me to be brave. (Not the best words to hear on your wedding day!)

Downstairs a ceremonial meal had been prepared and laid out upon tables; barley cakes and honey, white cheeses, sweet almonds, figs and pomegranates, and the dark wine of Media. Sara's father, Raguel, came towards me. Taking my hand he said, 'Eat, drink and be merry, for it is meet that you should marry my daughter.' He turned aside, then turned back to me and clutching at my arm again said, 'I will declare the truth to you. I have given my daughter in marriage to seven men who died the night they entered her.' He was a brave man and he looked me in the eye as he said it.

And perhaps it was this that made me answer as I did. 'Nonetheless I will eat nor drink nothing until the agreement is sealed between us as to the marriage of myself with your daughter.'

Then Raguel called Edna, his wife, and he ordered parchment to be brought on which he wrote an instrument of covenant and sealed it. And when the covenant was signed and sealed I spoke again.

'Have no fear,' I said, though for my part fear was turning my bowels to water. 'For this day my cousin and I shall be married.'

Then Raguel called his wife and said, 'Sister, prepare the chamber and bring our daughter to it.'

Edna rose, wiping away her tears, and said to me, 'Be of good comfort. May the Lord give you joy for your sorrow.' Then she sent servants to spread the bed in the wedding-chamber.

I looked about but Azarias had departed so alone I climbed the stairs to the chamber in the high tower.

5

They talked until the sky through the balcony window began to show not fire but pale gold. *Oro pallido*. It crossed Julia's mind to offer that Toby lie down on the bed. But their conversation had been somehow too intimate to suggest it.

'More tea?' she asked and then, 'Oh, no go, I'm afraid. We're out of milk – unless you like it black?'

'We can go out and get some? There's an all-night machine near the station.'

'Of course, if you'd like to.'

He seemed to want her company for he did not suggest going alone.

Julia, who had spent her student days in law-abidingness,

speculated that this sort of dawn raid was what she had missed in her tame Cambridge life. They walked through silent streets to the station to find the machine empty. 'I'm sorry. I shouldn't have dragged you out. I get restless. Drives Sarah mad!'

'Toby, where might Sarah be tonight?' She had not mentioned Carlo. Her sighting of the man she loved outside Sarah's door had ceased to seem important. She was ashamed, amid such tragic matters, to have made such a fuss. Why mention it anyway – it could only muddle things? Given Toby's story it was unlikely Sarah had slept with Carlo – unless her experience with her father had given her some sort of father-fixation. Somehow Julia doubted it. She remembered now that Sarah had asked her, pleaded with her almost, not to mention what she had seen that morning.

But where was the girl if not with Carlo? 'Could Sarah be with your architect friend?' She did not reveal that this was where Sarah's note had suggested she would be.

But Toby didn't think so. Aldo, he explained, had a difficult mother who was unlikely to welcome a young and attractive female guest.

So she was right about Aldo; Sarah's hint of his fascination with her was another of her lies. Perhaps when there was something you could not face, you wove a fiction around yourself to keep the unbearable from you? And then, when you needed it, where would you find a place where you could ever be truthful again?

'I tell you what,' said Julia after a while. 'Let's walk to the chapel. What do you think?'

'Sure, yeah.'

They walked along the Grand Canal. In the greenish light a green boat chugged by, with a man at the wheel in green overalls and a green cap. It was the second time in three days she had walked across the city. The first, the morning after the party, when she had found Carlo leaving Sarah's house. Now she was completing the circle.

What had really occurred the morning she had seen Carlo leave Sarah's apartment? Toby's account had convinced her that whatever it was she had drawn a false conclusion. It was her own mind which had woven the net she had become entangled in – which was only justice, when you thought about it – though it didn't, to be sure, say much for her mind! When you point a finger, Harriet had said to her once during an argument, remember there are three fingers pointing back at you! (A remark which she had dismissed at the time as 'Tosh!') She couldn't even remember what the row was about. Stella's cat-litter, she thought. And now Harriet was dead and beyond apology. The book she had been reading suggested that the story of Tobit might include remnants of a legend called The Grateful Dead – which she half recalled as the name of a band the children at school had gone crazy over. How could the dead express gratitude? Harriet could not be grateful to her any more – only she could be grateful to Harriet.

They walked on in silence past the Papadopoli Gardens. Julia wanted to ask if she could take Toby's arm; the ache in her hip had become more severe. But he walked on, always slightly ahead, with a remoteness she felt too diffident to breach. Why did old Tobit care so much about the dead bodies which lay about in Nineveh? Why not let the wild dogs strip the corpses' bones? To have one's body devoured by nature's hunters didn't seem such a bad thing.

They had come to the bridge which crosses the Rio Nuovo and Julia put out her hand to halt Toby. 'Would you mind? I need to catch my breath.'

'Sure.' He stood against the bridge, rolling another cigarette.

I'm glad I do not have children, Julia thought, watching him. Impossible not to mind when they did themselves harm.

The sky was beginning to flush as they turned into a tiny *calle* which came out by the bridge across to the exotic Carmini – where Carlo had shown her the Cima altarpiece: another version of Tobias and Raphael, respectful attendants on the infant Christ who lies, tiny and naked, among admiring shepherds in the gold-leafed countryside of Cima's Conegliano. The artist has painted Tobias as a mere child, an open-faced boy who carries the fish with him as a proud boast to his pals and not as a powerful remedy against devils. Julia's mind wandered absurdly to Sarah's fridge and the tin of anchovies. Maybe they should have brought it with them – as expedient against more modern forms of evil!

They walked on along the canal which becomes the Rio dell'Angelo Raffaele. The site of the Chapel-of-the-Plague lay across the water.

Halfway along the *fondamenta* Julia stopped. 'I'm sorry,'

she said. 'I seem to have a stitch now. I'm getting to be a hopeless walking companion.'

'It's OK.'

They were close to where the nobleman's palazzo would have been. 'Toby, do you know the story of the Chapel?'

'Yeah. It was built for a woman who survived the plague.'

'But did you know she was a Jewess? At least, that's what a friend of mine told me.' It was all right to call the Monsignore a friend.

'Hey, that's cool! Technically, me and Sarah's Jewish 'cos our mums are. It's Uncle Herb, their half-brother, who's put up most of the money for the Chapel. Herbie the Wallet, Sarah calls him. That's how we're on the case. They only use Venetian restorers, usually.'

'You should be flattered.'

Across the water, according to the Monsignore's story, was where the young Levantine must have stood, patiently hoping for sight of his mortally sick beloved. Now, six and a half centuries later, she was there in the company of another lover. But the object of his love – where was she?

They had crossed the bridge and were passing now through the archway which led to the tiny hidden *campo* where the chapel, hedgehog-like, stood: a small dome with scaffolding spines. Toby stopped.

'Do you have a key?'

He nodded. 'Yeah. We've one apiece.'

'Do you want me to stay outside?'

In the gathering light she could see his pale eyes; the black encircling rings gave them a faintly demonic look. 'No. You come too.'

Needles of panic attacked her stomach as he unlocked the padlock which secured the green bronze handles of the doors. What if Sarah were not there? But, then, what if she were? Perhaps it was better if she had, after all, spent the night with Carlo and was taking comfort in his paternal-seeming arms. The tale Toby had told of the maleficent therapist was unspeakable. And in the Devon barn the body of Sarah's father – hanging in despair. She hoped he was safe now, buried deep in the fastness of the earth – if that was permitted these days to suicides? Old Tobit was right: kindness to the dead mattered: it was not better to be left to the scavenges of animals.

Toby had switched on a torch and was walking ahead into the dark. She could just make out the scaffolding which stood behind the altar.

Julia stood in the blackness in which he had left her. Her stitch had returned and she held her breath – whether for cure or superstition she did not know – counting to a hundred. One, two, three, four, five, six . . .

'Sarah? Sarah, it's me! Are you there?' The tremulous torch beam roved round the chapel's curving walls, weaving between the watery-grey pillars.

. . . thirteen, fourteen, fifteen . . .

'Sarah! It's Tobes!'

. . . twenty-one, twenty-two, twenty-three, twenty-four . . .

'Sar! Answer me, if you're there. It's all right. No one's angry with you.'

. . . thirty-one, thirty-two, thirty-three . . .

Then it was she saw him again. On the upper reaches of the scaffolding, a sheerness of presence, no more. It was as if he took the space from the air about him and against the darkness was etched, like the brightness which seeps through a door ajar, hinting at nameless, fathomless brilliances beyond, the slightest margin of light. Impossible to look too closely, but some way below, beneath where the long feet might have rested, she made out the girl's huddled shape, her arms folded over her head like some small, broken-winged, storm-tossed bird.

Then Toby's voice. 'Sar, I can see you. Stay where you are – I'm coming up.'

She sensed rather than observed the boy climb upward, for her being was wholly held by the extraordinary lucidity with which she suddenly saw the pathos hidden at the heart of the girl's terror.

For a knife-edge moment the lighted air at the top of the scaffolding hovered. Julia, as she stood watching, half wondered if she saw it linger almost tenderly over the crouched form; then, just a fractional shift and it was gone, the doorway into the impenetrable brightness closed up, and she was left, gazing into the shuttered dark.

Toby was shepherding someone towards her. 'Hey, Sar, it's me and Julia. It's OK. You're safe now.'

But Julia Garnet, out of the extraordinary incandescence

which suddenly lapped and enfolded her, cried voicelessly after the vanished presence, 'Thank you, thank you.'

⁊

And now comes the strangest part of my story. At the top step I found Kish waiting for me, his ears pricked and the hair on his spine raised. In my hand I found I had the bag which contained the liver and heart of the great fish which Azarias had instructed me to preserve — and in my mind were the words with which he had instructed me what I was to do with them.

Sara lay on the bed naked. It was the first time I had seen a woman naked and I remember I looked at her with a kind of curious wonder. I saw a compact body, small-breasted and narrow-hipped, with an arrowhead of dark hair marking where I supposed I must enter her. Was ever man more afraid of making that entrance?

But in times since I have wondered: maybe that is what it is like for all men? Maybe it always feels like death whenever a man first enters a woman's body and goes into the dark? (This, you may imagine, is not a thing I could ever ask my father!)

There had been a fire burning in the room. I took the heart and liver of the great fish and in a kind of trance I went over and laid them on the perfumed ashes of the fire.

And at that Sara turned on the bed – but it was not me she looked at, it was Kish.

Kish walked towards her, his head lowered, tail swishing, and he growled a long-drawn-out guttural growl. At that minute Azarias appeared out of nowhere. At the same moment Sara groaned and her back arched on the bed and there came on me a blinding sense of what it would be like to penetrate her and feel myself inside her.

Then she cried out a long, awful, anguished scream and I cried out too and suddenly the room was full of a vile stench and smoke, I was coughing and retching and then I must have passed out; and when I came to the room was filled with the scent of myrrh and frankincense and spikenard, and Azarias was gone and Sara lay on the bed, her arms flung up and over her head, as I had seen her in my dream.

6

Cynthia, answering the phone, said at once, 'Of course you must come and stay in our spare room. I don't know why you ever involved yourself with that absurd child. She looked to me unstable. You should have asked us, Julia.'

Julia – waiting for Charles, who had insisted on ordering a water-taxi – looked at Sarah lying in the bed. Toby, beside her, held her hand. 'Shouldn't we get a doctor?' She was remembering the leather-jacketed *dottore*.

But Toby had not wanted to disturb the girl. From time to time she made smothered, snuffling sounds, like a sleeping child or an animal, but mostly she lay, her hands flung back over her head, apparently unconscious.

Then Charles was there manhandling down the stairs her case and bag which, fortunately, she had left packed.

'Hey, thanks,' said Toby coming down the stairs to see her off. 'I wouldn't have thought of . . . you know, her being there. I don't know why.'

'I expect she went knowing you often slept there.' Had remorse finally led Sarah to the chapel? 'Will you let me know how you both are?' Julia asked, not wanting to presume yet unwilling to be parted.

The taxi driver, with Venetian promptness, had begun to unfasten the boat's painter. 'I'll ring you,' Toby promised. 'When she's better you must come round.'

'That was kind of a daft place for you to stay, Julia,' Charles ventured. 'I know you Brits are tough but the stairs would have killed me. And we are thrilled to have you stay with us. Cynthia says to be sure to tell you that your room has its own bathroom.'

Julia, thinking of the twins in their eyrie, felt how much she would prefer to have remained with them. But they needed no one but themselves for the time being.

Later that evening, as she sat with Charles and Cynthia on the balcony looking across the water to the iced-cake front of the Gesuati, a half-dormant resolution took shape. 'Do you by chance have the number of your friend Aldo?'

'He has a dragon-mother,' said Charles.

'If I were you I'd let Charles ring for you. He butters her up.' Cynthia smiled, secure in her own place in her husband's facility with women.

But Julia did not want assistance. 'No, it's all right,' she said. 'I'll brave the dragon-mother.'

Aldo himself answered the phone so any soft-soaping was uncalled for. Aldo was chatty. He explained to Julia he would be coming over soon to see the Chapel with the *Soprintendente*. The ugly one? Julia nearly asked but instead said, 'Which?' It seemed they were both coming to inspect the work – he, himself, was looking forward to seeing how it had turned out. He gave no sign of knowing anything of Sarah's allegedly imminent departure.

'Aldo, can you do me a favour?'

Immediate politeness. 'Of course.'

'Your friend, Carlo. I have mislaid his card.' At the bottom of the lagoon, in fact; tied in his handkerchief with a stone and the dead marigold! 'Could I trouble you for his number?'

Aldo was all obligingness, and the conversation ended both pleased with their mutual affability.

Now the real steel was required. Quickly, lest she lose the impulse, she dialled – part-praying there would be no answer.

But he was there. Deep breath. 'Carlo, it's Julia Garnet,' and at the other end of the line a second's silence.

'Julia, how delightful to hear from you.'

Her voice wanting to shake, she forced herself to say, 'It's such a long time since we saw each other properly. I was wondering if, well, we might meet – for a meal or something.'

Another pause but when he spoke again she thought she

detected relief. 'That would be most agreeable. Where shall I take you?'

But about this she was clear. 'No, please, this is my invitation. I owe you so much hospitality. It must be my turn.'

Toby rang the following morning. 'Sarah's much better. I'm keeping her in bed but she's drinking brandy and eating like a horse.' There was an indistinct shout from the background. 'Sarah says to tell you we're getting married.'

'Toby, that's great! How marvellous.'

'When she's up and about you must come over and celebrate.'

Julia pondered, waiting by the Redentore for the *vaporetto* to take her across the water. Did Sarah now understand the evil which had been perpetrated on her father? What was the name the Zoroastrians gave to the evil spirits which carry corruption? The Nasu. The wretched therapist (such an unappealing title!) who had wreaked havoc in that family's life must be a latter-day Nasu.

The restaurant she had appointed for her meeting with Carlo was an osteria, hospitable enough, but unremarkable. She did not wish to be reminded of their previous relationship by one of their former, more glamorous haunts.

Carlo looked older, she thought. He declined prosecco and they both drank mineral water. Blandly, they discussed neutral topics, mostly his professional commitments which had taken him travelling since the spring. There was a van Dyck he had run down and he described his plans for disposing of it, perhaps to a banker in Los Angeles. The dialogue was hard work. Nothing could be less like the easy familiarity of their previous exchanges.

'I was surprised to learn you were still here?' She sensed question in his voice and his eyes looked timidly, almost beseechingly at her so that the words of the Monsignore came back to her with the scent of dark roses: *I think it must also be the case that your friend liked you for yourself too.*

Confused, she flung off, 'So will you try London with your van Dyck?'

But at this he seemed to colour and, seizing the moment, she said, before she should stop herself, 'Carlo, did Sarah show you a painting on a panel in the Plague Chapel? Of an angel?'

Even before he had flushed darker red she knew the idea which had been unleashed inside her had hit the mark. Her hunch was accurate: whatever Carlo's proclivities it was not the lure of sex which had prompted his visit to Sarah under cover of darkness; it was the angel panel which had drawn him.

Mustering courage she pursued, 'It's a wonderful work, isn't it? I'm so glad Aldo is bringing the *Soprintendente* of paintings along to see it next week. Sarah's not been well but she'll be better by then, I hope. She'll want so much to be there when the painting is shown.'

She had worked it out during the long hours she had spent on the Cutforths' terrace, watching the boats weave and ply the water. Sarah had distracted her attention with a play of a sexual entanglement. Two plays, in fact: Toby's alleged girlfriend and her fake involvement with Carlo. How shrewd of the girl to have picked out her, Julia's, blind spot! Doubtless Sarah had divined, too, the hidden feelings for Carlo (and that was how evil made its way into the world, she suddenly understood: through the cracks of our ignorance and weakness) and used it to draw the wool over her eyes. What deal had Sarah struck with Carlo over the painting that morning she had surprised them? That Sarah had intended to use her as a witness to lay a trail of the painting's disappearance to Toby was something they both now had to deal with. But would the girl remember the labyrinthine duplicities by which she had planned to betray, not just her, Julia (who after all was no more than a casual acquaintance), but the boy, her twin, who had loved her so steadfastly? That some such dark compact had been forged was horribly apparent before her now.

Carlo was staring down at his coffee, endeavouring to compose his expression. But there was steel in him too; for he mastered his face to show polite expectation. 'I am so pleased. Sarah, of course, as she has clearly told you, invited me to see the painting and to get my advice. I thought it was not safe to keep it in those conditions in the chapel. How it got to be there in the first place is a mystery, of course.'

So he was unaware he had been spotted taking the painting from Sarah's apartment. Well, that truth was safe enough with her. And as to how the panel had been mislaid all these years, she thought she knew the answer to that too as, letting him off the hook, she turned the conversation to the Cutforths. 'They have been so kind taking me in,' she said. 'And me a sojourner and a stranger.'

'I am sorry?' She was acutely aware how desperate he was to leave, how every further minute in her company was now a horror to him. But, just for a second, she forced him to stay looking into her face, uncertain of quite what it held for him.

'It's from the Bible. The Old Testament. It's what Abraham said when he came first to the promised land. You will think this funny but my friend from England sent me a copy of the Bible and the Apocrypha and I have been reading them both.' She had had her small revenge: he would never be sure how much *really* she knew. But she owed him something too. 'Actually, it's you I have to thank because I wanted them for the Book of Tobit. You introduced me to the story – do you remember? – all that time ago, as it seems now, in the Angelo Raffaele? It has become very dear and important to me: I shall be eternally grateful.' And it was, after all, true: Carlo, who could never have given her love, had incidentally brought her something more abiding.

'Ah, you English ladies, you are too deep for me,' and he said it with an air of a dog being let off a leash. 'Forgive me, it has been so good to see you and catch up. But I must go: I have a call I promised to be at home to receive.'

He did not stay to escort her to the water-bus stop. Instead she walked alone past the Monsignore's *calle*. It was too late to bother him. She imagined the priest sitting up in bed, perhaps with his teeth in a glass, drinking brandy, the pug dog asleep. He would be glad the angel panel was secure.

Before he left Carlo had enquired, casually, where Sarah was to be found. 'Of course I do not want to trouble her while she is unwell, but there was a number she wanted from me. A contact in the art world. I must call her sometime to give it to her.' So no doubt a means would be constructed for Carlo to return the stolen panel.

She walked on, past the Bridge of Sighs, past the Doge's Palace, where she was glad to see her old doge, with his naval cap, back ensconced in his former quarters, past the column of St Theodore beside his crocodile and the winged lion who keeps them company, into the Piazza.

And all this too will pass, she reflected, if man does not find a way to keep it from sinking back into the sea. The great basilica gleamed in the lamplight, testifying to the power of man's creation. All beauty can be saved, she thought, if we learn to fight, to keep it from the forces of corruption and darkness. Which are, she concluded, often no more than indolence and fear, greed and cowardice, although that quaternity can do harm enough if one thinks of the Nazis – or the Nasu.

The Nasu spread their plague across the vistas of the years, centuries after centuries, since as long as men had learned to kill and cast blame and seek power over others. But alongside them, undeclared, came too the angel whose name means 'God's healing'. And today the victory had been to him.

꒚

 'Sara! Sara, my sister, my beloved. Sara my wife.'

IV
THE FEAST OF RAPHAEL

1

It took some time for the letters to catch up with Julia at her quarters at the Cutforths'. Signora Mignelli had given the post to Nicco who had called by and given it to Toby who had put it aside. He was apologetic when he rang.

Julia, trying not to mind that she had been forgotten, said, 'Come over, if you would like it – or I can come to you . . . ?' and waited.

Toby sounded unsure. 'Um, I'm not sure if Sarah . . .'

'Of course,' she said, smoothing over his unease. 'If it's not too much trouble for you why don't you bring them over here?'

As it happened the Cutforths were both out when Toby

arrived and she was able to take him out alone onto the balcony. 'Wow,' he said, gazing across. 'Cool view.' He was definitely nervous.

'Some tea, Toby? We've drunk enough of it together!'

'Tea'd be great. Thanks.'

She allowed him to settle outside while she made herself busy with the tea-things. Having him there, so like his twin (and she could not get out of the habit of viewing the pair of them in that way), reminded her of the times she had spent having tea with Sarah.

Poor girl, it had all been lies; lies on lies. Sarah's father had died — hanging from a rope — because his daughter had believed a lie: one of those rational-seeming lies which pose as morality because human beings like to think the worst of each other. And Sarah had had to justify the atrocity, peddling more falsehoods to keep the frightful knowledge from herself. And so it had gone on, gathering force, until the lie had permeated all she did. What was it Harriet had used to chant? 'Beware, beware of those who ''care''.' If only we human beings could learn, Julia thought (pouring boiling water onto green leaves in the Cutforths' elegant china teapot), to leave each other alone.

Outside, Toby was smoking one of his roll-ups and the sight of his hunched shoulders brought an access of tenderness. Setting the tray down she said, with a sense of taking bulls by horns, 'It seems an age since we did this together.'

'Yeah. Look, Julia, oh, thanks —' he slurped noisily — 'what I said to you that night . . .'

'It's all right. I shall tell no one — have told no one.'

'Thanks.' Visibly he relaxed. 'Only she's touchy about it. She asked if I had talked to you and I'm afraid I said I hadn't.'

'It's all right,' she assured, 'it can be our secret.' She was becoming quite a repository of secrets. 'Toby, have you found the panel?'

And at this he brightened. 'Yeah! It was in the passage. Sarah forgot she had put it back there.'

'The passage?'

'It's where we found it in the first place. There's a passage runs down the side we think led to an old palazzo that was there once. It was blocked up, full of stones and rubble and that, and when I was clearing it I found the panel high up in an alcove, wrapped in a blanket. I was knocked out when I discovered it!'

The Monsignore's passage. So she had been right about that too. 'Why didn't you report it at once?'

Looking sheepish he said, 'Yeah, I know. I wanted to say about that too — if you wouldn't mind keeping quiet about how long, you know, we've kind of known about it.' All those years her taciturn self had had nothing to 'keep quiet'; now every silence might conceal a veritable treasure-house! 'That was what the row was about, as a matter of fact. Remember the day you asked us to tea and I went off? You must have thought me rude.'

'I thought it was a girl.'

'Yeah, well, it was in a way. Sarah. She wanted us to hang on to the painting — she kept saying, "Let's keep it to ourselves just for a while – our secret." I didn't know what she was playing at and I got really worried. That's why I showed it to you.' His love wasn't as blind, then, as her own had been for Carlo – Toby had guessed something of the nature of Sarah's plans for the panel. 'We had this massive row about it and I went off to England – I felt like jacking the whole thing in, if you want to know. I love her but, you know, a priceless picture . . . she could have got us both into deep shit!'

'I'm glad you showed it to me. It meant, well, I got involved in something which mattered – for once in my life.'

And how she had been rewarded: that unforgettable, limit-less gaze she had witnessed in the chapel.

'Yeah – the painting mattered – matters. I dreamed about it while I was away. It's why I came back – it and Sarah.'

. . . *the nearest thing to heaven I'll ever see on earth*, he had said to her. 'Toby, did I see you once at the Madonna dell'Orto?'

Toby went crimson. 'Oh? Yeah, I went there some times. I sort of like her.'

'I should think she's comforting.' The stone Madonna with the kind lap. This is a tragic phase of civilisation, Julia thought, where we are ashamed to be found to pray. 'I saw you at the airport too!'

'Hey!' he grinned at her and she saw again how attractive he could be. 'You must be my guardian angel – following me around. I certainly would never have gone to the chapel that night if it wasn't for you.' Toby's manner had lost its nerviness and become confiding – like the night they had sat on the double bed and talked together. She could never tell him that this was the sole occasion in her life she had passed a night with a man! 'Funny thing,' he said. 'She saw Plush.'

'Plush?' But she guessed what was coming.

'Yeah, Uncle Bill's Dalmation. He had to be put down after, you know, Bill . . . Sarah swears she saw him that night in the chapel. Guess she was pretty spooked.'

'But she's all right now?' The vision of the pathetic broken bird she had seen that night — that was what she must hold on to.

'She's doing fine. It all came out, all the tales she'd been spinning. She's guilty as Hell, of course, over her dad's death — that's what it's about. I've been telling her she has to forgive herself. I hate those creepy ''therapy'' terms but it's true, you have to forgive yourself or you can't go on.'

'Self-indulgent not to, perhaps?'

'Yeah, I reckon. Anyway, Bill shouldn't have done what he did. He should have stuck it out — sued, got the mad cow struck off from her professional body, or whatever it is you do to these people, taken her for all she was worth — but I didn't say that to Sarah.'

'Yes, it's giving in to it, isn't it?' And maybe that was the way: you didn't give in to a lie — you found resistance to it by establishing your own truth. 'And the panel?' She could not rid herself of a protective feeling for the fragile painted wood.

Toby explained that Aldo had brought the *Soprintendente* in charge of paintings along to see it, and he had almost fainted away so great was his excitement. It had been provisionally identified as one half of the diptych by the fourteenth-century anonymous master who, according to local legend, had with his own eyes seen the Angel Raphael in the little chapel. ('And when you look at it,' said Toby, 'you kind of believe that don't you? He's so *real*!')

The news was to be released to the press when all the appropriate tests had been carried out but there was no serious question that it was part of the treasured diptych believed to have gone missing during the war.

Julia, sipping gunpowder tea, wondered whether to mention the Monsignore and decided against it. 'There'll be quite a to-do then, in the press?'

'Yeah. They thought the Nazis had got their mitts on it. I've asked them to hold the press release till Sarah's really better. I want her to tell the story.'

'But it was you who found it?'

Toby shrugged. 'Yeah, but I hate publicity. Anyway, I kind of want it to have been her — call it a betrothal present!'

'Oh, your marriage! I was forgetting. That's the most important news of all. Are you going to get married in the chapel?'

But Toby thought not. 'I don't want us to wait and I reckon we should go home for it anyway. We might do it in a synagogue — smash glasses!'

'That would be fun!'

When he had gone she opened her letters.

One was from Vera who had decided to retire to Hastings. *The property there is very reasonable,* she wrote, *and there are* not too many Tory voters, thank God, in those parts these days.

A second letter was from the bank and the third, rather bulkier, contained a note and a further envelope inside it.

The note was from Mr Akbar.

Dear Madam,
I would like to purchase from you your very nice flat. If you would accept an offer from me I would pay £170,000. Please let me know if your are interested.
Yours faithfully, A. D. Akbar.

Included with Mr Akbar's offer was another letter, from a firm of solicitors who informed her that probate had been completed on the will of the late Miss Harriet Myra Josephs and that shares and bonds to the approximate value of £228,000 formed the portion of the estate which had been left to Miss Julia Ann Garnet.

Julia had surmised that Harriet had planned to leave her something in her will because from time to time her friend had alluded to what she called 'my Post Office savings'. 'I'm saving up for a rainy day,' she had used to say. 'And if the weather holds out till I retire, then "What larks!" Otherwise, you must have the larks for both of us.'

In the aftermath of losing her friend Julia had forgotten these elliptic remarks of Harriet's, but had she thought about them she would have assumed they hinted at no more than a few thousand pounds. Harriet's brother's boy, a tall young man with specs, had called at the flat, slightly awkward in his role of his aunt's executor, and removed the shoebox into which Julia had packed Harriet's few obvious valuables – her gold watch, a mother-of-pearl cigarette case, some earrings and the diamond-clasped double string of cultured pearls. Julia's own accumulated building society savings had been sufficient to cover her stay in Venice; after that (she had been putting off the thought along with her return to England) it was to be a resumption of a lifetime's habit of frugality. Now with this influx of Harriet's undisclosed wealth, everything was altered.

Harriet, dark horse, must have been dabbling in stocks and shares. No, that was patronising, it was more than 'dabbling' – clearly she had been proficient in her management of the money market. And no doubt she had been too mindful of her companion's socialist principles to let on what she was at.

What an ass she had been! And how merciful life was that it bestowed opportunities to change one's mind.

Swiftly she calculated. Almost four hundred thousand pounds. Along with her pension, more than enough to live out her days here. There was no need to return to England and narrow loneliness. Suddenly she saw that her friends were here too: the Cutforths, the twins, the Signora, Nicco, the Monsignore, even Aldo – more friends than she had made in England in a lifetime. She walked inside and took up the pad of paper which lay on Charles's desk.

Dear Mr Akbar, she wrote.

 It is many years now since I travelled to Media where I found Sara; she who lives now as my wife in Nineveh speaks only occasionally of her home in Ecbatana. But telling you this story has caused me to ponder: it is in my mind that when my father leaves us to cross the bridge to the other life, I shall take my wife and our children and go at last to the holy city of Raghes, by the far sea, where I once was to travel to collect my father's debt.

I never did get to Raghes, for at my father-in-law's request we stayed fourteen nights (twice the customary period for feasting) in celebration that I had survived my wedding night and his daughter was at last married.

My father-in-law dug a grave for me on my wedding night so sure was he I would die! You could see how like he was to my own father in this — always harping on death. For myself I learned something during those days which I kept in my heart and never told my father.

It was Azarias, as ever, who showed me the way. That first morning we came downstairs, Sara laughing and her parents weeping, her father ready to thrust half his wealth on me, I looked about for Azarias. Later, the maid came with a message that I should go outside.

Azarias stood there and I opened my arms to embrace him but he stepped aside. 'Brother Azarias,' I said, 'I owe my life to you I reckon, and what is more I owe you my wife!'

Azarias smiled one of his smiles. 'You chose well, brother, for you chose life.'

I didn't understand this but now I remembered about the evil spirit who had possessed the body of my wife. 'Azarias,' I asked, 'what happened in the bed-chamber? I remember you were there and . . .' for suddenly I recalled there was another there with us. 'Kish was there too. Why was that?'

Azarias fell silent; it was as if we stood an hour or a day or a week with nothing said between us. Then he spoke and now all this time later I feel the awe which his words aroused.

'You know of one Lord whom you worship and that is right. But He has an Adversary, and against that adversary a man must struggle each day of his life; in this life every good thing is matched with its opposite. The evil spirit was known to me and I to him. The smoke of the fish has baffled him and he has fled to the utmost part of Egypt and there he is bound. But a dog was needed to smell him out.'

'Kish?'

'Dogs have good instincts – better often than their masters. That is why they are man's friends.'

'Azarias, who are you?' For by now I knew in this matter, too, the master's instincts were lesser than the one who served him.

But Azarias just smiled that smile of his and said, 'Enough questions. If I am to get to Raghes to fetch your father's debt I must go and see to the camels,' which made me feel shame as I had forgotten all about the debt and that my father and mother must be counting the days to my return.

But for the time being I had enough to occupy me; it

came to me that whatever the nature of the baleful spirit which had been dislodged from the body of my wife, it had left place for more passion than was usual in a virgin!

2

The twins' wedding was to take place in late August and Julia decided to use the occasion to return to London. There were matters to attend to: the solicitors, Mr Akbar. And it's right too, she thought as the plane taxied out at Marco Polo and up and off over the sea. There is a life to close down.

London was dirty and hot after a cold July, and Ealing particularly stuffy. Mr Akbar, however, was overjoyed to see her.

'Madam, come in, come in,' he gestured hospitably down her own hall. 'It is wonderful that you have come.'

He made sweet mint tea and they sat on the balcony overlooking the gardens. The gardens, which had been a source of pride to Julia during her years at Cedar Court, looked seedy: the turf parched and the flowerbeds municipal. 'These I love,' said Mr Akbar, pointing at a pair of bedraggled mallard ducks which had wandered onto the lawns.

'Do you, Mr Akbar? Then I am happy you are going to buy my flat.'

'You accept my price?'

Julia had taken the precaution of visiting a local estate agency before their meeting and had gleaned that the sum he was offering her was rather below the market value. She had come intending to be firm on this point. But the eyes of Mr Akbar, looking pleadingly at her, made her waver. She had bought the flat for a thousand pounds, after the original landlord died leaving her with a sitting tenancy. It seemed greedy to take advantage now of her own good fortune and besides, had Mr Akbar not made overtures to her she might never have had the idea to sell up. He did not have the appearance of wealth. And the hassle of selling the place elsewhere would delay her. Anyway, she owed him something for putting the idea of her permanent remove to Venice into her head. Him and Harriet.

Thinking of Harriet, she glanced through the glass doors into the sitting room which she and her friend had shared for thirty years. It hardly resembled the flat they had known, so adorned was it with coloured rugs, with brass ornaments, and pastel portraits of improbably nubile young women.

Mr Akbar was watching her with anxious attention. 'It is a good price? It stretches me, I promise, dear lady, to –' he demonstrated with eager hands – 'as much as I can afford.'

'I accept, Mr Akbar.' He was probably lying but who cared? A sense of enormous and expansive freedom had begun to seep through her.

'Madam, I thank you.' Mr Akbar rushed inside and came out with a bottle of sparkling wine. 'Champagne!' he said, untruthfully. 'We must drink a toast for luck. Listen, I play you my Elvis album.'

It was, she reflected later, travelling back on the Central Line to Holland Park, no less remarkable, in its way, that she should sit on a balcony in Ealing sipping sparkling wine with a Lebanese businessman (the nature of Mr Akbar's business remained obscure to her but it seemed to involve party novelties) to the accompaniment of Elvis Presley's 'Suspicious Minds', than that she should be looking out across the lighted waters of Venice.

Mr Akbar had insisted on telephoning his solicitor – who, he explained, was also his cousin's husband – there and then. It was all she could do to explain to him the fruitlessness, at that hour in the evening, of her ringing her own firm in High Holborn, with whom she had the slenderest connections. But she promised to be in touch with the solicitors first thing in the morning.

'We are friends,' Mr Akbar declared at the door as she declined more mint tea. So she had made another friend.

Harriet's solicitors had made their communications with Julia's, so she was able to combine the two operations when she called at Derbyshire & Mills the following day. In the past Julia's concerns had been dealt with by an overworked assistant solicitor called Sita. But on this occasion Mr Mills, the junior senior partner, met her in the vestibule and led her into a roomy office.

'Do sit down. Some tea, coffee – or something stronger as a celebration?' Mr Mills smiled, showing dentures.

'Coffee, please,' said Julia, perversely since it disagreed with her.

Mr Mills read out forms, laboured points and repeated himself several times until Julia's nostalgia for Sita mounted. At the end of it all, as inwardly she was fairly screaming to leave, he said, clearing his throat, 'Ahhhm, your own will. Forgive the liberty but should we not, in the light of all . . . ?'

Julia had not thought about her own death which, with hindsight, surprised her. 'Goodness, Mr Mills, I suppose you are right. How thoughtful you are.'

Mr Mills, unused to this client, was uncertain how to take her tone. 'It is generally advisable,' he continued. 'And your being overseas and so on . . .' he laughed with nervous unhumour.

'My health has never been better than since I went abroad but of course I shall consider what you say most carefully. May I write to you about it? I suppose any necessary documentation may be posted along with the contract?'

It was agreed she formulate her bequests and write from Venice, and at last she was permitted to go.

'Goodbye, Mr Mills. Do give my love to Sita. I'm so sorry to miss her but you filled in beautifully.'

So, she thought, boarding the Tube, wealth has brought me Mr Mills. What else will it bring, I wonder?

The Tube was hot and claustrophobic; she got out early at Notting Hill Gate and made her way on foot to the hotel. The heat and the unaccustomed coffee had fagged her and she felt a stitch coming on again in her side.

Recuperating on the bed, in a modishly pastel-coloured room with matching en-suite bath and shower, and hearing the sound of traffic outside, she experienced an acute home-sickness for the noiseless, peeling dilapidations of the Campo Angelo Raffaele. She had visited Signora Mignelli before she had left for England and put to her the proposition which she had conjured up on the Cutforths' balcony. 'I would so much like it if I could rent your apartment for the year.' And she named a sum for rental which she hoped the Signora would be unable to refuse.

The Signora had been enthusiastic in her acceptance. She regretted that she had Germans coming for the whole of August. 'But September is free,' she said emphatically. 'My tenant from America cancel — so it is good for both of us. Good for me because I keep deposit — and good for you because you move in more quick!'

The following morning, teeth rather gritted — for, unde-niably, there was something about London which disinclined one to make effort ('But really I must!' she insisted to herself) — she rang Vera from the hotel room.

'Julia! You should have said you were coming to England!' Vera, as ever, was reproachful.

'I didn't know myself,' said Julia, not wholly untruthfully.

Vera lived in a mansion block near Marylebone High Street. It had in fact, Julia surmised (her sense of such things heightened by her recent forays among the Ealing estate agents), risen in value to become a 'desirable' property. But Vera, she noticed, was enamoured of its drawbacks.

'Of course this will be very difficult to sell,' she said when Julia raised the topic of the proposed move. 'The noise from the traffic.'

'But handy for theatres,' said Julia, refusing to join in Vera's sense of deprivation.

Vera looked displeased. 'I'm sorry there's nowhere decent to sit down,' she said, moving papers from a perfectly comfortable armchair. 'Was the lift all right?'

'I think so – it got me here!'

'We've had such a time with the porter. He's not quite, you know!' Vera, lowering her voice needlessly (for after all who but herself was there to hear, Julia noted with irritation), tapped her head significantly. 'Bats in the belfry,' she mouthed. 'I dread to think what he might say to the purchasers!'

Julia, thinking fondly of Toby's bats in the Chapel-of-the-Plague, hoped the porter might make lewd suggestions to Vera's potential purchasers. 'I wonder if I could trouble you for some of my books?' Before her departure to Venice she had packed her books into a couple of boxes which Vera had offered to keep for her.

'They're in the spare room, I'm afraid.' Vera sighed as if foreseeing some overwhelming challenge.

'I'm so sorry to be a trouble,' said Julia, not sorry at all.

The boxes were under Vera's spare bed and after making much of pulling them out she left Julia to go through them and went off to make lunch. 'Take whatever you like.'

'Yes, I will, thank you,' said Julia, amused at being invited to take so freely of her own.

During lunch she tried to make amends for her behaviour by reading to Vera, from one of her rescued textbooks, about Garum, an ancient remedy, much prized by the Romans and made from the decomposed innards of an exotic fish.

'What do you want to know about that for? I should think it was more likely to give them food poisoning,' said Vera huffily. 'Still, I'm glad to see you're back on history again. Thank heaven you've given up all that Bible-reading caper. I thought you were going potty.'

'Like your porter?' Julia asked and was glad when she saw the time made it possible to leave without further rudenesses on her own part.

After Vera's determined pessimism it was fun taking a taxi to St Martin's Lane. There was a bookshop she wanted to visit — one she had seen in passing on her occasional trips to the Coliseum with Harriet. Dear Harriet! They had sat in the amphitheatre — 'the Armpit', Harriet had called it, on account of the sweat-inducing heat, and eaten home-made cheese and pickle sandwiches and drunk tea from a flask in the interval. And all the while Harriet had been a wealthy woman. She would be glad about the taxi.

Later that night, the traffic making the pale pink hotel furnishings judder (like blancmange, Julia thought), she ordered tea and sandwiches from Room Service – in memory of Harriet.

She hadn't looked at her old Atlas of the Ancient World (removed from under Vera's bed) since her student days, and opening it and finding Nimrod she felt a pulse of pleasure. This was how she had felt when, as a schoolgirl, she had planned her escape from her father's house by reading history at university. Below Nimrod, a short way south down the River Tigris, she found Nineveh, Tobit's city, or rather the one he was forced to inhabit after his conquerors had annihilated Israel. So this was Assyria? But it got its comeuppance in the end, for Nineveh was taken by the Medes and their allies the subtle Persians, and like the ten tribes of vanquished Israel it too vanished to become history. Old Tobit would have been pleased!

Turning the page to find the Persian Empire she found a bus ticket: 3d – the price of a ride along the Cambridge 'backs'. Thruppence. She had forgotten the little twelve-sided coins with the clump of thrift, or the portcullis of the Bank of England, on the back. A coin you used to give to children who were good, or for washing your windows or fetching coal. You lived as though a way of life would last for ever, and when it went, it vanished, even from your own memory.

But her Tobias – where had he travelled? With her finger she followed down the Tigris. Ecbatana, the capital of Media, Sara's home, was well east of Assyria, over the Zagros Mountains, and nowadays it seemed to be the town of Hamadan. And Raghes, by the Caspian Sea, where Tobias was to collect the family debt, looked as if it might have become the modern city of Tehran.

Opening the door of the fridge-bar she took out a miniature brandy and unscrewed the cap, imagining what her father would make of his daughter 'taking', as he would have put it, 'to the devil drink'? *'The fear of the Lord is the beginning of wisdom!'* he had said, striking her across the shoulders, as she sat, refusing him the satisfaction of seeing her weep. The Proverbs of old Tobit's God, Yahweh. *'The backslider in heart shall be filled with his own ways,'* portentously her father had also uttered, not at all understanding, she guessed (and feeling, at this, the need to pour more brandy), what those words might mean.

The twins were to be married in Devon and on the train (first-class, courtesy of Harriet) Julia read the book she had found at the bookshop near St Martin's Lane. Gaspar, Melchior and Balthasar, she learned, were all a Christian fancy. The Magi, it turned out, were not kings at all but from the priestly tribe of the Medes, who did not consider a journey to a humble oxen's stall beneath their sacerdotal dignity. Their gold and frankincense and myrrh would have been ritual gifts, appropriate to the saviour born of a virgin whose birth was predicted by their prophet, Zoroaster. And Zoroaster's holy city proved to be none other than Raghes!

Excitement gripped her heart, making it flutter and jump. There, she knew it! That was why Tobit wanted his son to go there to collect a debt. What was a debt anyway? Something of yourself you needed to have restored. And it was Raphael, after all, who collected the debt from Raghes in the end. Unconsciously, the old boy must have known a change of heart was the Tobit family's best hope! No wonder the funny, charming story, that had so impressed the artists of Venice, was excluded from the Protestant Bible: it was not really a Jewish morality tale at all but something far older — kinder, in fact. In her notebook, bracing it against the train's centripetal force, she wrote: *The Zoroastrian priests of Media (later Persia) would bring a dog to the bedside of a dying man — for him to feed the dog a morsel and so be led by it safely after death across the Bridge of Separation to be judged.*

Here she stopped and thought about judgement. The laughing Zoroaster apparently believed our world was a battleground between the forces of light and the forces of darkness. Perhaps he was right. It no longer made sense to her to think in the old rigid pre-Venice days about 'good' and 'bad' but maybe life was a matter of having to makes choices. (Though how did you know which was which? And how had she fared in that test?)

And the Nasu — that seemed to be the Persian name for the corpse-spirit, the executive of evil. The dog — which didn't make Jewish sense — she understood, now, why it was there. The train was fairly hurtling along so she took her notebook onto her lap, cradling it.

If the Median part of the Tobit story is, as I think, really Zoroastrian, that explains why the dog is there — to rid the girl of the destructive spirit which has got into her.

She thought a bit more, then wrote: *The dog is there to smell out death and the death-dealing spirit. So the dog has two functions: (i) he represents natural instinct — Tobit lacks this which makes him morbid but his son has it in abundance, which is why (with the right help) he can sexually penetrate the girl where others have failed; (ii) the dog leads to life after death — whether physical death or death of a moribund way of being (i.e. the girl's and Tobit's).*

But of course, we all have a spirit of destruction in us, reflected Julia Garnet, as the train swayed into, then braked at, Totnes station.

If the notion of a synagogue had ever been raised it had been discarded, for the wedding was to take place in a church close to Sarah's family home. Whatever was Jewish in Sarah had been overlaid by the Anglicanism of her father's family.

And perhaps that is as it should be — out of respect, Julia decided, smoothing the skirts of her lilac dress as she extricated herself from the taxi and rearranging Harriet's cream silk shawl around her shoulders as she took in the Englishness of the churchyard before her.

The wedding passed off as weddings do: the church was picturesque with its square Norman tower and wagon-vault roof; the vicar's sermon was affable, the hymns cheerful and Sarah looked fetching in lace. But there was none of the mystery and passion, nothing of the anguish and drama (which is, Julia speculated, surely also the prerogative of marriage) she had found in the Venetian services. Half way through the ceremony she became conscious that she was disappointed. Everything was in good taste, but the sum of it was insipid.

It is all too *pink*, she decided later: the salmon, the raspberries — even the vicar, who had divested himself of his dog-collar and was demonstrating his pliancy by jiving with one of the ladies in charge of the tea. Lucky her departure on the following day had given her an excuse to leave early.

'Forgive me,' she said, going across to Toby. 'It has been marvellous, but I'm getting old and I have a train to catch.'

'You're not old, Julia — you look dishy in that dress. I'd marry you myself if I weren't hitched up with a beautiful woman already.'

'Flatterer!' For the first time in her life Julia flirted back.

'No really, I'm serious. I won't forget our midnight walk.'

'Hardly midnight!'

'Well, dawn walk, whatever. Don't be such a schoolmarm! Look, I've never said —'

'Well don't!' Julia was crisp. 'Least said soonest mended, if you want me to be a schoolmarm. Anyway, I have a present for you both. I couldn't find anything I thought you would like so I've got you something I like instead.' She handed him a flat package.

'If you're really off I'm going to open it. I should wait for Sarah but looks like she's tied up with Uncle Herb.'

Julia looked across the field to where the marquee was pitched. Sarah stood at the entrance, her arm round a short, powerful-looking man with a top hat and long grey hair. 'Goodness, he looks terrifying! He's your mother's brother?'

She had been introduced to Sarah's mother, a grey-haired, sparrow-boned woman who looked as if she was struggling between grief and joy. And her husband, Sarah's father, Toby's Uncle Bill, was he around somewhere to see his only daughter safe at last? Or had that astonishing remediate gaze in the chapel dissolved all remnant of darkness before it?

But (giving herself the faintest peremptory shake) this she was never likely to know; such a matter was for the privacy of the marriage bed. 'Half-brother,' Toby cut in. 'Grandma married twice. He's OK. Rich as Croesus. It's thanks to his wonga we're able to do the chapel.'

'I remember you said. What made the money?'

'Cocktail biscuits,' said Toby and, explosively, they both started to laugh.

'Biscuits and pizzas!' Julia, holding on to the arm Toby didn't have round her, had to resort to Harriet's handkerchief. 'The modern mainstays of restoration.' Then, more soberly — the slight tension dissipated — 'She's all right, then, your Sarah?'

Toby, tanned, looked well. His shoulders had straightened out, become broader, somehow. Shading his eyes to look across to his wife he said, 'We have our days but she's riding again, which I reckon's good for her.'

In her mind's eye Julia saw the long, intelligent noses of the bronze horses of St Mark's. 'Much better, I should think, than any "therapy"!'

'Hey!' Toby had unwrapped the parcel to reveal a red-bound book. 'The Apocrypha. This looks cool!'

'I thought you might like to read the Book of Tobit. We nearly spoke of it once and, well, you'll maybe see why I like it.'

'Hey,' said Toby. 'Then I guess we'll like it too!'

The sun had retreated by the time Julia reached Plymouth station and she was grateful for Harriet's shawl. The buffet was closed so she couldn't even have a cup of tea and she had to make do with the comforts of her book until the train arrived. When it did she banged her shin on the step up to the carriage and, rubbing it, recalled the day she had arrived in Venice and met Cynthia and Charles. It was England where she felt a stranger now.

Her eyes were tired and she had some difficulty finding her seat number so that when she at last plumped down with her back to the engine (a placing which did not best please her) she did not immediately observe the dark-haired girl opposite.

'Would you like a cup of tea?'

Julia, who had withdrawn into her book, looked up to see that it was her fellow passenger who was asking the question. 'How kind of you — I'm fairly parched.'

'Well, if you wouldn't mind guarding my things I'll get us both one, unless there's anything else you would like?'

Julia thanked her but declined anything but tea. Within minutes the girl was back, carefully carrying the two beakers in their plastic handles. 'Disgusting looking, I'm afraid — bright orange but at least it wets the whistle.'

'My father used to say that!' The girl's friendliness was unexpectedly soothing.

'Did he? That's funny, mine does still. Cheers!' The girl smiled and raised a beaker towards Julia who drank gratefully. The day had been more of a drain that she had expected.

After a bit the girl said, 'Forgive me if I'm prying but I was looking at your book.' She gestured at the book which Julia had placed, cover down, on the table between them.

'Do look if you'd like.' Julia half-shuffled the book about the Magi towards her newly-met companion.

The girl opened the book and began to read the introduction. She handled the pages with care. Watching her Julia became conscious of a feeling she would not have recognised nine months ago: she was envious of the girl's attractiveness, her capacity to engage so easily in conversation with a stranger. It was a facility she herself had never had, would never now have and yet, as she watched herself watching the girl, she had the strangest sensation. She felt she was almost clinically observing a small insidious squib lodged inside her, which for years had poisoned her associations with others.

'Are they the same Magi then who followed the star?'

The girl seemed really to want to know. She might have been my daughter, Julia speculated; and the unlooked-for thought was warming. 'Yes. The same. I got oddly interested in them because of one of the books of the Old Testament Apocrypha: the Book of Tobit. It's only partly a Jewish story – the Jews, I've been working out, took it over from something much older.'

'Is that the one about the angel? We did it as a play at school.'

Is he here too, wondered Julia Garnet; between Plymouth and Paddington on the Great Western Railway? Perhaps he's everywhere if one cares to look.

'Yes – there's an angel. From what I've been able to find out, the subject of the Tobit story goes back to the time of the Medes and Persians. The Medes had a priest tribe, called the Magi, who became followers of Zarathustra – Zoroaster to us. The "Good Religion" they called it.'

'Don't all religions think they're "good"?'

'I expect they do. But he seems particularly to have liked life, if you know what I mean? In fact he believed we had a duty to enjoy ourselves. But he thought we had to be vigilant, too, against . . .' What was it? Excess and deprivation, the Iranian prophet had counselled against both – perhaps moderation in all things, including moderation, best summed it up? '. . . I suppose the things which conspire against the life-force – anger and brutality and dishonesty – he was particularly hot against that! It was the dominant religion in Iran for hundreds of years before the Muslims virtually wiped it out. A pity because it seems so sensible to me.'

'And the angel?'

'There's a dog in the story I got interested in,' said Julia, not wishing to speak on the other topic. 'The dog was part of Zoroastrian ritual, which is why Muslims hate dogs still.'

'My father says all religious practice is founded on political utility.' The girl had long hair which she had wound up into a silver comb – like Sarah's the day they had met at the Cutforths' party.

'I used to believe that,' said Julia, suddenly longing for the golden dimness of St Mark's. 'But I suppose what you believe or don't believe is a choice too.'

'I don't even know your name,' Julia (visited by a rogue sense of devastating loneliness) had declared as the train pulled into Paddington, and the girl had written it out, with her address, on a piece of coloured paper she had found in her bag.

Before retiring to bed in the blancmange hotel room, Julia looked at the piece of paper again to copy it into her notebook. 'Saskia Thrale'. A memorable name. It was not likely she would ever meet the girl again; but the meeting had crystallised something for her.

❧

Soon for me there will be time no longer and I must make my way beneath the earth. Therefore I must at last come to tell how my son Tobias returned to me.

The Rib and I waited two moons, and I counted each day of his journey. Every evening before sundown the Rib went out, pretending to deliver laundry – but I knew in truth she was lingering by the banks of the river, watching and waiting.

Until a day came when I lost patience (it was ever my besetting sin) and I turned to her and said, 'Is my kinsman dead and no man there to give them the money or what is it?'

At this the Rib started up. 'My son is dead. Now I care for nothing. I have let go the light of my eyes.' And so on.

'Hold your peace,' I said, angry that she was giving voice to my own fears. 'Doubtless they have been detained by some distracting business.'

But she would take no comfort from me and went out every day sorrowing and I pictured her following with her eyes the road they had gone. However much I tried to assure her our son was safe, in my own mind he had perished and all her searching after him was chaff before the wind. There would be none would care for the Rib after I was gone nor no one to bury my body in the earth away from the jaws of the carrion-eaters. And I cried as King David did, 'O my son, my son!'

But there came a day when the Rib went out to the banks of the Tigris and came running home, shouting.

I stepped out from my place in the porch to the courtyard wall. 'It's him,' she was calling. 'I saw them. Him and that man who went with him. Tobias is home. They'll be with us soon.'

Suddenly at my feet and around my legs I felt a warmth and then a dampness pressing itself against my calf. It was that blessed dog back again! I could feel the way he pricked his ears sharp, and the wagging of his tail.

And I swear I felt the coming of them too, through the arched passageway into the courtyard, as if it was the first day — my boy and the man who went beside him; for ever before my boy spoke to me I had called out to him, 'Tobias, son of my heart,' and I stepped away from the wall out towards him, and stumbled, my arms open to enfold him, my best treasure — an old man and blind.

I heard one word as I stumbled into the dark, 'Father,' and then 'Courage, Father!' and a vile stinging in my eyes and a foul stench, such that I almost vomited and I lost consciousness and fell to the ground.

And then a tall dark young man, with a beard, was helping me up, and wiping my face and pulling something away from my eyes and I saw I had a clutch of purple leaves in my fist and a broad fair man stood aside of him; and the young man with the beard said again, 'Father.' Then he added, 'See! I have come home again!'

3

I n October the rains came and those who knew the significance of such matters cast calculating eyes at the mark on the base of the campanile in the Piazza which measures the height the waters reached on November 4th 1966.

Acqua alta, the curse of Venice, for the waters which rise ever higher from the levels of the lagoon become lethal when driven by a following wind. In the Piazza San Marco the raised trestles, by which visitors and natives make their tottering or practised way round the square, were already in place.

Julia had accepted an invitation to dine with the Monsignore. She had set out and returned to put on green rubber boots, the hallmark of those native to the city. Before she turned into the Calle Lunga, she stopped to post some letters. So that was done; Mr Mills would be pleased.

A yellow crane, supported on a wide red barge, was sinking piles into the water. Men in thick leather gloves and woollen hats hauled and steadied the piles, beating them deep into the bed of the canal with tremendous mallets. Another passer-by called out a joshing greeting to one of the men who had recently married. Some banter ensued concerning the amount of time the bridegroom had been spending in bed. Listening amused, Julia realised that she understood the gist of what the men were saying.

Along the familiar route over the Accademia bridge (she could walk it, she had written to Vera – trying to make amends for the visit – in her dreams) she met the woman in the emerald hat whom she had last seen in the little chapel of St Mark's. The woman, gleaming in patent boots, bestowed a regal nod of recognition as they passed.

'You come prepared for the deluge!'

She had taken off her boots and the priest had taken her, in her stockinged feet (too late she remembered she had forgotten slippers) into a study which resembled a painting she had first seen with Carlo.

'Thank you for these.' She deposited a parcel of books on the table. 'This is like St Augustine's cell!'

'Too big a compliment. I fear I do not have the saint's resistance to his own shadow. But Marco, here, is a model for Augustine's dog!' The pug had come wheezing forward to greet her.

Julia bent down to reciprocate. 'I've been doing some detective work on dogs. Do you know, I used not to like them.'

They dined in his panelled hall – pigeon cooked with peas in rich gravy, the crystal glasses tawny with wine.

'The wine of the Veneto for winter,' said the Monsignore, refilling her glass. 'Good for the belly and the heart.'

'And the spirit?'

'That too. But better not talk too much about the spirit. It is shy.' He spoke as if of a quick-hearing presence. 'However, tonight we might make a toast, you and I.'

'Of course?'

'*Ottobre ventiquattro* – The Feast of Raphael – that is until some imbecile in the Vatican dumps it in with Michaelmas! But always before, today is his feast; and myself I always honour him this day.' He raised his glass to her across the table.

So that was why she had been invited. She raised her glass in answer and they drank in silence.

'The books you kindly lent me –' she had become quite a regular in his library – 'you know, I think he –' she did not like to speak the name – 'is far older than the Old Testament even.'

Oh Raphael, thousands of years ago, on the high grasslands by the Caspian Sea, ever before there was a Moses or a Christ or a Mohammed, was it you showed the laughing Zoroaster his vision of a world poised between truth and lies?

If she had hoped for surprise from him she would have

been disappointed. 'But of course, such as these have always been; since the beginning. It makes sense!'

Marco, from his place by the fire, came across to her chair and she offered him a scrap of pigeon. 'Do you mind my feeding him? Sorry, I should have asked.' The priest, who had been staring into the fire, only shook his head. 'I expect you knew this, but I didn't, that dogs were sacred once. I have been wondering if that's why, you know, there's a dog with him in the painting?'

The Monsignore, turning back, began to help himself to cheese. 'I wish you would take some of this Provolone. Or the Gorgonzola is excellent with the wine. It is an odd dog, this one in the Tobiolo story. The only good dog in the scriptures. But as you say these stories are far older than our religions.'

He seemed not to wish to say more but there was something which had bothered Julia and, obstinate, she pressed. 'Monsignore Giuseppe, what happened to the other part of the diptych?' Sometimes in the night she woke puzzling. Had the companion picture gone with all the other undiscovered treasures with the Nazis? Or had Sarah stolen that too? Was it still in Carlo's possession, waiting for an opportunity for him to sell it to some discreet millionaire? Yet Toby had spoken only of discovering the angel panel – had said nothing of its other half. 'Do you think it will ever turn up?'

'You are troubled for the picture or for yourself?'

Would the angel panel be able to 'cure', now it was buffered by the sleek powers of modern security and no longer in the safe quiet of the little chapel? So far as she knew the priest had never disclosed to anyone but her that it was he who had hidden the diptych in the passage. An idea began to quicken in her mind – perhaps the other part was still . . . ? but the blackbird eyes were looking levelly and her half-formed question died away.

'Some more wine?' He offered the decanter. 'Then I will finish it. I never tell you, I think, my story about Pope John.'

'The day you told me about . . . ?' They had never spoken of what he had seen in the chapel either.

'Just so. All popes are appointed by God but some, let us say, come to us more as His friends. For myself having known Pope John, I learn a little more about the force of light. You understand?'

Marco snuffled at her chair and she fed him a piece of bacon. 'I think so.'

'He was, you see, always –' the Monsignore made a gesture with his fingers as if crumbling pastry – '*light* himself. So, I tell you: it is one time in Paris and Pope John is invited to a dinner. Sophia Loren and her husband Carlo Ponti are also invited – to give His Holiness some company from home, I suppose, because being a peasant Pope John speaks only Italian. Miss Loren is a little late – a habit of hers – and when she arrives she is very décolleté. But very! And at once around her, from all the people from the Vatican, there is an atmosphere.' The eyes looked malicious glee. 'After a while Pope John says, "I feel sorry for Signora Ponti – she is dressed so charmingly. But when she enter the room no one looks at her – all of you look instead at me! Where are your manners, gentlemen?"'

The Monsignore rose from the table. 'Do you feel like a little promenade? Marco had better accompany us. You are getting fat, Marco, like your master, and the *dottore* tells me we must pay attention to the heart. No need, I think, for your muzzle tonight.'

The moon was full and hung over the shallow lake which the *acqua alta* had made of the Piazza San Marco. Not another soul was in sight to witness the liquid silver on the water's surface.

'You see,' said the Monsignore, 'one of the truly lovely sights of Venice and also the most dangerous.'

Carlo had shown her the height reached by the last flood – a jot below his own. 'See,' he had said. 'If I had been standing there the waters would almost have covered me!' – and she had wanted to cover him instead with her own body.

'Someone told me that it was only because of the time of the year that the city was saved.' The time of the neap tides, Carlo had explained, when the gravitational force of the sun and moon pull in opposite directions. 'The floods are becoming more frequent?'

'Certainly. The ice is melting at the pole and adds daily to the level of the sea. And each day Venice sinks by just so much of a fraction.' In the moonlight she saw him move his hand in a gesture of annihilation.

'But is there nothing can be done?'

'Oh yes. They say gates can be constructed to keep out

the water which blows across the Adriatic. But I wonder if we can ever really turn back the tide.'

He turned back towards the lagoon. 'I will call my boatman to escort you back to the Angelo Raffaele.' She was about to say it was unnecessary when he laid a restraining hand on her arm. 'No, no. Do not protest. It is my pleasure. You know you were talking of the old religions? Everything has its time. All of this . . .' he waved backwards at the drenched vista of the Piazza '. . . was once green fields and vineyards and a canal ran beside the church which was St Theodore's, before Marco's body was brought to put his nose out of joint. Like so much of Venice, he too was stolen from the East!'

Julia looked up at the displaced saint with his crocodile. A rhyme the children at school had used to chant in the playground was running in her mind. *See you later alligator — In a while crocodile*. She pictured the anonymous author of the Book of Tobit, perhaps in Egypt, writing down on his papyrus the tales of the Persian soldiers as they visited the Egyptian garrison, and mixing them in with his own race's pieties. A 'splendour of miscellaneous spirits' Ruskin had called Venice. He might as well have meant civilisation! A hotch-potch, anyway. Perhaps the crocodile had travelled from Egypt along with the body of the Evangelist? 'He was the Patriarch of Alexandria, wasn't he — Mark?' It was the only piece of information she had retained from the Reverend Crystal.

'Indeed. Also something of a coward, which is why Marco, here, is named for him. Come, Marco. Enough of these sad sights. You and I must go home.'

And in the mind of Julia Garnet rang these words: *East, West, Home's best!*

᠈

 I no longer worship the great God Yahweh though I do not tell my father this. But I think my father understands because he changed too, that day. Who could not, seeing what we saw?

It was a slower business travelling home to Nineveh: I had my wife Sara and her maids to attend to, and all the goods her father had heaped on me for a dowry, and out of gratitude for what I was supposed to have done, which took many packhorses, mules and camels.

Azarias did not walk with me but ahead or behind with the muleteers – he liked animals best, I have thought since. But Kish remained at my side, and for all I was so engrossed with my wife I was glad of his company.

It was exciting when we reached the banks of the Tigris again for then I knew we were only days from home. And that night, before I went to Sara's tent (for we never spent a night apart), Azarias came to me by the fire.

'Tobias,' he said, 'have you the gall of the great fish I told you to stow away in your bag? When we come close to Nineveh let us go ahead before your wife. Your father will come out to you. Now listen and I will tell you what you must do to cure his blindness . . .'

I told my wife I would go ahead to prepare my parents

for her arrival and my heart was quick with the thrill of this and of seeing them again and guessing their joy. My stride had lengthened since we first set out and now I kept pace easily with Azarias along the river bank. It was good to be back there beside him by the fast-flowing water.

Azarias was whistling as we walked and I felt some awkwardness because there were many things I wanted to ask him and for the life of me I didn't know how.

I must have been grimacing because he said suddenly, 'Don't look so gloomy, man. Don't you know care's an enemy of life?'

Well, this was a new idea to me – but then Azarias was always full of surprises. 'How so?'

'Humankind has a right not to be miserable,' was all he said, and walked on.

Kish, who had come with us, had run along ahead after his old foes the water rats but he turned back now and settled into trotting at Azarias's heels.

'Azarias,' I said. 'You told me once I may find out who or what you worshipped when we got to Ecbatana. Might you tell me now?' I had been thinking about the tribes of Israel and how they had deserted their God for the old leafy shrines. I had been thinking, since I left Ecbatana, I might have deserted too.

'How would courage and truth and mercy and right action strike you?'

'But those are not gods,' I protested.

At this Azarias stopped stock still and Kish stopped beside

him. I remember a long loose chain of flamingo flying behind his great curly head. They looked like flaming angels in the rose-coloured evening light.

'Tobias, for heaven's sake, what do you think a god looks like when he works in men?'

And to that I had no answer, so we hurried on without more talk towards Nineveh.

4

*I*t was past midnight when the Monsignore's boat drew up by the wide, weed-covered steps which led up to the Chiesa dell'Angelo Raffaele.

Stepping out Julia Garnet looked aloft to see the group of stone figures: the fish, the dog, the boy and, over and behind all, the figure of the Angel Raphael.

She thanked the Monsignore's boatman and watched his shoulders square as he took the boat up the *rio* and round the corner out of sight.

In the light of the moon she could see the wrinkled stockings of the Archangel and looking up she winked at him, '*Ciao, Raffaele!*'

The moonlight fell especially bright and unable to sleep,

or to shut the beams from her room, Julia rose and made herself a cup of tea. What was the meaning of the Monsignore's story tonight? To distract her? How he loved to talk about women's breasts! Perhaps it had no other meaning.

Opening her notebook she read what she had written on the plane home, after the twins' wedding: *Despite the hazards the Magi trusted their vision and followed it, even to a strange land (and a stranger god!).*

The Magi, the 'wise men', had followed the star where it took them, and, in the persons of Nicco and his friends, she had followed them. So perhaps she was an honorary Parsi after all?

Long ago she had decided that history does not repeat itself; but perhaps when a thing was true it went on returning in different likenesses, borrowing from what went before, finding new ways to declare itself; and always there were the Nasu, and the Nasu's accomplices and inheritors; but always too, beside them, the Angel Raphael. Even old Tobit saw him in the end.

There was the end of a pencil by the telephone and taking it she wrote in her book: *Let the dead bury the dead!* Maybe that was the point of the Monsignore's story: a belief in your own rightness was a kind of death.

Sleep seemed to be eluding her that night: her arm had begun to ache again and she was overcome by a restlessness in her limbs, making her want to stamp them. Outside the Chiesa dell'Angelo Raffaele shone obliquely. Across the way she saw a shape and, imagining at first it was a cat, she made out at last a small dog nosing around the wellhead.

Still there was no desire to sleep and her legs felt so restless she almost wanted to dance. Setting the notebook aside she slipped her tweed coat over her nightdress and pulled on the green wellingtons. Then, recalling her father's dictum, as a last-minute gesture to health she put on Harriet's hat.

Outside the dog had vanished, but alone in the square it was peaceful with the moon for company.

'I will walk around the *campo* three times and then back to bed,' she announced to herself. But after the third perambulation, still feeling unusually wakeful, she stole over to the bridge which crossed the *rio* by the church.

The peculiar moonlight must have brought others out from their beds, for, across the bridge, she saw an old man with a beard.

The old man lifted his hand and waved to her as if he knew her and she waved back — companions in the night.

Ah, the dog must have been his, for suddenly she saw it, a black shape pattering noiselessly over the bridge, and walking across the bridge herself she saw Harriet.

'Harriet?' she said.

Behind Harriet, in the blue shadow, framed in a brightening doorway, stood another figure; and looking into his eyes she beheld myriads of infinite whirlpools pulling her towards the end of time.

 I knew already, before Azarias told us, before
he made the revelation. All the things he had
spoken of on our journey, all the strange
events which had transpired, dovetailed in my
mind before he spoke the words.

'I am Raphael,' he said, 'one of the seven holy angels
which go in and out before the glory of the Holy one,' and
he said it so lightly, casually you might say, that I wanted
to laugh. But my heart hurt, as if it was melting in a fire.

He took us, me and my father, apart to tell us; while my
mother was embracing my wife and weeping and asking
questions about the journey and her parents in Ecbatana.
Kish was there too. Kish howled as Azarias left us, a great
yearning howl, and then whimpered and fell silent. I think
Azarias might have been sad at leaving Kish.

My father has gone ahead now. He has crossed the Bridge
of Separation and I know he will be judged fairly – Azarias
will see to that. He was a good man, my father, and tried
to live by his own lights. Today, for the first time, I found
myself able to read what I know it took him all the remainder
of his days to find a way of writing down.

My belief is it changed him: for one thing, from that day
he recovered his sight, the day when Azarias charged him
to write down what he had seen, my father left the dead
alone.

For myself it changed everything: I gave up the idea of
a jealous god (for I had walked and slept and talked and
argued with Azarias, and the god who had Azarias to serve

him could not be jealous). I have come to think that the only true god must be one who allows for all manner of ways of worship and who fosters all parts of creation: after all – fish, dog, man, woman and angel – I met each of these on my journey, and in the end each proved their necessity.

And also this changed nothing for me – for I have come to see there will always be the same things in this world – the water, the land, the skies, and fish, flesh and fowl to inhabit them; and humankind which mis-takes things.

And until time ceases altogether there will be the spirits ready to take us from ourselves, and, if we are fortunate, those as well to aid us in recovery.

5

*E*xtract from the Last Will and Testament of Julia
Ann Garnet:

To my friend and comrade Vera Kessel Flat 2 36 Har-
swell Road Hastings Sussex I bequeath my collection of
books on the Socialist Movement
To Signora Beatrice Mignelli of Dorsoduro 1710A Venezia I bequeath a year's rental for the apartment in the
Campo Angelo Raffaele where I have passed such happy
times
To Niccolo Concetti of Dorsoduro 1728 Venezia I
bequeath the cost of two return air tickets to London

together with the sum of one thousand pounds for his stay there

To Cynthia Cutforth of Whitelands 1169 Franklin Boulevard Philadelphia USA I bequeath my hat with the veil

To Saskia Thrale of 12 Wells Rise London SW10 I bequeath my copy of The Magi of Persia with thanks for an invaluable meeting

To the Venice in Peril Fund I bequeath in trust the remainder of my fortune in monies and in shares the Fund to oversee its appropriate allocation to works which contribute to the shoring up of the foundations of Venice to delay its decline into the sea in small thanks for all they have done for the city which has taught me to learn and enjoy at this late stage in my life

Further I request that my body be cremated the ashes to be scattered in the lagoon of Venice and that Sarah and Toby Traherne of Elm Cottage Summerton Devon be commissioned and reimbursed to carve on a stone to be placed in Putney Vale Crematorium beside the stone of my companion Harriet Josephs a likeness of a dog together with these words

UT MIHI CONTINGAT TUO BENEFICIO POST
MORTEM VIVERE

Valde te rogo, ut secundum pedes statuae meae catellam pingas . . .
ut mihi contingat tuo beneficio post mortem vivere.*

PETRONIUS

* I ask that you paint a small dog at the foot of my statue
. . . that by your kindness I may find life after death.

AUTHOR'S NOTE

The Book of Tobit has been part of Jewish literature for over two thousand years. Although it is set in the aftermath of the first Jewish holocaust, when the ten lost tribes of Israel (a separate country from the longer-surviving southern kingdom of Judah) were deported to Assyria in 722 BCE, it was probably not written down in its present form until the last quarter of the second century BCE. Speculation about its likely date varies: some scholars believing it was composed during that early period, some seeing it as deriving from the time of the later, more famous, exile from Judah to Babylon, and yet others seeing it originating from the Jewish Diaspora in Egypt.

The Apocrypha (from the Greek word meaning hidden or stored away) is made up of those books of Jewish scripture which the translators of the 1611 King James Bible, the 'Authorised' version, excluded from the Anglican Old Testament. In this the translators followed the Hebrew Bible which had come to place these books outside the Jewish canon. But there exists an older version of the Jewish scriptures, the so-called Septuagint, the ancient Greek translation of around 250 BCE which predates the much later Masoretic (traditionalist) decision to keep certain well-established books from the Hebrew Bible. Many of these 'apocryphal' books were part of Jewish Wisdom literature, often considered too holy or precious to be made commonly available. That the Book of Tobit was certainly in use as a holy book among the Jews around the first century CE is confirmed by its discovery among the Dead Sea scrolls finds. As the Eastern Orthodox Church still uses the Septuagint translation for its Old Testament, the Book of Tobit remains in currency there; as it does in the Catholic

Bible, which, following St. Jerome's translation, has Tobit blinded by swallows' rather than sparrows' dung!

The origins of the tale remain obscure. Although set in Nineveh, in the period of the Assyrian Empire, the most dramatic and mysterious part of the story takes place in Media and many scholars agree that key features contain strong hints of Zoroastrianism, the old Iranian religion adopted by the Magi of Media and later by the powerful empire of the Persians (from whom the Parsis of today are descended). From my researches into the story I formed the view that the dog, which in its positive representation is unique in Judaic/Christian literature, could be explained by an earlier Zoroastrian foundation to the story, a supposition which is borne out by the fact that Raghes, to which Tobit travelled in his youth, was known as 'Zoroaster's city'.

For the Zoroastrians the dog was a sacred animal whose function was twofold: the dog was one means by which the bodies of the dead were disposed of, a practice which makes good practical sense in a hot climate but which, for the Zoroastrians, had the more important religious function of sparing human contact with dead matter. The Assyrians, in fact, like the Jews they took into captivity, practised grave burial. Tobit's preoccupation with burial of the dead is made more intelligible if seen to be set against the Magian practice of exposing the corpse to wild dogs and carrion-eating birds of prey.

More crucially, the dog was used in Magian ritual to exorcise the 'corpse spirit', or 'spirit of corruption', and to help guide the departed soul across the Bridge of Separation. In the Zoroastrian religion this defines the moment of judgement, when the sum of a person's good or bad deeds is weighed. It seemed to me likely that the dog might equally have been used to heal the mortally sick, or in cases of psychological possession, such as that of Tobias's Sara.

This idea was reinforced when I discovered that Asmodaeus, the evil spirit who inhabits the body of Tobias' eventual bride and has caused her to strangle seven men before him, probably takes his origin from Aesma daeva, the arch demon who is given 'seven powers' to destroy humankind in Zoroastrian demonology and whose principal feature is wrath or anger. Just as the Archangel Raphael is pitted against Asmodaeus, the counter or opposite to Aesma is the immortal being Sraosha, who is central to Zoroastrian angelology.

Both Judaism and Christianity owe much to the vision of Zarathustra (more commonly known to us by his Greek name, Zoroaster); not least among the ideas we have inherited is the concept of a hierarchy of 'Bounteous Immortals', supranatural beings who aid mankind in the fight against destruction and evil and towards health, happiness and right conduct. These are almost certainly the originals of our Judeo/Christian angels. Among them is Sraosha, whose remit was specifically to protect the body and to escort the departed soul to the 'Bridge of Separation', where he also acted as a benevolent final judge of a person's life. Sraosha seems to be associated with a dog (as are other psychopomps, or soul guides, in ancient literature) and this not only reinforces the parallel with Raphael in the Book of Tobit but also provides another explanation for the presence of the dog in the story.

The Talmud tells us that when the Jews returned from their exile in Babylon (encouraged by their tolerant new masters, the Persians) they brought with them from captivity the names of the angels. My hunch is that Raphael, whose name in Greek means 'God's healing', was imported then into Jewish lore, but that he appeared first as Sraosha, one of the Bounteous Immortals, and that the Book of Tobit is really an old Magi tale which has been overlaid with Jewish pieties and strictures. Nor is it commonly known today that the three 'wise men' (who, in Christian mythology, followed the star to Bethlehem) were in all likelihood Zoroastrian priests, their famed gifts of myrrh and frankincense being typical of the sweet woods and resins used in the ritual practices of the religion whose founder, perhaps fifteen hundred years before the birth of Christ, had predicted the virgin birth of a world saviour.

Salley Vickers